SIRI, WHO AM I?

SIRI,

WHO

AM I?

Sam Tschida

QUIRK BOOKS
PHILADELPHIA

Copyright © 2020 by Sam Tschida

Library of Congress Cataloging in Publication Data
Tschida, Sam, 1979- author.
    Siri, who am I? / Sam Tschida.
    LCC PS3620.S44 S57 2020
    DDC 813/.6—dc23   2019051818

ISBN: 978-1-68369-168-6
Printed in the United States of America
Typeset in Brandon Grotesque and Adobe Garamond

Cover designed by Andie Reid
Cover illustration by Carolina Melis
Interior designed by Molly Rose Murphy
Production management by John J. McGurk

Quirk Books
215 Church Street
Philadelphia, PA 19106
quirkbooks.com

10 9 8 7 6 5 4 3 2 1

To Lila, who ate so many frozen pizzas while I was busy writing this book. And to Daphne, who learned how to make macaroni and cheese and a mean scrambled egg. I love you girls!

CHAPTER

ONE

It seems as though I'm the kind of person who lands in the hospital in a cocktail dress on a Tuesday night with no ID and no friends. The doctor says I've been in a mild coma for the last two days like Peter Gallagher in *While You Were Sleeping*, a movie I seem to remember every word of. As for my name? No clue. All I know is that I hate my hair. Maybe it's just coma hair (medical-grade bedhead), but still. You'd think they would have washed out the blood, not to mention a crust that feels like bridesmaid-level product build-up, but Brenda the day-shift nurse explains, "This ain't a spa, honey. We only do blowouts on doctor's orders." And then she laughs. When she hands me an oversize cup of water a minute later, she looks at my hair like it's the first time she's noticed it and says, "You know, it's actually cute." Just being nice, I think. Either that or she has no taste. I can't judge because I've only seen her in scrubs.

The doctors say that, amnesia aside, I'm mostly fine, but that doesn't seem true. I definitely feel like I almost died. I mean, I didn't see any of my dead relatives welcoming me to the other side but that proves nothing; if I can't remember who I am, I probably wouldn't recognize them either. That's probably what happened—God sent Uncle So-and-So to pick me up and I just assumed he was a perv and missed the ride to heaven.

Though circumstantial, the evidence of my attempted murder is highly convincing:[1]

- Blunt force trauma to the back of the skull.
  (Let's hope that's why my hair looks bad.)

- Cocktail dress. (This should factor in, I think.)

- Blood alcohol of . . . I don't know what the
  numbers mean, but mostly Grey Goose.
  Funny how I know what I drink, even if
  I don't know where I live. #priorities.

- Someone (anon.) called an ambulance for me but
  didn't wait around to hold my hand on the ride in.

I'm just going to assume someone tried to kill me. That's what it feels like. Eight out of ten on the pain scale with a side of abandonment. If I find out I just slipped and did this to myself, I'm going to be really disappointed.

Halfway through *Keeping Up with the Kardashians*, which

....

[1] Am I a lawyer?

I've been binge-watching on the small TV in my hospital room ever since I woke up, my medical team walks in. They all smell like Purell, even though current research tells me they're probably mostly spreading germs. Bad hair won't be my only problem if I don't get out of this place soon. And I'm pretty sure I'm not even a germophobe. I have a feeling that I'm really well-adjusted. Who the fuck knows, though. What does well-adjusted even mean? I might as well say that I love all kinds of music, even country. But no one loves country.[2]

Brenda, who ordered me a special gluten-free, vegetarian meal because I "just look like a vegetarian, honey," explains the facts to the neurologist, Dr. Patel. He'd be attractive if he didn't look so much like a neurologist. If *Queer Eye* ever got their hands on him, they'd get rid of his rumpled, secondhand clothes and truss him up in a sexy, fuchsia shirt and slim-fit pants in his actual size. (You are not a 34-inch waist, Dr. Patel.)[3]

"The patient can't seem to remember her name," Brenda says.

Kim, Khloé, Kourtney, Kris, Caitlyn, Kanye, Kendall, Kylie, and all the assorted babies . . . I know *all* of their names. But who the hell am I?

The neurologist interrupts Kim, who's talking about permanent lip liner with zero expression on her face. "How are you doing?"

....

[2] Except for "Jolene."

[3] I might be a fashion expert.

Why can't I tune Kim out? It's like my brain is hardwired to focus on her. Because she's pretty? Because her problems are dumber and therefore less stressful than mine? Because of her butt? "I seem to be having trouble focusing," I say to Dr. Patel. "I don't know if that's normal for me."

Patel finally looks up from my chart. "Time will tell. Before I explain your test results, do you mind if I do a physical examination of your head?"

I might not have all of my memories, but I have a feeling I've been asked that before.

"As for the physical trauma," he says, "MRI and CT are negative for signs of intracranial bleeding. The swelling in your brain must be going down, which is why you woke up. The headache probably won't go away for at least a week."

"How about my memory?"

"Your memory—" He stops for a second to look at an incoming text on his phone.[4] "You have what's known as traumatic amnesia, which means your memories will likely come back to you as your injuries heal. But there's no telling when— and you might struggle for quite some time."

The light-headed feeling hits again and my peripheral vision starts to blur, but I lean back and shut my eyes. *No passing out.*

"For now, I think you should try to reconstruct your life as best as you can. If you can get back into some old routines, you will increase your chances of remembering. Once you

....

[4] Or is he just reciting this off of WebMD?!

10

get home, surround yourself with familiar faces, go back to work—you might begin to remember things."

Home. Routines. Wasn't he listening? I don't even know my own name or who cuts my hair.

———

"Girl, you gotta cheer up," my nurse, Brenda, says. "I have good news."

"Tell me it's a cure." Or an invitation to live on her couch. I'll take either.

"Definitely better than anything the doctors are gonna do for you." She looks up, waiting for my full attention.

"Go on."

"Well, I still suspect you're a vegetarian, so you've got that to deal with—"

"How do you know?"

With a shake of her head and a *If you have to ask, you'll never understand* look, she says, "I charged your phone. The intake nurse thought it was broken but I gave it a little check-up. It's cracked, but it works." She holds it out to me.

An iPhone, cracked to hell and splintered. I won't be able to click on anything in the upper third of the screen, but only my banking and weather apps are up there. The important stuff is all at the bottom, within thumb's reach.

My desktop background is a picture of myself. I've got good hair in it, at least. Gwen Stefani blond, all sirens-of-the-silver-screen glamour on one side and a buzz cut on the other, but salon quality; it doesn't have that *I buzzed it myself in a dimly lit bathroom* vibe—I don't think. I hold out the phone to Brenda. "Does this hairstyle seem like a weird choice to you, or is it just me?"

Brenda lets out a startled laugh. "Little weird. Can't say I'm surprised."

"Whatever, Brenda. You love me."

She raises an eyebrow. "And you love quinoa."

"Take me out to lunch and we'll find out." I look at the screen. It's a lifeline to all of my friends and family—everything that matters. I mean, it's one thing to lose your memory but another thing altogether to lose your phone. Email, texts, Facebook, Twitter, Instagram . . . Does it even matter that my memories aren't in my brain? Everything that counts is on my phone. Hard data and digital evidence.

Including my name . . .

CHAPTER

TWO

As soon as the facial recognition software locks on my features, my phone's screen unlocks. (Someone finally fucking remembers me!) "Siri, what's my name?"

"Hello, gorgeous. Your name is Mia."

"Siri, did you mean Elizabeth?" I feel more sophisticated than a Mia. Mia sounds like someone who plays the flute or volleyball. A girl who earns two hundred fifty dollars every summer babysitting. Someone who likes strawberry ice cream and always has her hair in a ponytail. Elizabeth—she sounds like someone with potential, like a chick who could run for Congress or become a doctor. I must be important if I had somewhere to go in a cocktail dress on a Tuesday.

"No, gorgeous, your name is Mia."

I frown at the phone. "Mia . . . Mia," I repeat to myself. "What do you think?" I look up at Brenda hopefully.

Brenda pats my hand. Her peppermint Altoid barely covers the smell of her coffee breath. "It's the first day of the rest of your life, Mia."

Maybe she really will let me sleep on her couch.

"Siri, what's my last name?"

"I don't know, gorgeous."

"Why does she keep calling me gorgeous?"

Brenda smirks. "You must have nicknamed yourself that, *gorgeous*."

I seem to have a healthy self-image.

Another nurse, Cindy, wanders into the room, apparently aware of the memory upload currently going on. I'm the major plotline on this week's episode of fourth-floor hospital gossip. "Just think, you could be anyone. Maybe you're a doctor or a lawyer or an actress or . . ." After an up-and-down look, she says, "I don't know why but I kind of think you might work for an airline."

"Uh, thank you . . . ?" Was that a compliment? Not to mention, these nurses don't understand memory loss at all. "Ladies," I explain, "it's not like I'm getting a chance to start over or something."

"Well, sort of. If I passed out for two days and woke up to find out I was a rocket scientist or a supermodel, I mean . . ." Cindy raises her hands in the air, as if that would obviously be the best thing that had ever happened to her. No wonder no one thinks my situation is a crisis. They all probably want to forget who they are, too.

"You could be royal. Like a princess who was visiting and got separated from her royal entourage. I mean, you were wearing a tiara when they admitted you. An understated one, like something Meghan Markle might wear to a polo-match afterparty, but still."

Okay. The nurses are watching waaaay too much TV. Most likely I'm going to find credit card debt and a mountain of student loans the minute I figure out my social security number. I mean, I woke up in America. But still, they've planted a seed of hope. I'm hoping I'm a college graduate at least. Even if I'm not, I know I'm important because that's what tiaras signify—importance (and glamour).

I look at the shiny black mirror that is my iPhone and click on the texts icon, but there are no texts. Not a single conversation is listed in the text message app. How could that be?

When I show the anomaly to the nurses, Cindy says, "Oh, you're one of those."

"One of what?"

"You must be super OCD about erasing all your messages."

"Why would I do that?"

Cindy looks at me like she's about to deliver one of those lines punctuated by a *dun dun* on *Law & Order* and says, "I guess you have something to hide." She follows up with a laugh. "Probably just sexts, unless you're a princess. You wouldn't want the paparazzi to get their hands on it and publish your private conversations in the *Daily Mirror*."

I think I'm just efficient, not a lazy bum with old conversations using up all of the space on my phone, space I could use for other more important things like . . .

I pull up my contacts list. "Where should I start?"

"That's easy. Check your contacts for 'boyfriend'"—she seems to glance specifically at my haircut—"or 'girlfriend'?"

"Boyfriend. I think." Boyfriend—if I have a boyfriend, I probably listed him under his actual name, meaning he might as well not exist. If he does exist, I might have to break up with him anyway. I mean, where was he when I cracked my skull? Something tells me I don't have a husband. (No ring.) Plus, the cocktail dress and Grey Goose don't scream married.

Brenda, standing with her hands on her hips and clearly not expecting me to find out that I'm a doctor or rock star, speaks up. "Check for Dad and Mom. That's who you need right now."

Oh Brenda, the voice of reason. There's no way I'm a princess or a doctor. If I were a doctor, I'd probably have a sham degree and dispense pills to anyone who asked. At least that's what the look on Brenda's face told me.

I scroll down to M. *Mom*—bingo! I take a deep breath and close my eyes. She's probably worried. She probably even filed a missing person report. I wonder if she smells like apple pie, or if she hates to cook and lives off Lean Cuisine. I can't picture her to save my life.

My pulse races as I wait for her to pick up. In one second I'll find out if I've won the amnesia patient's lottery. I silently pray, *Come on, Big Mary! (Or is it Big Money?)* and *Dear God—please let my momma save me.* Come to think of it—do I believe in God?

One, two, three, four rings. I start thinking of the message I'll leave—"Mom, it's me, Mia . . . I'm in the hospital, but I'm okay." Hopefully she'll fill in the rest: SAT score, favorite food, ex-boyfriends, and—dude, where's my car.

An automated message cuts off my train of thought. "We're sorry. The number you're trying to reach has been disconnected."

Fuck.

Brenda and Cindy look at me expectantly. I announce, "I don't have the right phone number for my mom." As if that isn't a giant red flag. It'd be one thing if I didn't have an entry for my mom at all, like we were estranged or she died. But to have the wrong number? That's weird.

I say, "Siri, call home."

An old lady with a quavery voice answers the phone. "You've reached the Nelsons. Hello." I imagine Auntie Em and my home in Kansas perhaps. "It's Mia."

"Mary?"

"No, Mee-uh."

"I'm sorry, dear, but I think you have the wrong number."

Don't I have any decent relationships? I'm a Millennial, clearly, but Millennials have mothers, too.

One more try. Someone from my contacts list must know me. I click on a recently dialed number—someone named

Crystal. Maybe she's a friend or a sister or . . . literally anyone who knows me. She has to know me. I talked to her for three minutes and twenty-eight seconds a few days ago.

She answers on the first ring. "Hello?"

"Hi, this is . . ." I pause. My name is strange on my tongue, not because I don't like it, which I don't, but because it's my name and it feels downright foreign. Like when it takes months before your cat really feels like a Marmalade instead of a Kit Kat, which in retrospect sounds like the more fitting name— not that I remember owning a cat or anything . . . (Am I a cat lady?) "I'm Mia." Might as well be Kit Kat. "I don't know if you remember me," I say. A tear leaks out.

A half second later, she answers, "What are you calling me for? I told you, I'm done."

The line goes dead. What. The. Fuck. I'm a disaster, a hot mess, exactly the kind of person you'd expect to land in the ER in a party dress on a Tuesday. I drop the phone in my lap and try not to look as straight-out-of-a-country-song desperate as I feel. I don't need Brenda feeling like she has to be my only source of emotional support, even though she totally is.

"I'm cool. Crystal and I weren't close, I guess." Understatement of the year. "I think I'll take a break." How much rejection could one girl handle right after surviving a major head injury?

Brenda looks at the clock. "Lunch time. What do you think, would you like to order something?" When I don't respond, she says, "The egg salad isn't bad. Not as good as a hamburger, but . . ." As if there's any saving things.

Who could think of egg salad at a time like this?

"It's really good, sweetie."

Cindy agrees. "It sounds gross, but everyone likes it."

"Does it have onions?"

Brenda shakes her head.

Anything for Brenda. "Okay. I'll have an egg salad. And could one of you turn on the Kardashians again?"

———

After another binge session of nearly a whole season of the Kardashians, a knock on the doorframe makes me look up—Dr. Patel, this time with his hair brushed and a few more hours of sleep, it looks like. I set down my phone, which yielded no more information—just a bunch of apps: a weather app, a banking app, Facebook (which I don't seem to use), and some kind of off-brand dating app.[5] "I ordered your discharge papers, Mia."

"Discharge papers?"

The doctor nods. "Yep. There's nothing more we can do for you, medically speaking. It's just a matter of giving yourself time to heal and, like I said, surrounding yourself with familiar people and things."

"Doctor, I don't know anything about myself." Except for my first name. I don't even have a first and a last name, unless you count "4Realz." Like an idiot, I use a cutesy nickname

....

[5] Rush? Whatever happened to Tinder? Not that I need a date anyway. Gonna start with food and shelter. 😂

instead of a real name on every app. I can't even Google myself. My phone is a digital trash can. No one has called me and I have nowhere to go, nowhere to sleep tonight besides this hospital bed. "Is there any way I could stay just one more day?"

Two hours later, Brenda wheels me out to the curb. I'm wearing the clothes they say I arrived in: a lemon-yellow cocktail dress. It's Prada[6] and has a fitted bodice with sequins scattered about, spaghetti straps, and a short skirt. The shoes and cape (you heard me right) are dyed to match. The cape, technically a capelet, ties with a big floppy bow over one shoulder.

I left the tiara at the nurses' station for Cindy. Maybe it'll give her a thrill. A rhinestone-studded clutch just fits my phone. Besides the phone, there's a receipt for a Smartwater, a bobby pin, and two keys to who-knows-where on a rabbit's foot key chain. My lipstick is Chanel (!) in a shade of red called Pirate. (Thank you, Chanel. I needed that.)

I look pretty good except for the bloodstains, mostly on the cape besides a rusty smudge on the hemline that doesn't look too gruesome. "Sorry we couldn't wash it, sweetie. It was dry-clean only," Brenda says.

I rise from the wheelchair and take a deep breath. The traffic blurs past. I might as well be a superhero trying to jump onto the roof of a moving train, but I'm just a normal girl (I assume) trying to hop aboard life.

....

[6] Am I rich or is this a Rent the Runway situation?

As such, I untie my cape. Minus the cape, which took the brunt of the blood spatter, the dress looks nearly perfect. With a sigh, I shove the cape into a nearby trash can. It's over-flowing with fast food cups so I have to jam it in. Good-bye, designer cape.

"You can do this, Mia," Brenda says.

Do what? is the question. I have to do something, though, even if it's stupid. I can't sit in front of the hospital all day.

"I'm giving you my number. Text me when you get wher-ever you end up going." Brenda wraps me in an antibac-scented hug. She's a big woman and I just want to stay there wrapped in her soft hug forever, which is pathetic. Brenda probably has a real family. Did I ever even ask?

"Thank you. I don't know what I'd do without you." As I say it, I know it has to be the weirdest hospital good-bye ever. She might only know my first name and that I might be vegetarian, but she knows me better than anyone else. I can tell that she knows it, too; the poor woman looks like she feels responsible.

When I glance over my shoulder for a final good-bye, I see Cindy prancing in my tiara in the lobby just beyond the sliding doors and Brenda making a cut-it-out motion. I'm tempted to run back and ask if I can just hang at the nurses' station, but I can't. It's just me and my phone.

———

In a stroke of brilliance, I look up my last Uber trip and enter in the same destination: the Long Beach Museum of Art. It sounds important, just like me.

The app shows a dot where I'm supposed to meet the driver. Like a cat following a laser pointer, I walk a few feet down the block, then across the street.

My UberX shows up—I got a random upgrade to a black shiny car with a driver who looks like Enrique Iglesias, except without the face mole. Speaking of which, how do I remember Enrique Iglesias's face mole[7] and not my own last name?

"Nice dress," he says, handing me a bottle of water.

Enrique makes comfortable chitchat, and I settle in and automatically open Instagram. (It's muscle memory.) And there I am.

@Mia4Realz . . .

Pictures of me with glitter on my face, me submerged in a milk bath. Is this super glam Insta feed for real? I mean, my profile name says it is.

Questions of why I'm in a milk bath aside—like, waaaaay aside—the rest of it looks pretty damn good. The bio isn't helpful. *@Mia4Realz. SoCal 4evah. GoldRush.*

Four posts down I find my house. #homesweethome is an adorable pastel brick duplex on a palm-lined street. My only question now: do I live in the blue brick building or the pink? I assume pink.

"Driver, I'd like to change my destination." I can scope out the museum anytime. Getting home is more important,

....

[7] Which he hasn't even had since 2003! (Ask me anything besides my name.)

and I could use a milk bath. Enrique without the mole doesn't recognize the pink brick façade but he's game to figure it out. "How about we check a few of my other Insta posts and triangulate?" I suggest.

It's worth noting that I seem to be good at problem-solving. Even Enrique appears to be surprised by my use of *triangulate* in a sentence. I definitely graduated from something.

Based on a few pictures, a shot of me with a FedEx in the background (the Ocean Boulevard branch) right across from the music center, and a postcard-worthy snap of some palm trees, Enrique drives south on Ocean until he finds my front door. "How come you don't know where you live?" he asks.

"Long story, and I don't even know most of it. I lost my memory." Should I be telling strangers this? Thankfully, Enrique doesn't strike me as a serial killer.

"How?"

"Don't know that either," I say, though I'm ninety percent sure someone tried to kill me. I don't even think I'm a drama queen. A drama queen would have already been way more dramatic about the memory loss.

"When's your memory coming back?" he asks.

"Mind if I roll down the windows?" I shut my eyes and breathe in the fresh air. The temperature is perfect with a light breeze. Long Beach smells a little like pee, but mostly like ocean. Enrique plays some top forty pop stuff and I want to tell him it's okay to play his own music. I mean, I know he's not really Enrique Iglesias but . . . maybe he is? Maybe he had to become an Uber driver to make ends meet after the world forgot about him—just like it forgot about me. Maybe we can start a support group.

"I'm not sure when my memory will be back," I say. I laugh like it's funny. If anything, I might be repressing my feelings. Totally not a drama queen.

Enrique looks at me in the rearview, checking to see if I'm full-on nuts or just pleasantly unhinged (if that's a thing).

I remember what Dr. Patel told me before he discharged me: "There's often a psychological component to memory loss. You were probably suffering emotionally and psychologically at the time of the injury, which might explain why you're having difficulties latching onto your sense of self."

Dr. Patel's diagnosis was amnesia as a form of identity crisis? Ugh. It made me hate California. If he'd offered me essential oils and a pamphlet for a meditation retreat in Big Sur, I would've lost it.

"Amnesia isn't easy to treat or understand," he'd explained. "Memories change over time. Some fade. Some become stronger. Everyone has different memories of the same event. Memory is just a story we tell ourselves, not an objective truth. That's why your sense of self, which is dependent on memory, is something that fluctuates and changes."

"So basically, you're telling me that I need to make up a new story about my life," I'd said.

"Well, not exactly, but . . . yes. At least until you remember the old story."

Thank God for Instagram. I'd already written a story for

myself, and damn if it wasn't pretty.

Enrique pulls up to the pink door. Impulsively, I ask, "You want to come in?"

He gives me a suspicious look.

"No pressure," I say in a thin, high voice. "I can walk in alone. I mean, it's my house, right?" I laugh awkwardly as Enrique gives me the side-eye.

Uber asks me if I want to tip him and I say yes, if only so Enrique doesn't think I'm a total psychopath. He could have easily ditched me but he got me home.

I pull the keys from my rhinestone-studded clutch and one of them fits perfectly in the keyhole. This is my home. Final stop on the crazy train. I'm so jittery I pause to talk myself up before turning the key, like I'm about to go on stage for a per-formance. This is my house, my refuge, not some rando from my contacts list who will hang up on me. I love this house and it is going to love me back. With a deep breath, I turn the latch and open the door.

It looks like the Property Brothers have been here. The floor plan is #openconcept with tons of #naturallight and let's just say: I must love throw pillows. French doors open to a courtyard in the back, and there's a freaking statue of a nymph or an angel in a fountain. #praisejesus.

Even better, there's a guy at the kitchen table: a sexy black man in glasses and a Star Trek T-shirt featuring a big picture of Spock. The shirt says TREK YOURSELF. Is this guy my boyfriend? If so, where was he? I can't give him a pass just because he's extremely hot. He looks surprised to see me and like he's not sure what to say. He must feel bad about not checking to see if I was still alive. I don't care how good-looking he is, dude better have a damn good excuse . . .

"I'm sorry," he says.

I want to say, *you should be*. But I'm not sure that's a great way to start the next chapter of our relationship.

"I'm Max. JP didn't say anyone else would have the key." Ah. Soooo . . . not my boyfriend. He stands and walks toward me.

"I don't know who JP is but I'm pretty sure I live here," I say with complete confidence.

He eyes me skeptically. After taking in my cocktail dress and matted hair—I probably look like I just completed a walk of shame and murdered someone along the way—he says, "Then why did JP hire me to house-sit?"

God, I hope he doesn't expect me to have an answer to that.

He repeats the question with added emphasis. "Why did JP hire me to house-sit if he knew his girlfriend was going to be home?" (I take the extremely sexy compliment back.) "And what is your name, by the way?"

"Mia," I say.

"He definitely didn't mention you."

My mind is blank. Like a genius, I let a "because" hang in the air while I run through a list of options in my mind:

- He's my husband and didn't want to worry me with the responsibility of taking care of all the miniature succulents and throw pillows.

- He expected me to be out of town, too.
  (Don't ask me where. Obviously.)

- I was the original house sitter and this
  guy is the last-minute replacement.

I freestyle an answer. "Um, I was supposed to be on vacation, too, but . . . I had to cancel because . . ." I turn around and lift my hair to show him the nasty gash, which the doctors stapled together. "I had an accident." (I am Meryl Streep.)

Max's eyes widen. "Whoa."

"Tell me about it." And that's when I know I'm in. Max is a nice person; he won't kick an injured woman out of JP's house (which could still be my house but the odds aren't looking good) and onto the street.

"What happened?" he asked.

"Not sure," I say. "Whatever happened knocked the memory right out of me. I just got out of the hospital an hour ago."

"And came straight here?" The confusion on his face is apparent. "Who drove you home from the hospital? And were they sure you lived here?" He looks around the room. "Where'd they go anyway? You have amnesia and they just dropped you off like it's no big deal?"

I laugh in a way that could become bitter if things continue this way. "I Ubered over. The driver was super nice and helped me find my address."

"Using what?" Max looks confounded.

I breeze past the question. I don't want to get into my Instagram sleuthing just yet. "Speaking of which, I should give him a review. He went above and beyond."

"Umm, five stars for sure. But . . . what . . . ?"

"It's totally okay." I comfort him about the uncertainty of my situation. "I just need to . . . Trek myself." I grin. "And my instincts say that I live here." Really, this place *fits*. There's a Degas on the wall and it doesn't look like a poster from Target. This is the kind of place where a girl with a designer cape would live. I Trek myself so hard.

Max looks down at his shirt. "Uhh . . . I don't think that's what this shirt means. I'm not trying to get rid of you or anything." He looks at me so sincerely I can't not believe him. "But I'm still not sure this is your house."

Okay. I trust him. I wish he'd quit with the details, though. I just need to lie down. But I can see he's still chewing on the issue. "You have a key," he says, "which implies that you've probably been here before, but that doesn't mean you live here."

"No, I'm sure it's my house." I can stretch a false sense of confidence pretty far.

"You could be the maid." He points this out as if we're in math class and everything is logical and makes sense.

"I arrived at the hospital wearing a crown." I gesture to my cocktail dress. "And this. If anything, I *have* a maid." Unless I'm J.Lo and this is a *Maid in Manhattan* situation, but I doubt he's seen that.

"Just saying. I have a key and I definitely don't live here . . ."

I collapse on one of the kitchen stools and rest my head in my hands. "Dude, JP is probably my husband." (At least in this version of the story.) "Who knows, maybe this is my house and he's my executive assistant."

He laughs hard at that. "I'm looking forward to when you call JP and ask if he's your secretary or your husband."

Apparently JP comes off as a lot more important than me. Go figure. That's when I notice the pile of mail sitting on the counter in front of me. I start brazenly flicking through, ignoring Max's side-eye. All addressed to JP. Nothing has my name on it, unless you count the ones marked for the "current resident."

Glancing back at the TV, Max says, "Well, whether you live here or not, you need somewhere to stay tonight. Want to watch *Our Food System* with me? Might as well settle in." He points to a half-eaten take-out pizza. "Help yourself, if you're hungry."

"Maybe I'll grab some chocolate." There's a bowl filled with Jacques-o-late bars on the counter. This chocolate is freaking everywhere these days. "Once you go Jacques-o-late, you never go back" is the company's slogan. The ads all feature women biting chocolate bars with orgasmic looks on their faces. I think it's . . . okay, as in I will eat all of it, even though it's missing a little something. I can't put my finger on it.

I should probably want to find out more about Max—I mean, what if he's lying? What if *he's* actually JP and he's just messing with me? What if *I'm* JP and we've never met in person before so he doesn't actually know what I look like? Can I trust him? What are my standards normally? "You're not a serial killer, are you?"

He yawns. "No one would say yes to that. Especially a serial killer."

"Oh my God. You *are* a serial killer."

He takes a while picking out the best slice of pizza, the same one I would have grabbed, with the ideal toppings-to-cheese ratio. "I'm black, Mia. Statistically, there's zero chance of me being a serial killer. As long as you don't call the cops and catch a stray bullet, you're good."

Too black and too cute to be a killer. And he shares pizza.

Before I move to the couch, I glance at the TV. The documentary playing in the background is about how humans are killing themselves with corn syrup and nitrates. At the moment, a slow death by trace amounts of anything seems to be the least of my concerns. "I'm tired. Can you point me to the master bedroom?" I say this as naturally and breezily as possible, hoping he won't say *hell no* and make me sleep on the couch.

He hesitates a second, glances at my head wound, and says, "Sure. We'll figure out what's really going on in the morning." He says this in a reassuring way, not a threatening way. Gotta love a sweet nerd.

While he carries a glass to the sink, I casually check out the bookshelves while munching on more Jacques-o-late. It's all fancy leather volumes or first editions with a few photos artfully arranged across the ledges of the shelves. An attractive man with dark, side-parted hair and a Prince Charming jawline is in several, along with people who might be his family members. JP?

I'm not in any of them.

Max leads me down a hallway filled with original art-work, lit gallery style, to a master bedroom big enough for a California-king-size bed. I check out the crown molding and a slightly domed ceiling painted to look like a soothing sky. The bedding is cumulus-clouds-level fluffy and the whole room smells like lavender. Navy-blue walls and a few manly paintings (originals, of course) take the vibe from spa day to European. It could be a man's or a woman's room. Long Beach is nice enough, but this place looks like it should be in Laguna or Malibu or France, even.

Max watches my reaction. "I missed this place so much," I say with a wistful smile.

He laughs because, really, who wouldn't?

After Max leaves, I search for any evidence of myself in the bedroom, some sign that I belong here, that it's "our" room and not just JP's. Condoms in the nightstand and a second tooth-brush in the bathroom (mine?), a couple of T-shirts that look too small for a man, depending on how tight JP likes 'em—and that's it. The nightstand on what is probably my side of the bed gives me hope. The *US Weekly* could definitely be mine and the book about a sexy vampire is a solid maybe, but who knows? I mean, doesn't everyone love celebrities and vampires?

I'm just going to say I'm home, but am I?

CHAPTER

THREE

I wake up on Friday morning in the kind of bed that swallows a person whole, surrounded by luxurious layers of comforters and pillows. It's the style of bed you normally only see on a showroom floor but never in real life since no one except for Real Housewives would ever buy all the stuff on the display model.[8] Sun filters in through the windows, casting everything in picture-perfect light, and a soft breeze ruffles the gauzy curtains. It takes a minute for me to remember I'm not at a couples resort in Jamaica. Pink house, Ocean Boulevard, cute house sitter who is hopefully not a serial killer. And me, whoever I am.

I reach for my phone, which is sleeping peacefully on JP's side of the bed, and give it a little tap good morning. It responds with nothing. No texts. No notifications. My phone,

....

[8] Am I a Real Housewife?

though useful, is not a generous lover. What I need is someone who knows me, my social security number, and where I keep all the cute shoes. My phone is one of those crushes that sucks up every ounce of energy and gives nothing back. Pretty sure I've had a couple of those. I can't remember the names, but I can feel the scars.

Like with a bad crush, I can't give up. I open up the texts app, knowing there's nothing. Email, however, is a different story. When I see that I have three new emails, I sit up straight and grip the phone tighter. This is it, someone who knows me sent me a message.

But no, two of the emails are from organic tampon start-ups, both boxed delivery services that solve all the menses-related problems a modern woman could have. The remaining email is from Jacques-o-late. *Once you go Jacques-o-late, you never go back*, the subject line reads. Jacques-o-late, it seems, wants me to try their new flavor: white chocolate. Ha! The mofos at Jacques-o-late must think they're pretty funny.

I delete all of the above in keeping with my practice. Inbox zero—my one accomplishment in life so far. It's a little weird that I delete texts too, but I guess I must have just KonMari'd the shit out of my life. And really, does any of this electronic communication spark joy? No. The fact that I disposed of them points to the fact that I'm highly evolved and not beholden to my phone like the rest of the world.

Decluttering isn't ideal in an amnesia situation, though. If I could go back in time and give myself a piece of advice before deleting all traces of my life, I'd whisper in my pre-amnesia ear, *Hey girl, props on being efficient and all, but you're gonna need those someday. See that email from those two chicks at MIT who know just what kind of wine you want—save that one . . . or, maybe, even one from a person you've met.*

Instagram, though, I didn't declutter that. Let's see what kind of guy you are, JP . . . At least a few of the shots on my profile page are with JP, who I recognize from the photos on the bookshelf.

1. There's a picture of JP alone and unbearably handsome in a tailored suit. It's captioned: "And he has a French accent!" 😍

2. There's a selfie of us at a winery, grapevines in the background and wineglasses in our hands. The caption: "Me and boo." 🍷 ♡

3. Finally, a picture of us in a group of hot young things dressed for the club. I'm wearing a statement dress with dramatic puffed sleeves that barely covers my ass. JP is giving me an appreciative look. No caption. His looks says it all. He wants me.

So . . . according to Insta: JP is my boo and he's definitely into me, or at least my ass. Even with a head injury, I'm smart enough to know there's a difference. This is all reassuring information and normal boyfriend stuff.

An incoming text pings and my heart leaps into my throat. *My first text ever.* The name pops up as Frenchie.

I miss you.

Can't say I miss Frenchie so I respond with a 👋.

The three dots appear and reappear a few times, indicating that he is typing and erasing and can't figure out what to say. Finally he writes, Is everything okay? U still mad?

Now I really want to know who this guy is and what should I be mad about. Attempted murder?

Sorry, but who is this? I lost my phone and all my contacts.

I'm sorry love! Relieved there's a reason u haven't called, tho. 😄

Glad that solves his problem, but still . . . WHO is this?

😂 Only the love of your life.

I'm thinking, *Then where the hell are you?!* but I write, And who might that be?, which I hope comes off as flirty.

Frenchie responds with a selfie, a mocking expression on his extremely handsome, made-to-play-a-doctor-on-television face. And my previous detective work pays off instantly. Frenchie is JP, not to mention—breaking news—"the love of my life!" Funny that I haven't left any of my stuff at his house, but I'll save that question for later.

Where are you? I ask.

Switzerland. U know that . . . r u ok?

Stupid me, just waking up. Feelin groggy. When r u coming back?

Sunday. I miss you.

Emotionless, I scroll back through our convo. JP misses me. Maybe he even loves me? At the very least, I belong to someone. I belong here in this beautiful bird's nest of a bed— not in the lost and found at the local ER, getting shooed onto the street without so much as a follow-up visit. I'm young, gorgeous, and shacked up in the lap of luxury with a hand-some rich dude. I need to keep it that way.

Except, who is he? What are we like together? Am I sweet (doesn't seem likely, but maybe)? Will he like me now that I'm damaged? (Even one day into my new experience of the world and I'm wondering what a man will think of me.) I shove that thought into the closet where I presume the rest of my middle-school insecurities are trapped and put on my big-girl panties. (Lacy, low-rise hipsters, thank you pre-amnesia self.)

Before I get any deeper into this convo, I consult my assistant. "Siri, who is JP Howard?"

JP Howard. Short for Jacques-Pierre. (Ooh la la!). Date of birth is 1983, which makes him . . . (I open my calendar app) . . . 2020–1983=37. A thirty-seven-year-old rich guy with a French name. So far, so good.

Better yet, there's a Wikipedia entry about him.

I stop eating the chocolate bar that is, at this very moment, on the way to my mouth. Jacques-Pierre, my boyfriend, is the creator of Jacques-o-late. *Once you go Jacques-o-late* . . . runs through my mind.

This is better than waking up as Meghan Markle.

Jacques-o-late, according to its website, comes in five flavors: dark, light, medium, caramel, and white. They all have nuts. Size: king only.[9]

And he's saving the rainforest, at least according to the

....

[9] Is JP compensating for something with his chocolate bars? 😱 🤣

website. Jacques-o-late only buys fair-trade Jacques-o-late beans from Honduras, Ecuador, the Dominican Republic, and Trinidad and Tobago. The company always pays three times the going market value, and twenty percent of profits go to buying back rainforest. A boxed inset on the website contains an interview with a dignified old man. The website calls him a Jacques-o-late farmer. In his words: "Jacques-o-late has saved my way of life."

What's more, JP was almost a capital-B Bachelor. According to the internet, JP is the one who got away from ABC executives, who desperately wanted him for *The Bachelor*. Since then, the show has tried to recruit him nearly every season and he's said no.

Wide-eyed, I look up from my phone. *The Bachelor* chose me? I woke up to a fairy tale. Cindy is going to eat this up. I'm going to have to drop by the ICU and report that I'm practically married to an almost-Bachelor who makes Jacques-o-late. Maybe JP and I can throw a lavish party for the nurses when he returns.

I click on a link to a podcast called *Dreamboats: A Podcast for Lovers of Sexy Yachts, Etc!* The link is purple instead of red because I've clicked on it before. It looks like JP was a guest on an episode called "Yachtastic Men!" Not much subtext happening here. I hit play and after a little intro music and "brought to you by" statement, the host starts in.

"OMG people. I'm sitting here with someone I've always wanted to meet. I'm such a fan! JP, I've been following you forever, even before Jacques-o-late."

"Why, thank you. It's good to be here, Jessica."

"So tell me about your boat . . ."

"Well, it's a 60-foot—"

The hosts laughs and cuts him off. "Just kidding. I don't really care about your boat."

Sounding confused, JP says, "Isn't this a show about boats?"

"Silly, that's just a pretext. Tell me about you. Tell me about Jacques-o-late." Just like everyone, she says *Jacques-o-late* like she is whispering it into her lover's ear.

He sounds sincerely flattered, which is cute. He's confident but not obnoxiously so.

"What do you want in a woman?" Jessica asks. "Just so we all know who to pretend to be." Then she titters.

JP returns a polite laugh. "Well, then, don't pretend. I want the same thing every guy wants. I want the girl next door, someone sweet who I can be myself around."

"Hmmm." The host sounds skeptical. "Now let's discuss the elephant in the room and I'm not talking about your Jacques-o-late bar . . ."

"What's that?"

"Your bank account, obviously. *Forbes* listed your net worth as $2.3 billion."

"God, is that what I'm worth? I only have $60 in my wallet."

"Come off it, JP. You are obviously not eating generic-brand mac 'n' cheese."

So far so good on JP. He's rich, handsome, a chocolate

lover, and he thinks he's the love of my life. That's not exactly the same as saying that he loves me, but close enough. I'm ready to respond.

I miss you too!

Don't ask me why I don't lead with the head injury. I guess I need more than a mansion from him. I want to know who I'm talking to before I confess my situation. He might be amazing, but he's still a handsome rich guy, and I know what that means, even without a brain: he can get away with anything.

Phew. Thought you might still be mad.

Huh . . . back to red flag number one. Should I be?

Hopefully it was just a run-of-the-mill argument about how big our next yacht should be. I mean, what else could we have to worry about? There must be a thousand dollars' worth of throw pillows in this room alone. I probably just toss them in the cart at the checkout like cash register mints at whatever luxury furniture store JP and I shop at.

No need to be mad, *cherie*. I'm going to make it up to you. Do you want to see a pic?

A dick pic? Is he *that* kind of guy?

Never mind. No pics. I'm making you wait.

Not that I mind a dick pic, but I'd prefer an actual present.

Let's just say your present is almost as sparkly as your personality.

Dear lord, a sparkly personality?! Just send me the dick pic. I'll take it over the lies. If only Brenda were here to walk me through this convo.

I text: 😂 Have you met me?

He responds with: 😂 😂 😂 ♡ You'll love it. Although might not work with your hair. 😜

I reach up and touch my hair. The undercut might be a little edgy for him, given that he looks like the crown prince of France. And let me tell you, it doesn't do much to cover up the staples.

Thankfully he can't talk long. He's all: Gotta go. Ttyl. 😘

I send him a quick xoxo, but I'm confused. I want to remember him, to feel my heart spark with feeling, but there's nothing. Before I set down the phone, I glance at the Instagram picture of us at the winery. I don't remember the day or why we were laughing in the picture. I'm pretty sure it doesn't matter, though. JP is definitely the kind of guy I can fall in love with all over again. We can have one of those "We fell in love twice" stories. I have until Sunday to prepare.

In the living room, Max looks like he's been up for at least five hours typing furiously at his laptop, even though it's barely past eight and he's wearing another T-shirt that I'm not sure I get. IT'S NOT YOUR LIMBIC SYSTEM, IT'S MINE, it says.[10] He's cute in that slouchy grad student sort of way, which makes me think maybe he is one. On a scale of one to ten, I'd give him a, "If he delivered my pizza, I'd probably invite him in for a slice." And by pizza, I mean pizza.

"Morning," I say with a little pose, like I'm making my entrance onto the set of an old-fashioned sitcom, pausing just long enough before my next line so the audience can applaud.

....

[10] Do I need a PhD to understand your T-shirts, Max?!

Max doesn't applaud, but he does look up from the computer. "Hey. You feeling better?"

"A little." I still feel like I had a major head injury two days ago, but how bad could it be? I woke up to a gorgeous home, a lifetime supply of Jacques-o-late, and a boyfriend with a net worth of $2.3 billion.

"Well, it's nice to meet you officially in the light of day, Mia." He holds out his hand and we shake like we're meeting at a networking event instead of the home of a super rich dude who neither of us really knows.

"Is there any coffee?" The question rolls off my tongue before I can think twice about it. Some sub-basement level of my brain knows what I need.

"I just drank the last cup, but I can make more." With that, he stands up and starts rummaging through the kitchen for coffee supplies. The smell of Italian espresso hits me hard when he opens a bag of beans with a swan on it. It hits me harder than texting with JP or opening the door to this house. I guess I know who I've had the longest relationship with, and I take plenty of cream and sugar with it.

Noticing my swoony expression, Max says, "He has bags of this stuff flown in from Italy. I'm pretty sure it's the best coffee in the world. It must be, if JP buys it."

I sit down in the space Max vacated, directly in front of his laptop. I see a Gchat window open and flashing, from someone named Fay, and catch a glimpse of her last message. Max, you're a liar.

Whoa. That sounds intense on several levels.

When he catches me spying, he reaches over the counter and shuts the laptop.

"Your boss?" I ask.

"That's what she likes to think," he says, his voice ninety-nine percent sarcasm.

"Ahhh, girlfriend." I don't need my memory to understand that dynamic.

"Ex, but we still work together."

"Yikes. What kind of job?" I give him a once-over and guess, "Tattoo parlor?"

He laughs. "Close. I'm a neuroscientist at USC."

That explains the T-shirts, I guess. "What does that mean? What does a neuroscientist do?"

"Well, I study how structures in the brain affect cognition and behavior."[11]

While talking to him, I google "annual salary neuroscientist" because it sounds like a fancy job, and I don't get why he's house-sitting. Google comes back with $82,240. "Sounds like a sweet gig. Shouldn't you own this house?"

He shakes his head. "That's a common misconception. I'm a postdoc, which means I'm still training, essentially. Eventually I'd like to run my own lab, but it takes years and a lot of publishing and funding to get to that level. Meanwhile, I still gotta make a buck. I don't have to tell you what the cost of living is in LA."

I can believe that one.

....

[11] All that and he still doesn't understand why his ex is mad at him.

"My research is aimed at coming up with a better lie detection system," he tells me, unprompted. I sit back and prepare for the elevator pitch that I see coming.

"Oooh . . ."

"Polygraph tests are shit. They just measure increased heart rate and respiration, but those are associated with anxiety, which can be caused by anything."

"So how's it going?"

"Fay and I are working on a mobile brain-imaging system that can be implemented in interrogation scenarios. Very specific structures in the brain light up when a subject is lying, so if you scanned a person's brain, you'd get a much better picture of their truthfulness than with a polygraph."

"So you're really into The Truth."

"Isn't everyone?"

I shrug. "No clue what I'm into. Mainly Instagram, from the looks of it."

That's enough science for me. "So, Max," I say. "Now that I'm *home* . . ." I really lean into the word, owning it, "I don't need a house sitter, you know."

He nods, taking his early dismissal in stride. "I'd like to talk with JP before I take off. He was very specific about how things should be handled."

Hmm. I'm not sure I want JP and Max talking about me. If I don't live here, Max doesn't need to be the one who tells JP that I've moved in.

"Never mind. It'd probably be better if you stayed. I'm going to be busy the next few days." And really, that feels a little safer. I already lost Brenda. I kind of want to keep Max.

"So what are you doing today?" he asks, glancing at my staples. "Do you have follow-up appointments or . . ." He trails off.

I shake my head no.

"Really? They just let you out?" He seems unable to wrap his mind around that. "But you don't even know who you are."

"As soon as I figure out my life, I'll be fine." I found the boyfriend and #homesweethome, but I have a lot left: my job, my friends, my family, and my own apartment. "I post a lot on Instagram. I'm pretty sure if I retrace my steps, I'll figure out exactly who I am, or at least all of the major things."

"What's your Insta handle?" he asks. I tell him and a second later he says, "Gotcha." He reads my bio aloud. "Mia4Realz. SoCal 4evah. GoldRush. What's GoldRush?" he asks.

"It's a documentary about gold miners in Alaska." My Google search result featured pictures of bearded men in hard hats. I have no idea why this doc would be important to me. Maybe I'm involved in filmmaking? This is LA, after all.

While I wonder if other people understand my bio, my phone pings. I have an Instagram notification that @BlackEinstein314 has just followed me. I smile at Max and follow him back with a "Let's do this baby" nod. I don't even know myself but I'm not sure if he can keep up with me, especially on Instagram.

His bio reads, *Neuroscience postdoc, USC. The truth is out there.* Which is like the most adorable thing ever.

@BlackEinstein314, though? Leaves a question mark over his ego. It might be outsize.

I see a picture of him smiling in front of a fancy microscope and a few pictures of a pretty girl further back in his feed. The captions couldn't be drier. Me and Fay at the 2019 Society for Neuroscience Conference in Chicago. Fay presenting her poster, "The Role of the Parietal Cortex in Deception."[12] There are almost no selfies. Ninety percent of my posts are of me, mostly with other hot girls. I don't know what that says about me.

I switch back to my profile. "Take a look at my last four posts. I'm trying to figure out what they mean." They include:

- A shot of a latte with a heart swirled in the foam on top. (Not very interesting, but it might be a spot where I hang regularly.)

- A picture of me on a yacht, in a sailor hat and bikini. A gorgeous girl, also in sailor-wear, has her arm slung over my shoulder.

- A selfie at the beach.

- Me at some fancy party kissing an ice sculpture of Cupid.

Max gives the posts a once-over. "That coffee shop from your first post is just around the corner. I recognize the cups."

....

[12] Note to self: google parietal cortex.

"Further proof that I spend a lot of time here."

"What about the rest of them?"

"Dunno. But I definitely need a car before I investigate further."

"Do you *have* a car?"

I smile wickedly. "I bet JP does."

He gives me a concerned look. "Serious concussion, amnesia, and no follow-up visits. I'm not sure if exploring LA in a Ferrari is the best idea. Reduced stress and extra sleep is literally the recommended treatment for you."

With a shrug, I say, "What else am I gonna do? My life isn't going to find me. And my doctor did say I need to get back into my normal routines. Can't do that if I don't know what my routines are."

"Do you even remember how to get around?"

"No one knows how to get anywhere. Google is the only one who knows anything anymore. My brain is irrelevant." It's true. Everyone was worried about Big Brother, but when he actually showed up, we all signed on and admitted we couldn't live without him. It was a full-on voluntary situation. Sorry, George Orwell! Also, why do I remember George Orwell but not my father?

"You do realize I'm a neuroscientist."

"I know," I say, nodding sympathetically. "I'm sorry about that. At least you're not selling DVDs."

"True, that would be worse. Speaking of my job . . ."

"I can't wait to find out where I work." I hope it's not a dumb job.

"Mia, has anyone called to look for you?"

"No, but I know I have a good job. I'm probably the boss, which is why my boss hasn't called." I gesture to my Prada gown. "And I drink fancy coffee." Speaking of which, I hold up the post of the beautiful latte I drank last week. "Forget JP's coffee. Let's get a latte before you head to work."

There isn't much at JP's for me to wear. Luckily my cocktail dress can go from day to night almost effortlessly, and it looks remarkably good considering I took an ambulance ride in it earlier this week. I throw on a jean jacket, which I think might even be mine. If I don't say so myself, I look like an '80s rock star and pretty much every other person wandering around Long Beach, except without a skateboard and a joint.

Based on the clothing selection, I definitely haven't moved into JP's yet. We are only toothbrush-level serious. How many clicks below marriage is that? Close enough to spend the cash I found in his sock drawer, that's for sure. I stuff it in my clutch and head out the back door. Coffee's on JP.

According to Max, who's easily impressed by cars, apparently, JP's Ferrari 550 Maranello is red. Actually, it's Pirate red, the same as my lips. My rhinestone clutch in hand, I hit the unlock button on the key fob (thanks for keeping your keys on the key holder by the door, JP!). The car beeps a hello and I hop in the driver's seat. "You coming, Max?" I say with a flirtatious smile.

Today, I will find my life.

———

At Cuppa Cuppa, a hipster coffee shop on the corner of Ocean and Linden, the woman behind the counter says, "Good morning!" like she knows me. "The usual?" she asks.

I say "Yes" like she asked me if I want a million dollars and puppy.[13] I'm a regular! I could scream it from the rooftops.

All efficiency, she boots up the machine and starts frothing milk for my usual (!) drink. I'm definitely rich, BTW, because it's an $8 maple latte. The maple syrup is probably sourced from Quebecois maple trees and smuggled across the border in a lumberjack's ass. Actually, no. I'll pay for standard transport. When the chaos of milk frothing is over, I move in closer and say to the barista, "So I know this might be strange, but I got in an accident a few days ago and lost my memory."

She gasps and claps a hand to her mouth. "My God! I just saw you a few days ago and you were fine!"

Excitement bubbles up. "If you could tell me anything you know, I would appreciate it." I look at the coffee. "Like, the only thing I know about myself is that I drink maple lattes."

"I'm sorry, but I don't really know you. You come in all the time but you just sit and look at your phone. Sometimes you go outside to have a conversation. On your phone." She thinks for a moment and says, "Every now and then you meet up with a friend."

"Do you know any of them?"

She shakes her head. "I'm sorry, but this is the most we've

....

[13] Am I a dog person?

ever talked except for that one time when you lost your phone
and I helped you look for it."

Hope blossoms in my chest at the speed of a flower opening in time lapse. Maybe she learned something about me.

"It was in the bathroom."

The flower of hope dies an even faster time-lapse death.

Max cuts in. "Let's just get some food. You'll feel better.
Blood sugar is directly correlated to optimism."

I blurt out, "Oh fuck off, Max!" I wonder if he knows
that's me flirting.

He laughs. "Good one." I'm filled with relief. I seem to
have a personality.

A sign on the front counter advertises a protein bowl with
quinoa and my heart sputters. "Could I have a protein bowl,
please?"

"Of course. Would you like chicken on that?"

"Uhh . . . I'm vegetarian," I say, in honor of Brenda.

Max gives me a funny look. So does the barista, but
whatever.

"Just guessing," I confess to Max, and he laughs.

"Why would you want to eliminate all the best foods in
your do-over life?"

"People eat 27.43 chickens annually, which I'm pretty sure
has far-reaching environmental consequences—maybe even
incidental rainforest destruction, which JP and I are both taking a stand against." Don't ask me how I came up with that.

Instead of calling me out for my bullshit statistic, he says,

"I feel like I might eat more chickens than that. Like, twice that many."

"I choose to let them walk the earth freely." I can feel my halo glowing. It's the first truly positive decision I've made, at least since waking up. And talk about selfless.

At a table on the back patio, I take a bite of my quinoa. Fuck if Brenda wasn't right. I love quinoa. It's hearty and flavorful, and I feel saintly for eating it. "Let's talk more about quinoa, shall we?"

Max takes a sip of his coffee and gets a little foam on his nose. "I feel like you're only doing this because there are more answers about quinoa than about your identity. But if you want to."

Without a second thought, I lean over the table and wipe the foam off his face. I lick it off my fingers while Max watches, his eyes lingering on my mouth. Does he think . . . ? I dismiss the thought and announce, "I was right. Totally not a germophobe."

"I wonder if you're normally this scattered. Did the doctor say anything about the recovery process?"

"Not really," I lie.

Expect to be confused and easily exhausted. Avoid any stress. Get plenty of rest and stick to a routine. Dr. Patel didn't mention that I would be energetic and highly curious about the food system . . .

"So, quinoa . . ." I scan my memory. "Obviously it's the most nutritious food on earth, and soon to be the most nutritious food in the galaxy. NASA is starting a quinoa farm in outer space. Have you heard?"

Max looks at me suspiciously. "Where exactly?"

"Like I remember. On a space station, maybe. Or Mars."

"I guess they had to think of something to do when Congress cut the space program," he says drily.

"The United Nations also said it might save Earth."

"I could talk about quinoa all day," he says flatly. "Buuuuut . . . I feel like you should go back to JP's and rest. A nap might even increase your chances of recovering your memory. How can you expect your brain to recall anything if you're stressing it out with all kinds of new information?"

Like facts about quinoa? I wonder if anyone has been derailed by quinoa before. As soon as I ask the question, I realize the answer is yes. Obviously. "You're right, Max. Enough about quinoa. It's so 2013 anyway. I need to focus on me. But first I have a question for you."

He waits attentively. For just a second I wonder what Max is avoiding in his own life. There must be something else he's supposed to be doing right now, but here he is, patiently listening to me prattle on about quinoa.

"Do you know anything about JP?" I flip back to an Insta post of us. My hair is styled. It's a cute selfie featuring my hair when it looked good, chic blond waves with an undercut. Hipster from one side, Grace Kelly from the other. JP stands next to the Grace Kelly side of my head, and I wonder if he avoids my bald side all the time. He seems more like a Grace Kelly kind of guy.

"Not much. I met him through one of the people in my lab. She was supposed to house-sit for him last time but had to cancel at the last minute. She didn't want to let JP down because she sits for him all the time and needs the money. I filled in because—"

"I get it." Max is a super good guy and stepped in to help some chick in his lab. He might be the nicest person I've ever met, besides Brenda.

"Plus he pays well and his coffee is definitely better than mine."

"Yeah, sweet side hustle. Have you ever met him?"

"We crossed paths once. He showed off his Scotch collection. After he found out I'm a neuroscientist, he told me everything he knows about the brain." Looking amused, Max says, "I can't say much, except that he's loaded and he doesn't know as much about cognition as he thinks he does."

I move the food in my bowl around. The avocado is already turning brown. "My quinoa bowl is missing something."

"Chicken," he says. After a dramatic pause, he adds, "Maybe you should focus on saving yourself instead of chickens, Mia."

I look up from the browning avocado and into his eyes. Does he genuinely think I'm in danger? And why? Because I lost my entire life? Because an unknown person conked me on the head? Or because I'm not following proper head injury aftercare? Ultimately, it doesn't matter. I can't take care of myself if I don't even know who I am or what there is to be scared of.

CHAPTER

FOUR

I think I'm the kind of person who always offers to give a friend a ride, so I tell Max I'll drop him off at his lab. I want to stay on brand. Plus, driving around the city will probably help me remember things. On Google Maps, Max's office, the Hedco Neuroscience Building, is practically next door.

"You have to take the 110. Are you sure?" Max says.

"Yep." I'm just that cool.

In the car, I learn that:

A) Max has always wanted to be a neuroscientist (which makes me think his mother planted the idea because no little boy would come up with that on his own, meaning that he must have very caring and invested, though slightly overbearing, parents, which in turn makes me wonder WHERE THE FUCK ARE MY PARENTS?), but on to the next point . . .

B) he believes that everything makes sense and can be logically explained,[14] and

C) his favorite movie is *The Matrix*. Don't get me wrong, I like Keanu Reeves, but I preferred him in *Bill & Ted*. In fact, I kind of feel like I've time-traveled to 2020, except without Ted. Or Bill. I can't remember which one Keanu played. Not that it matters. They should remake the movie with me and Keanu.

As I park in front of Hedco—did they misspell head?—I ask, "What kind of mad scientist, hypnotized monkey experience do you have going on in there?" The building is made of nice-looking red brick with art deco features and looks nothing like how I'd imagine a brain research center. In general, it looks like all of the other buildings on campus, but this one is full of attractive scientists arguing about transgenic mice and dating around. Someone should get a camera in there and start recording.

"No monkeys, just data," he says. "But it's some good, juicy data."

Juicy data? Max is living a lie, but I'm not going to be the one to break it to him. "Have fun doing math with your vindictive ex," I say.

"I always do," he replies in a *see you later, honey* tone.

"I'm off to find my mind. It looks like I might have left it at the beach." That's where all my Insta posts are taken, at least.

....

[14] Isn't that cute! I, of course, respectfully disagree.

With a worried look on his face, he says, "Call me if you need help. Anything."

I smile and nod at his needless concern. He should be more worried about himself and his own drama den. I've got my life handled.

"You had a serious head injury and don't even know who you are. You can expect periods of profound exhaustion and confusion. Unexpected nausea and vomiting aren't out of the question."

I posted a selfie this morning and got 220 likes already. If that doesn't say near-full recovery, nothing will. "I'm fine, Max. Plus I have Siri. My digital assistant's got me covered." It's like he doesn't understand it's 2020. "You just do your thing. I'll pick you up after you're done studying brains." I don't have time to linger; I have two posts to investigate: 1) sexy beach selfie, and 2) yacht selfie.

After I drop Max off, my phone buzzes. Dear God in heaven, hallowed be thy name, thy kingdom come, thy will be done: my texter's name is Kobra. (And I might be Catholic?)

Hey Sweetcheeks, Crystal ain't answering my texts.

Me either. How could I forget Crystal of the *What are you calling me for? I'm done* phone call. Unless I know tons of Crystals?

I'll go check on her. Have plans tonight for a private boat ride to Catalina. Don't want her to miss out.

Damn! Sounds like a lucky girl.

It's in the cards for her. 💰 🐍
Go get 'em, Kobra. 🤍 🐍
Oh, I'm a big bad snake. 🐍

I'm guessing Kobra is from a trailer park and has chipped at least one tooth opening a beer bottle. Still, he sounds okay . . . I think.

Good luck with Crystal, dude!

I wonder if I know Kobra for real. Maybe he and Crystal and I are super awesome friends. I search my Insta friends for Kobra and . . .

There he is. @TheBigSqueeze562. He's almost naked in his profile photo, undoubtedly to show off his bomb tattoo. A life-size python coils around his torso and extends down his arm, ending at his wrist. The snake's jaw is unhinged and it appears that Kobra's hand is coming out of the snake's mouth. Rad tattoo, dude.

His posts feature him fronting like a gangsta all over LA, plus some close-ups of the tattoo. What appear to be stripes from a distance are words, and when I look closer, I can make out a Bible verse. *The serpent was more crafty than any of the wild animals the Lord God had made.* Then, more directly, *I am the devil. Take the fucking apple, Eve.*

As far as Bible translations go, I'm giving him props: creepy but clearer and more accessible. Way to bring Genesis into the modern world.

His Instagram bio actually says, *Snake charmer. Preacher. DM me ladies.*

Crystal might be out of her mind. Either that or Kobra is

not as creepy as his tattoo makes him seem, which is common with tattooed guys. Hard to tell till you meet 'em. That's why you can never trust online profiles.

Back to me and all my selfies . . .

According to the tag, my beach selfie was taken on Long Beach. Based on the island in the background, it was taken next to the third lifeguard station in. It looks like any other California beach except for one thing: the island just offshore looks like the lowest-price-point Lego set, an overly simplified version of what an island should be. It has one palm tree, one glass building, and no people. Creepy.

Just like the rest of the town of Long Beach, the beach itself is filled with people on the raggedy edge of California. Lots of young and beautiful people who look like they might be on drugs and could benefit from a shower. Not quite as square or polished as Pasadena. Not as much money as WeHo. Not as glitzy as Sunset. Also, more drugs in plain sight.

In my selfie, a breeze is ruffling my perfectly highlighted hair, the sideswept bangs covering one eye like I'm Marilyn Monroe. The nearby lifeguard station hints that I might be on the set of *Baywatch*. As for the push-up bikini top—it's doing its job and then some.

I trudge down the beach to find lifeguard station three. I don't expect to find anyone there but I'm going one hundred percent Veronica Mars on this investigation and not skipping a single step. Maybe I'm a PI or a cop! Who knows. When I find the spot where I took the picture, I'm right outside some public restrooms. In front of the restrooms, a homeless guy who appears to be tweaking hard (on meth?) has built a semipermanent structure. Was I really smiling like I was on a Hawaiian vacation right in front of him? Maybe it wasn't even a selfie. Maybe this guy, or someone like him, took my picture. Maybe I simply don't *see* the homeless. That's what they always say about rich people. Have I been walking through life oblivious to the human suffering around me?

The homeless guy takes out his earbuds and walks over. "Yo Mia, you got a couple of bucks? I need bus fare."

"What?" My jaw drops. "You know me?"

"Duh."

"How?" Do I volunteer my time at the soup kitchen? Do I regularly give spare change to panhandlers?

"Like you don't know?"

"I don't."

"Thursday free lunch at that church." He squints harder at me. "What are you on today?" I volunteer to feed the homeless! God, I love myself. "What about bus fare?"

I give him $10 of sock-drawer money because I'm that kind of person.

He fist-bumps me and gives me a "thanks," and then, with the confidence of someone who believes he'll actually see me around, he says, "See ya around."

I pull out my phone and check out the next post to investigate. My yacht is just a ways down the shoreline at the Long Beach Marina. Or it could be a friend's yacht, or just one of the many yachts I frequent in my daily life. I tagged it #TheGoodLife. The yacht's name, I suppose? Did I pick that name?

The Good Life is not hard to find. She's parked on the end of the first dock. Or is it a pier? IDK.

When I catch sight of her, I feel all sparkly and effervescent and my breath catches at her beauty. I laughed at Cindy when she said I might wake up to a dream, but she was right. I'm *living* the dream. The Good Life is probably the fanciest boat at this particular dock. She's big and white with lots of decks and undoubtedly stocked with more martini glasses than flotation devices, like any good boat should be. "Maybe this is where I had my accident," I say as I scan the decks. I could have reenacted *Overboard*.

I study the Insta post once more. I'm with a girl I didn't tag. We look like models having the time of our lives, and really, why wouldn't we be? Young, beautiful, rich, on a yacht—what more could a person want?

I step onto the boat and turn a full 360 degrees to take in every inch of the view. It's so pretty. I can't believe I own a boat?! Well, a skeptic like Max couldn't believe it. *I* can because I'm open to joy and wonder in my life. Glass half full. Heart half full. I kick off my heels. The gentle rocking of the boat doesn't work well with stilettos. Neither does sand. I would give anything to find my wardrobe soon. If not, I'm tracking down my debit card and buying some more shoes.

The cabin is unlocked so I wander in. The fridge is stocked with cheese and olives and other things I like. I open the olives and eat four or five. The owner of this boat also has a jar of chocolates, another food group I enjoy. I open a bottle of expensive fizzy water and plate up some snacks, take them up on deck, and lie down in a deck chair. Luckily I found a hat in the cabin because the sun is strong, threatening to turn my skin into a raisin. If there's one thing I know, it's that I don't want wrinkles. And water is the answer. No one can ever drink enough.

I want to share this moment with Max, in addition to everyone I don't know. So after I post a picture of myself on Insta, I send the same photo to Max and write, I found my boat. I like it. Gonna take a nap on it now. Zzzzzzzzz you later.

The gentle rocking of the boat, the sunshine, the olives . . . Soon, I let myself drift to sleep aboard *The Good Life*. I can see why I wanted a boat, unless my parents gave it to me or I inherited it. As I'm dozing off, I make a mental note to walk over to the marina's office later. Maybe they can help me find a key so I can steer this thing to Baja. Or they can give me the name of the captain I normally hire. I must have one.

What feels like a million years later, a male voice jars me out of my sleep. "Hello!" It's not a friendly hello; it's an "explain yourself" hello.

I open my eyes to find a middle-aged white guy dressed in an outfit that screams *I own a boat!* It makes me want to run the other way, but I'm cornered. He's standing aboard *The Good Life*, staring down at me.

I reach for my phone, ready to dial 911. Strange man, in my space. I'm not messing around.

"Do you know the Olsons?" he asks.

"Uhh . . ." I don't know anyone, obviously, but I say, "Yes." It seems easier than the truth.

He relaxes just a little.

"That's good to hear. I've been trying to look out for them while they're gone."

"Their boat?"

"Yes, Dave and Mallory Olson from Arizona."

"How long have the Olsons been gone?"

"Months," he says.

I could be the new owner. This guy doesn't know everything. Either that or the Olsons have a twentysomething daughter.

"Someone threw a party on deck last week."

I glance at my Insta post. It's from last Sunday. "Was the party on Sunday, the twelfth?"

He thinks for just a second and nods. "That sounds about right."

"That must have been me," I say. "You should have dropped by."

He gives me a *really?* look. And I can see him trying to figure out if I'm so confident because I'm right or because I'm just that brazen. When it comes down to it, though, he's probably collecting the hottest yacht club gossip. I bet he's just pretending to be friends with the Olsons so that he can get all nosy with me. In fact, I'm sure that's what's going on. This man is *so* not friends with the Olsons.

"That was my boat-warming party," I say, and who knows. It might have been. "You don't happen to have the Olsons' number, do you? I lost my phone and wasn't able to upload my contacts." The lie slips off my tongue before I can even think it through. It's so easy.

The guy gives me the Olsons' number and I shoo him along with a smile and a declaration that I need to continue my beauty sleep. He might contact the Olsons, but not before I do.

I immediately call and leave them a message. "It's Mia. Please give me a call about *The Good Life*. I have a few questions."

They're probably not answering their phone because they're in Switzerland and it's midnight there. Everyone who's anyone is in Switzerland this week.

I can see that the Nosy Neighbor is headed to the marina office. I don't particularly want to answer questions I don't know the answers to, and it's not like I'm one hundred percent sure about my boat ownership. More like seventy-five percent sure I own a boat. So, it's off to the next post. I say good-bye to my darling yacht and head down the pier back to the beach.

The next post is a picture of me kissing an ice sculpture Cupid at the art museum. It's time-stamped at 11:11 on Tuesday night, which means that this was probably the last place I was before the hospital.

I send Max a text: Status report: I own a yacht and volunteer to feed the homeless. I hope you're doing as well as me. 😉 Want to grab lunch?

If I had my memory and a life, I'd probably find it weird to text Max such frequent updates, but given the situation, the guy is basically my best friend.

CHAPTER

FIVE

I think about changing my Insta bio to *Texting and Driving a Ferrari* because that's what I'm doing. Well, not exactly texting—just checking notifications on my phone when I'm at a stoplight, so whatever, bitches. Stop hating. Everyone who's anyone texts at stoplights. (Quote me on that.) Anyhoo, I'm on my way to the art museum where I almost died.

Back to my latest notification . . .

I click on it and a post from @Mia4Realz pops up. What the fuck? At first I think it's a memory, one of those "one year ago today" reminders, but it's not. (A memory would be nice, by the way, motherfuckers!)

But supposedly I posted this *today*.

I did not. This picture does not look familiar

As I look at the post, my heart speeds up and I get that weightless feeling when adrenaline starts to flood your body and your muscles are ready to run, leaving your brain behind, like in those Warner Bros. cartoons when Road Runner is about a mile ahead of himself. That's me. Someone is messing with me.

Well, in reality, I'm still in the Ferrari. Someone lays on the horn behind me and I realize that I'm sitting through a green light. The horn guy passes me on the right. As he swerves around me he yells, "Get off your phone, bitch!"

I set the phone down and just focus on getting to the art museum. It's two blocks ahead on the left. I'm so close, but I feel like someone is breathing down my neck rather than just messing with me online. A left-hand turn in busy traffic is almost more than I can handle.

When I finally pull into the art museum lot, I stare hard at the screen. I think I've been hacked. Whatever this is, I definitely didn't put this up.

It's a promo. There's a picture of me with an *I have a secret* face and, might I add, perfectly blown-out hair. The caption reads, "ANNOUNCEMENT COMING SOON!"

It gives me chills. Is some creep messing with me? Maybe the person who conked me on the head is playing games on an epic scale. Maybe they want something. If so, I wish they'd just come out and say it. They probably don't realize they're messing with an amnesiac.

I'm the only one freaked out, though. My followers immediately start liking it.

Ooooh!!! Tell me. 😍 ♡ ☺

I wonder if someone is trying to blackmail me. I feel like I'm about to receive a text asking for a million dollars or they'll announce some dirty secret I don't want the world to know. On the flip side, if they reveal my dirty secret at least I'll know something about myself. That'd be nice for a change.

But I'm practical, and I don't like being a sitting duck. After I share the post with Max via text with an appropriate WTF! message (because this is the kind of news you need to share with your BFF), I go about figuring out how to solve the problem. After finding Report Something and then Hacked Accounts in my app, which feels like a Veronica Mars–like accomplishment in and of itself, I explain the issue: I'VE BEEN HACKED! SAVE ME! Et cetera, et cetera. It's so satisfying fixing problems without talking to people.

I'm crossing things off my to-do list like one of those women who answers emails while on the treadmill.

———

The Long Beach Museum of Art is housed in a decaying million-dollar beach house. It looks like a house flipper's wet dream, like you could buy it for one million, fix all the chipped paint, and then sell it for ten. Never mind the fact that a good chunk of California's 109,000 homeless people camp out on the beach below.

A ticket is going to cost me too much of JP's sock drawer money. The dude at the admissions counter looks exactly like who you'd expect to work in an art museum: underfed and pale.[15] He doesn't look like a reliable witness, unless you want to know where to score dope, but I give him a chance. "Do you remember a party here on Tuesday?"

He gives me a snooty look and says, "Would you like admission to our special exhibit as well?" He proceeds to tell me about the exhibit, something about the evolution of self-portraiture, blah blah blah. It's called *MySelfie*.[16]

I'm pretty sure I could tell him a few things about selfies.

"So about Tuesday," I say. "Were you working?"

"Tuesday . . ." He taps his pen and squints. "Tuesday . . . hmmm, I wasn't working. I can check to see who was, though." He pauses to think. "Maybe Ben, I don't know. Are you asking about that thing that happened?"

"What thing?" My pulse quickens. Maybe this derelict will help me before I even have to pay the admission fee.

"There was a fancy party for the opening of *MySelfie*. Some mystery chick left the party in an ambulance."

Me.

A little girl starts screaming like I would if I were to express how excited I am about the clue. Her plight to get another juice box—I'm not feeling that. Her parents are urgently digging through a diaper bag as if the world will end if they don't

---

[15] Definitely not an art person. I seem to have deep-seated prejudices against art people.

[16] I could have thought of that. Maybe I did. I should check to see if I work here.

pop a Capri Sun in her mouth. As soon as she stops screaming, I'm going to find out what happened to me.

The mom, thank God, finally solves the problem by handing the kid her phone—thank you forever and ever, Steve Jobs—and my guy starts talking again. "My boss was all freaked out. He thought she might sue the museum for whatever happened."

"What happened?"

He shrugs. "At first the story was that she slipped and fell, but now there's a rumor circulating about the executive director's mistress and his wife getting into a fistfight at the sushi table. Last I heard, they were both pregnant."

When he catches the look of shock on my face (Mistress? PREGNANT?), he says, "Who knows what really happened. Might have just been performance art. Really, that's probably what it was." He smiles.

I touch my stomach, which does not feel pregnant. There's no way this Prada gown would fit me if I were pregnant. Not to mention, Dr. Patel definitely would have mentioned a pregnancy. I am decidedly Not. Pregnant.

He makes eye contact with me, as if he's going to say something important. "I wish someone had invited me to the party. I'm a bit of an actor."

I have to stop myself from rolling my eyes. "You don't have a guest or donor list, do you?"

"I was in a commercial last year. Maybe you've seen it . . ."

OMG. "What was the commercial for?" I ask through clenched teeth.

"It was for this surf shop in Huntington Beach." He pulls up the party guest list on his computer while telling me about how he was "in the commercial, but not the star of it." I stare at him with a frozen smile. "Who do you want me to look up?" he asks.

Obviously I was there, but I ask anyway. "Are there any Mias on the list?" I bet I'm a regular on guest and donor lists around here.

"What's the last name?"

"Um, not sure. I don't know her that well." Understatement of the year.

"Uhhh . . ." He scans the list and announces, "No Mias."

Frustration threatens to cloud my optimism but I square my shoulders and literally put my chin up. I've only been out of this coma for a little over twenty-four hours. I'm gonna get there.

"How about JP Howard?"

He scans the list again. "Oh, he's *always* on the list. He donated a Rembrandt or something last year. I don't know how much it's worth, but it's a lot." Then a big lopsided smile takes over his face. "And here's my duuuude." He nods with appreciation and I see the name Frederick Montcalm.

"Your dude?"

"My boss, as in knocked-up two chicks and caused a fist fight. I want to be him when I grow up."

I channel Veronica Mars[17] again and sidle up next to him. I need to see that address.

....

17 I love you, Kristen Bell! #marshmallows #VeronicaMars

"Umm . . ." he says. "What are you doing over here?"

I get it. I'm on the wrong side of the desk, but if he wants to be a ladies' man like that boss he thinks is so cool, this is his chance. While he tries to figure out if my flirty smile and proximity mean that I'm into him, I sidle up even closer and scan the list. Frederick Montcalm lives on Balboa Avenue in Laguna Beach.

Before he can pull out his phone to show me his commercial on YouTube, I sneak away, leaving him to watch himself not starring in a commercial. A "hey" echoes unanswered in the cavernous lobby when he realizes that I am definitely not that into him. I've already moved on to the exhibits.

I should be sort of happy—I mean, I'm closer to finding out more about myself, but a feeling of existential dread is eating at the frayed edges of my tentative happiness. I'm just a nameless woman who got her head smashed in at some party where I wasn't even a guest. I was probably JP's plus one. No big deal, but . . . who am I? It's not like I'm some 1950s house-wife who goes by Mrs. JP Howard and lives in the shadow of my husband. I'm a Millennial with a decent Insta following and an undercut.

I pick up a pamphlet for the self-portrait exhibit. It's a bunch of touchy-feely mumbo jumbo about the artist becoming the spectator to her own art, and about how that places the artist in a position of extreme vulnerability, becoming the audience of her own suffering (because that is what art is—a tangible representation of suffering).

These idiots have no fucking clue.

The exhibit pamphlet goes on to say that self-portraiture is a way for the artist to supercharge her artistic growth. Being the audience and the creator at one time is like adrenaline for the creative brain.

Pretentious much? I just want to know if they sell earrings at the gift shop. Or maybe a scarf.

I wouldn't want to make any of these artists jealous, but I think I'm struggling more with self-representation than they are at the moment. Being a spectator to my shitty existence is causing way more pain than the guy who painted himself in glasses and hung it on the wall. But mostly, if I don't get a sandwich soon, I'm going to die.

Thank God they have a restaurant. Claire's at the Museum looks fancy, with yellow umbrellas on a patio overlooking the beach with lots of #locallysourced ingredients and Mexican dishes everyone is dying to eat, but sprinkled with Himalayan salt for fanciness reasons.

This is where the party was, where I (the mistress?) fought the executive director's wife and lost my memory. But this story doesn't sound true, and I've already determined that there's no way I could be pregnant. Again, Dr. Patel would have to be really bad at his job to let that fact get by him.

The event area where the party must have been is behind the museum, a grassy suburban backyard that looks ripe for bocce and lemonade but located on a cliff overlooking the beach and harbor. It's not far above where I took the selfie next to the meth head who is now presumably on a bus to somewhere $10 away from here. Directly ahead is a resort-y looking island, the same one I noticed from the beach.

A girl—or, more accurately, a waitress—walks up to me. "Did you know that island is just an oil well in the harbor? They put a glass-brick tower around the well to make it look like a hotel and planted a palm tree next to it," she says.

"Really?" I look at the waitress. She's wearing a white shirt with one of those aprons that has shallow square pockets, one for the bill and one for who knows what else. Forks? I've never been a waitress, I guess.

"That is so weird," I say, looking at the island. Now that she's mentioned it, that's all I can see: an oil refinery in a cheap disguise. The harbor is filled with these fake islands. A few tankers are headed in to dock at the Long Beach Pier, a giant undisguised oil refinery.

I'm not picky, though. A fake view is fine with me.

"Do you want a table?" she asks.

Until now I've been staring at the harbor, but when I turn and tell her, "No, thanks," a funny look passes over her face. She stares for a second, as if to place me. When it hits her, she exclaims, "Oh my God! I'm so glad you're okay! I thought you might be dead."

I snap to attention. #eyewitness—and this one appears to be ready for the stand. I scan her name tag. *Azalea.*

Azalea examines me, wide-eyed and, I think, legitimately surprised. I'm definitely the most exciting thing that's happened to her today.

"I'm okay. What happened? I don't have any memory of that night."

"*Dios mio!* I've never seen that much blood." She puts her hands to her heart.

Azalea is definitely exaggerating. I'm wearing the same dress the massacre occurred in, so it couldn't have been that bad, bloodwise at least. The cape did look pretty bad, though. I'll give her that.

"I didn't see much. I heard an argument, though." With a snicker she says, "Well, I mean, *everyone* heard an argument."

"What about?"

"Something about a guy. And I heard someone mention GoldRush."

"GoldRush?"

"You know, that dating app for rich guys."

So it's *not* a mine in Alaska, and it's something worth arguing over? It still doesn't ring a bell.

"I don't know what the argument was about, but I heard someone yell 'GoldRush!' which I thought was funny. I just read about this chick I went to high school with. She got engaged to some high-fructose gazillionaire from Iowa." The California-speak edges into her voice the more emotional she gets about not having her own millionaire. When she says, "I mean, Iowa!" she might as well be in the Valley twirling her hair. "They met on GoldRush. I was totally thinking of signing up. I mean, it'd be like winning the lottery, but girl, I've earned it."

Her eye makeup game is solid, if that's what she's getting at. More important, maybe that's how I met my millionaire.

I mentally flag this to research later; I need to get every bit of info out of Azalea while I can.

"Anyway, when I heard yelling, I came running . . . totally dropped the tray I was carrying, which would have pissed my boss off, if he'd noticed. Before I got to the screaming, I saw you falling toward the ice sculpture. In a split second you'd smacked into it and were sprawled on the ground."

"Ice sculpture?" She must mean the Cupid I was kissing in my last Insta post. Good thing he didn't actually kill me. That would've been crazy morbid, definitely worth one of those "Last post before she died" slideshows on BuzzFeed.

"Yeah, it was this cute sculpture of Cupid. In retrospect, that arrow was probably too pointy."

"Did someone push me into Cupid or did I just fall?"

"Pushed. I saw you being propelled backward into the statue. *That* I'm sure of, but I don't know who pushed you. There was a commotion and whoever did it took off."

Someone pushed me into Cupid's arrow. Talk about messed up. Did my attacker choose the statue intentionally or was it just a random act of symbolism?

"I gotta get back to work," she says.

"Cool, can we exchange numbers or something, though? In case I have any more questions?"

She gives me her cell. "I'm also @TheRealChicaBonita on Insta if you want to look me up."

I add Azalea's phone number to my contacts; she is one of two people in my phone whom I know IRL. If I get married anytime soon, she'll have to be a bridesmaid.

I watch Azalea head back to work. She's going to look great in my wedding photographs at least. The girl is adorable— cuter than me, even. Luckily, it doesn't seem like I'm a competitive bitch. #girlpower.

In the parking lot I scroll through her Instagram. On Tuesday, she posted a selfie with her eyes brimming with tears, just the right amount to make her look sad-pretty and draw attention to her improbable lashes. There's no way those are natural, right? And what filter is this? Rise? It's really flattering. I scan the caption: Saw a woman die tonight. Hold your loved ones tight. Any moment could be your last. 🙏 😲

Really, Azalea, talk about jumping to conclusions. I definitely wasn't dead. I roll my eyes at the comments below the picture:

OMG Zizi! I hope u r OK! All my ♡!!!!!

Stay strong gurl!!!! 💪 💪

♡ ♡ ♡

🥺

Plus about twenty more.

Excuse me. I didn't even get flowers. Not a single condolence or visitor to the hospital. This post was like my obituary starring Azalea.

The morning after my supposed death, she posted a picture of her butt in tight jeans.

Azalea is officially out of the wedding.

I need to get out of here, but on the way out of the museum I walk past *MySelfie*, the new exhibit. Fuck them. Fuck their pain. I'm going to give them a goddamn self-portrait. There's a selfie booth with a very PhD-esque description of the self-ie as today's version of the self-portrait, and a few sentences about how in the past only the rich could experiment with self-portraiture, versus these days when every asshole can take a gazillion self-portraits a day. Was this the democratization of self-obsession? On another note, I'm totally saving the line about democracy for the next time Max looks smug when I take a pic in front of him.

I'm not sure if the commentary about the inherent power of choosing how to present yourself to the world jibes with reality. The wall of self-portraits is filled with shots of girls with heart crowns and Barbie-fied faces. Does a Snapchat filter that gives you kitty whiskers, makes your ears sparkly, and erases your zits carry power? Is there power in choosing to be fake? In choosing to conform? Online anyone can look like an ideal woman, but only online.

The exhibit's selfie booth is a teenage dream. It encourages runaway selfishness. There are backgrounds, props, hats, Venetian masks, and party beads to pick from. A college intern is posted next to the booth to assist. None of the computerized backgrounds (hot-air balloon and cotton candy scenes) work for me. I'm not in the mood for any cutesy bullshit, so I stand in front of a blank wall without any props, not even a fake smile, and snap a pic. It looks like a mug shot.

"Whoa, I like what you're doing here," the intern says. "You're moody AF."

Like my mood is part of a costume. "No, bitch. I just hate the world for real at the moment. Do you have a black Sharpie I can borrow?"

He nods. "I feel ya. The world is a cesspool."

I can see Audi keys in his back pocket. I think his world is a candy store, but whatever.

He wanders off to find me a Sharpie. After he prints my moody AF photo I write, *If you have any information about this woman, please message @Mia4Realz on Instagram.*

"That's deep. I mean, really profound."

I give a half smile and hang up the picture, right in the center of all the other selfies. I'm the only mug shot in a sea of adorable girls being adorable. "I'm serious. I just want information. I need someone to tell me who I am." I jam in an extra pushpin so it doesn't fall off. "As soon as possible."

"Don't we all," he says, totally missing my point. As I walk out, wearing my mood (if that's what he wants to call it) harder than Lady Gaga wore that sliced meat dress, he says, "I hope you enjoyed the exhibit."

Maybe my ego is out of proportion, but I think I am the exhibit.

Finally, Max texts back. Lunch sounds great. Ready when u r.

I stare at the text a little longer than necessary, like it's a message in a bottle from that Nicholas Sparks movie. You know the one. It's just a text about lunch, but to me it's a lifeline. I need to show him Azalea's Instagram, look up

GoldRush, and show him my yacht. Max better buckle up 'cause I've just drafted him as the Watson to my Sherlock.

Google says it'll take thirty-nine minutes to get to the lab. I text back, Pick you up in 25.

CHAPTER

SIX

With traffic it takes more like an hour to get to Max's lab, but at least I look fast. I park the Ferrari in a handicapped spot out front on the theory that if I follow my instincts, I'll find my true self faster. All of my random impulses are probably who I am at my core. We all get through the day on muscle memory for the most part. If I don't think and just do, I might arrive at my true self.

So there we have it: a bright red Ferrari in a handicapped spot when there are, like, five other spaces available. Am I in a hurry all the time? I reapply my lipstick and walk into the building, my heels clacking on the sidewalk. Devil may care in Pirate red. And I was a cape wearer. If I wasn't me, I'd want to be my friend.

The inside of the building is covered with posters from every scientific conference, and the people walking around look like they're filled with purpose and a sense of belonging.

Max fits in perfectly. Could I ever fit in at a place like this?[18]

Speaking of Max, I catch sight of him coming toward me and I exhale. The yacht, the art museum, the freeway . . . I didn't realize how tightly clenched I've been until now.

I realize his clothes are pretty wrinkly, as if he's been looking through a microscope in one position for too long. He could also use a haircut and a trip to the mall, something I'm pretty sure I could help with.

"I have so much to tell you," I say.

Then I see his face. Something truly awful has happened in the last few hours. He looks like someone just told him that Congress defunded the space program for a second time.

"What's the matter?" I ask.

"Ugh. I'll tell you in a second. I have to get some stuff out of my lab. I'm clearing out of here for a couple of days."

It must be bad.

I follow him up to his lab, which is a cross between a high-end hospital and an office building. The lab echoes the look of the lobby—cool, clean, and painted in shades of gray. The only thing that saves it from being totally boring is the printouts of memes, comics, joke pictures, and takeout menus pinned to the walls. That alone makes me want to hang out with these twentysomething geniuses, telling jokes and eating Chinese delivery. How is there not a sitcom set in a lab? Or a romantic workplace drama starring Max? Totally bingeable TV, in my opinion.

....

[18] No other cocktail dresses on premises. There's one cape, but it has more of a D&D vibe. Wearer probably refers to it as a cloak.

A couple of lab girls who are cute enough to make me question if they're neuroscientists say, "Ohmygod Max! We heard the bad news. Fay is such a bitch." Apparently science girls also speak Valley because their accents are *strong*.

"I can't believe Eric is firing you," one of them says.

Max exhales. "Me either."

Fay, who I recognize from her Gchat profile picture, walks up to the group. She's even prettier in person. She and Max were probably the power couple of the neuroscience department, with Nobel prizes and modeling contracts in their future.

"I don't know why you're leaving, Max," she says. "I was just making a point."

He laughs bitterly. "That was not a point. That was straight-up sabotage."

"You're just being sensitive. You don't have to throw away your job. Just fix the damn software."

I'm on the edge of my seat. Tell me what you did, Fay!

Max sets down his box, as if he needs all his focus to say whatever he's about to say and can't also hold a box. "Eric made it very clear that both of us are fired because of what *you* did, Fay!"

While Fay starts going off about how he did some shit too, I ask one of the lab girls who Eric is.

"He's the principal investigator," she says. "Our boss."

I'm piecing it together: Fay got up to some sort of science shenanigans because she's pissed about the breakup, and now both Fay and Max have been fired.

Fay puts her hands on her hips and gives Max a piercing gaze. "And you're being dramatic, Max. You're only fired if you don't fix it."

Looking exasperated, Max says, "And what am I supposed to fix? You destroyed two years' worth of work and I have a few days to figure it out and save my job. It's over, Fay."

When Fay says, "You're not even trying, Max," I think she's talking about more than his job. I guess he didn't work as hard at being a boyfriend as he did at being a scientist.

Max picks up his box. He's done talking. I recognize the look on his face. He needs some time to process his sudden career change and office drama.

Fay looks in my direction and sizes me up. "Nice dress," she says. "I'm Fay, Max's colleague."

"Former," Max says.

While Fay and I shake hands, she rolls her eyes at Max. "Former colleague is actually true."

"Mia's my new girlfriend," Max says.

"Mmhmm," I say, and sidle up to Max, wiggling up against him like he's catnip, which he basically is.

Fay looks back and forth between the two of us. "Good luck with him, Mia." Still completely composed and wearing a smile, she says, "He's a big fat liar."

This neuroscience lab show is better than the Kardashians.

"I've never lied in my life and you know that, Fay."

Fay flips her silky ponytail over her shoulder and raises her eyebrows. "You think that through while you're fixing the software."

Max kisses the top of my head. "Let's go, Mia." He calls out to no one in particular, "I'm leaving."

"What is going on?" I ask.

"Fay fucked with our software and put in a bunch of bugs just to prove a point, something about me. Eric, our boss, told us we're fired if we can't fix it. I don't know what the hell she did and she's not talking, something about how 'if I really knew her, I'd be able to fix the project.' Can you believe it?" He glances my way to make sure I'm following and understand just how crazy Fay is. "There's no way I'm playing that game."

"You'd rather lose your job and give up on your dreams than play Fay's game?"

"Yes."

Max is apparently so stubborn that he will throw away his whole career for this.

"We're fired until we prove we're not all just messing around."

They *are* messing around, and I love it—it's so much more interesting than whatever lie-detection system they're trying to build. I don't say that to Max, obviously.

"I don't know why Fay's not embarrassed."

"She's proud," I say. I can't wait to find out what she did.

On our way out, Max has to do "one more thing." He walks me down the hall to a room with a lot of warnings on the outside about high-powered magnets. DON'T WEAR YOUR WATCH OR BRING CELL PHONES IN, reads one sign, as if anyone has a watch these days. "I have a test subject in the fMRI," he says. "I'm not going to be able to use this data, so I might as well let her go."

SAM TSCHIDA

I follow Max into the room after ditching my phone in a basket outside the door. In the center of the room, there's a girl in an outfit that features a bolo tie and short shorts, wearing a very large metal helmet. It looks like a prototype of the first scuba diving gear and I'm grateful that her neck is strong enough to hold it up. Max points at a big computer screen displaying a picture of a brain.

"Hers?" I ask.

"Yep, I'm taking pictures of her brain while she's lying." He points out the amygdala on the screen. "You can tell this chick is a good liar because of all the extra white matter. Her brain is good at making connections quickly. You need to be pretty smart to be a good liar."

"How much are you paying her?"

"Twenty bucks an hour. She's been here for two already."

I nod with approval. I'd totally tell some lies while wearing a helmet for forty bucks. Too bad his project is over. That sock-drawer money is going to run out soon.

"Thanks for your help, Clarice," he says to the girl, handing her forty bucks in cash.

"I bet you got some good data today," she says. "I spent the whole time creating a fake online profile for Bumble. Like, for real. I'm going to use it."

I chew on that for a minute. "I don't know," I say, "is lying online even lying?"

Max looks shocked at that suggestion. "Of course it is."

"I don't know, exaggeration on dating websites is pretty much expected."

84

Max raises an eyebrow. "That's actually a good point. Exaggeration to impress a potential mate might not be lying exactly, but . . . I need a break." He loses steam mid-thought, probably because he just remembered that he's giving up on science and leaving this all behind. "Wanna get some tacos? And maybe a beer?"

I'm human so tacos sound amazing. "As long as they have a vegetarian option," I say. JP might be bachelor of the year, but so far Brenda is the real love of my life.

"Got it. How was your morning?" he asks. "Any news?"

"Tons. Have you ever heard of a dating site called GoldRush?"

"This morning you said it was a documentary about mining in Alaska." He gives me a suspicious look as he picks up some stuff from his desk and ushers me out of the lab.

"Turns out I was wrong. This chick at the art museum mentioned something about it being a dating app."

Max doesn't slam the door to the lab on the way out but he lets it close loudly, which is pretty much slamming for him. When we get to the parking lot, he says, "Mia, you parked in a handicap spot. That could be like a $200 fine!"

"Oops, I didn't notice." Max doesn't need to know that I'm discovering my true self by following all my impulses, which, on second thought, might not be the best idea. If I follow my impulses will I just find myself at the bottom of a Cheetos bag?

"Max, do you think we are basically just an amalgam of all of our bad habits?"

"Um . . . only if you don't engage in any other behaviors or aspire to more."

A guy behind the wheel of a Kia at the stoplight next to us is side-eyeing me. I've only been driving a Ferrari (at least that I can remember) for a couple of hours, but every dude who wants to speed down the Pacific Coast Highway has come out of the woodwork to rev his engine and challenge me to a race right through the middle of LA. I don't have enough testosterone for that, so I let him burn rubber down Vermont alone.

"This car feels more like an asshole magnet than a chick magnet," Max notes drily.

What does that say about JP? Does he spend all day zooming around in his penis-complex car while I: 1) wear a sundress and file my nails, 2) go to work at a fulfilling job, or 3) resent him because I've sacrificed my own hopes and dreams to ride his coattails?

I think I'm the girl behind door number one. That would be fine, as long as we're racing to a getaway in Baja or something along those lines. I'd even take a nice lunch on a patio. I want to live #TheGoodLife, just like my boat says.

"So about GoldRush, I take it you haven't used it?" I ask.

"I prefer to date my coworkers," he says.

I laugh.

He directs me to a spot five or ten minutes away from his lab on Figueroa. USC goes from college campus to skid row in less time than it takes a girl to take a selfie and pick a filter. The taco truck is wedged between a gated parking lot (armed security and barbed wire fence—yikes!) and a strip mall with a bodega, a wig shop, and a place selling Mexican corn. Some of the wigs are cute and, come to think of it, would cover my staples.

"Here we are," he says, pointing to a taco truck with a handwritten sign out front that reads L'EMPIRE TACOS.

I wrinkle my nose. "Are you sure they have a vegetarian option?" Now that I see this taco truck, two things are clear to me: 1) It's in a slum, and 2) I doubt they have a vegetarian option. Going veg is a pretty bougie thing to do. Brenda knew it the minute she saw me: I come from a place where people worry about the welfare of chickens and wear glasses for style reasons.

The line outside of the dirty taco truck is a mile long, so we just sit in the Ferrari for a minute. Noticeably, we are the only Ferrari in the parking lot. That's not to say that we're the only fancy car—just the only fancy car that isn't a drug-dealer-mobile. The smell of—goddammit—savory meats and spices is making my mouth water.

"Can't you smell that?" Max huffs the air like it's a can of paint.

"Yes, all those roasting vegetables smell so good," I say even though the only vegetable I can smell is garlic and it's probably in a pork marinade. Being a vegetarian is both the worst and only decision I've ever made. At least Brenda didn't tell me I was a committed virgin or a Scientologist.

After putting on just the right pretaco playlist for this situation, he leans his seat back and puts on a pair of sunglasses. I commence Googling as we wait for the lunch rush to die down. If I had an argument about GoldRush right before I was nearly impaled on an ice sculpture, it must be important.

The internet informs me that GoldRush is a dating app for millionaires (at a minimum) to find "sophisticated and elite Californians interested in long-term, committed relationships." Basically what Azalea told me.

With a laugh, I say, "No wonder you haven't heard of GoldRush, Max. It's an app for super rich dudes looking for arm candy."

"Are there any super rich women looking for poor men?" he asks. "I'd sign up for that. I'm on the market and about to be poor."

"That's not a thing," I say.

"That's sexist. I mean, I could be arm candy."

"You could definitely be arm candy," I confirm. "Maybe you should file a complaint with the person in char—" My mouth drops.

"What is it?"

OMG OMG OMG OMG OMG OMG OMG OMG OMG OMG OMG OMG OMG OMG OMG OMG OMG OMGOM GOM OM OG OM GO GM MG OOOOO GOGOGOGO MOMOMOMO MGMGMGM

My overexcited neurotransmitters can't complete the connection from thought to speech, which is fine. Finally I utter a single "OMG."

"Is it your head? Are you having a stroke? Mia—are you okay?"

I gather my wits. "I'm fine. It's just that . . . *I'm* the owner of GoldRush. At least according to the internet." I point him to a very exciting article from the SoCal Lifestyle website listing me among the "Top Ten Entrepreneurs Under 30 in Long Beach." It was published last week. I am the hot news in SoCal.

Mia Wallace,[19] a Long Beach resident, started the Gold-Rush dating app because, she says, "California's most important resource is its people, in particular, all of its hot women. Sadly, this resource is being wasted on losers who graduated from California public schools working at taco trucks and selling smack. I decided to step in and solve the problem. Gold-Rush matches California's best and brightest women with the men they deserve: high-net-worth individuals from Switzerland and Japan—really, anywhere but Long Beach." Ms. Wallace's idea has taken hold. After two years in business, she is on the brink of brokering her first engagement at the whopping price tag of $250,000. She has set up countless dates for between $10,000 and $35,000. It's good to be young, single, and female in Long Beach.

It's official. I woke up to the best life ever. The Good Life—both the yacht and the life—is definitely mine, which reminds me. I need to access my bank accounts, for practical reasons, not to mention for good-news reasons. I can't wait to see just how much I'm worth. As soon as we get back to JP's I'll do some accounting in front of Netflix with a glass of wine and some Jacques-o-late.

Max scans the article. "Whoa. Are you sure that's JP's house and not yours?"

....

[19] My last name, finally! 😜

I shrug. Damned if I know anything. It definitely sounds like I can afford my own mansion.

"Tacos are on me." Actually, they're on JP because I don't have a wallet or ID or credit card. Obviously I have a ton of money, though.

I hope I remember how to be CEO of one the hottest businesses in Long Beach. I have so many questions. How many clients do I have and how much help do they need? Do I have an office? How do I run a business?!

"Do you have the clients take a test to match them up, or do you get in touch with the universe and light a candle?" Max asks.

"Damned if I know." If I have matchmaking skills, it's news to me.

"It's extremely interesting how you only forgot facts about yourself. Why do you think that is?"

"You're the expert. What do you think?"

"I have to say, the pattern of your memory loss indicates that it's definitely psychological," Max says.

"No, Max. Someone shoved me into a frozen Cupid. Azalea said so."

Max doesn't even bother to ask follow-up questions. "Even if it was triggered by physical trauma, I think the symptoms you're showing now are psychological."

Damn. Do I look that nuts to everyone? "That's basically what the doctor at the hospital said."

"It just means that you're dealing with some sort of trauma. It could be anything. All I can say is that it was too much for you to handle. Essentially, your brain used this as an excuse to shut down."

Max's talk of trauma and psychology is making me uncomfortable so I look at my phone without really looking at it. What could possibly be bad enough to force me into shutdown mode when my life is perfect in practically every way?

The answer is obvious: someone I care about shoved me into that ice sculpture.

CHAPTER

SEVEN

The question of murder will have to wait. I push that and visions of my bank account to the side because my real life is calling. JP is FaceTiming me. Max and I are still sitting near L'Empire Tacos on a block of cement next to a dirty parking lot and a wig store, but with tacos now (the line was heinous!). There's a dumpster behind me and Max is with me so it looks like I'm on a date with a hot guy in a slum.[20] Also, I haven't checked my makeup in about five hours. I start to panic. I mean, it's good news. My boyfriend is calling. He's the only person who actually knows me from before my injury—except for that random guy on the beach who knows me from the soup kitchen.

My physical reality is messier than my online one. Currently it's mostly about nervous sweating and mild hyper-

....

[20] Am I?

ventilation. "I bet this is how people feel when they meet their future spouse the day before their arranged marriage."

"You should want to talk to him because he's your boy-friend," Max says. "Plus, he knows some shit about your life. If nothing else, he's a resource."

"But it's freaking me out."

He thoughtfully digests that information for a minute. "Probably because he knows almost everything about you, I would assume, and you know nothing about him. And, sure, he's your boyfriend, but who knows what kind of relationship you have?"

Max is right. JP and I could be fuck buddies or we could be in love for real. Maybe we haven't gotten married because the commercial nature of weddings would cheapen what we have.

I rub the change in my pocket leftover from the sock-drawer money and send JP a text.

Call back in 10. 😘

JP gives it a big white thumbs-up.

I can't have salsa running down my chin when I talk to him. And I need to collect myself. *After* I finish this taco, I will show my face. And the taco is definitely worth finishing; it's maybe even better than the quinoa. Without thinking, I set it on its wrapper and pull out my phone to take a picture. It's muscle memory at this point.

Max grabs the phone. "You're not allowed to post that. Consider this an intervention."

"What? I've hardly even posted anything since I woke up." There's no point pretending to have an amazing time eating tacos when I'm actually panicking about JP. I want to, but I see Max's point.

"Plus, should you be posting if you've been hacked?"

"I don't know." How can you care about something if you don't understand the consequences? It's basically the same as every other problem facing planet Earth. "The hacker will have to share the account with me for now," I announce.

He looks at me like he can't even with me if I don't follow the rules. "Call JP back."

"Just one more pic," I tease. Before he can stop me, I snap a picture of him in front of the taco truck. He's reaching for me and my phone. If he had to pick a photo for a dating profile, this would work. He looks like the kind of guy any girl would want to hang out with: unpretentious and cute. And he looks happy, like he's enjoying being part of my crisis.

"Why are you putting off calling him?" he asks. "Just get it over with."

He's right. I am putting it off. I have dental-visit levels of anxiety over this FaceTime.[21] JP is a major piece of my life, and I'm not sure if I should trust him or if he'll know something is off with me. "Honestly, I'd like to just go on living in his house while he stays in Switzerland," I say.

Max laughs. "Wouldn't we all."

"I'll just give him one more Google before I call."

....

[21] Pretty sure I prefer sedation.

A few seconds later, Siri answers in her comforting robotic tone: "I found this information about JP Howard." Up pop all the Google results I looked through yesterday morning, but also a file. It's an inactive GoldRush profile. "He was on GoldRush?" I say.

Max and I read it together. There's a picture of JP smiling and looking off camera, a glass of wine in his hand.

The headline reads, I am looking for a woman who loves staying in just as much as she loves jet-setting, a woman to share the quiet moments as well as the triumphs of life, a woman who love Jacques-o-late.

Okay, I'm warming up to calling him . . .

There's some old news (at this point) about his billions and the fact that he's thirty-seven. Then, hobbies: Skiing and saving the rainforest—really. I'm sure I've personally saved an area the size of Delaware so far just by eating Jacques-o-late.

"I have a Jacques-o-late T-shirt somewhere," says Max.

Of course he does.

"I want to hate him, but I don't," Max says.

"He seems so good." I sit up and take a deep breath. "I don't know if I can be responsible for this," I say gesturing to the profile. "He's so, so . . . perfect." Like a white dress that I want to buy but know I shouldn't. I can't be responsible for dry-clean-only Chantilly lace.

"That's ridiculous. He's a jet-setting billionaire and you just checked out of the hospital with a head injury and don't know who you are. He's the one who should be concerned about taking advantage of you."

"But still. He's so perfect. What if I wreck him?"

Max scoffs. "Who knows if he's even being honest?"

This is coming from the man who only believes a person if they take a polygraph test, and not even a normal one. It has to be the one he invented. Funny that Fay called *him* a liar. Maybe truth is like memory—shifting depending on perspective, one thing to Fay and another to Max.[22] One thing's for sure—Max doesn't believe he's ever been on the wrong side of the truth.

"Call him," he says.

I pull up the FaceTime app and call JP. My face pops up, which reminds me to wipe the smear of salsa off my nose and reapply my lipstick in a hurry. For good measure, I adjust the phone so that it gets me from a more flattering angle. No up-the-nose shots for JP.

"Hello?" I hear his sleepy voice first and then I see his face, which has that vulnerable little-boy quality that I seem to recognize—and respond to—right away. (Even if I can't recall any of my former partners or their wake-up faces.) His hair is messed up but that just adds to the attractiveness. Rumpled hair and a stubbled Prince Charming jawline. He brings to mind that guy who played Jon Snow, but with a French accent and hair just beginning to gray at the temples, which somehow makes him look more trustworthy. He's a mature, French Jon Snow. Any girl in her right mind would want to wake up next to him.

....

[22] Don't tell Max I said that.

But I can't help thinking, however briefly, about the unfairness of his easy attractiveness. Why do men get to be boyishly cute in the morning while women have to look like sex kittens the minute they open their eyes? I guess that's because girlishness is bound up with sexuality at a much younger age? (No wonder I run a dating empire.)

"I'm sorry," I say. "What time is it in Switzerland?"

"Don't worry," he says. "I'm just glad to see your face, Mia." He sits up and props himself up on one elbow. He's shirtless. Dear God, my previous decisions all make perfect sense.

He rubs the sleep from his eyes and puts on a pair of tortoiseshell acetate glasses. Why do they make him look even hotter? Maybe because his vision isn't 20/20, he's flawed enough to be mine.[23] Plus it makes him look smart, which is undeniably sexy. "I'm sorry about that fight," he says. "It was stupid. I hated leaving like that."

"It's okay." Whatever we fought about, it was probably my fault. JP is clearly the better human of the two of us, all of his goodness and inner beauty grown in a hydroponic, pest-free environment and nurtured by unconditional love and reasonable expectations. Just like all the best weed. (OMG—where did that come from? Am I a pothead?)

"It felt like you were still mad this morning," he said.

"I just don't like being bought off."

With a laugh he says, "Could have fooled me."

I smile. I guess I am into being placated with diamonds.

....

[23] #ClarkKent.

I've spent less time with JP than with myself, but somehow he seems easier to understand.

Max sips his horchata and I reach for it. Suddenly I feel parched.

When JP says, "Who's with you?" I realize that was stupid.

I move the phone so that he can see Max. "Just the house sitter," I say.

He opens his eyes wider. "Really? Max?"

Max nods.

JP doesn't miss a beat. Apparently he doesn't consider someone who house-sits competition. "Why aren't you in Sonoma?" he asks, as if it just occurred to him. "I thought you were scouting out a date for some client."

I shake my head. "A lot has happened . . ." I'm just about to explain everything to him when he says, "So sorry, sweetie, but can I call you back in a little bit? Jerome is buzzing me." With an exasperated exhale, he says, "How many times do I have to take out these Sprüngli execs and tell them they're pretty before they sign? They know they need Jacques-o-late."

Jerome, Sprüngli execs—JP sounds incredibly important. "Of course." I can tell him I lost my memory later. "I have a few fires to put out with GoldRush, too," I say.

He laughs. "I bet you do." In a softer voice he says, "I'm so glad you're not mad, love." Then he remembers Max is there. "Oh, and thanks for watching the house, Max. Hope it didn't give you any trouble." He blows me a kiss and then hangs up.

A gorgeous billionaire just told me he loves me. Who am I even?

Max and I sit in silence for a few seconds. It's hard to fill the sacred space just vacated by JP, a god on Earth. What could anyone say that would do the moment justice? Instead I take a moment to meditate on his perfection, i.e., scroll through all of our couple's shots on Instagram. We are beautiful and perfect. I'm not arm candy; I'm part of a power couple. I'm a legit businesswoman who is dating a legit businessman.

Max sighs. "He seems . . . nice."

Talk about an understatement.

"Except where's his respect for Sprüngli? That's like a three-hundred-year-old chocolate company. Jacques-o-late—who does he think he is?" He dips a chip in the salsa. It makes his eyes water and he takes his horchata back and chugs.

"Hey!" I protest. "I stole that fair and square."

"Not all of us can be JP," he says with a hint of bitterness.

"Don't be jealous of JP!"

"I'm not jealous," he says, too emphatically. "Anyway, I was thinking . . . JP signed up for your dating service . . ."

"Looks like."

"And you set him up with yourself?" His voice is filled with subtext.

I raise my shoulders in a *you caught me* gesture. "No one said I was stupid."

"That's for sure."

He has a point, though. If any of the other women on the

app realized I took JP for myself, they'd probably smack me upside the head and leave me for dead. I repeat this out loud to Max. It seems like as good a theory as any. I create my list of suspects:

- Art museum president's wife

- Angry chick who wanted JP for herself

- Disgruntled art collector whom I randomly fought for the last spicy tuna roll

"You never know, but I'm guessing it's not door number three," he says.

"You have a PhD so you're probably right."

"That means it's the president's wife or an angry chick."

It strikes me that I have quite a bit to do between solving my attempted murder and running a hot business. Speaking of which, I don't even know how to run a business. Have I been missing calls and emails? Do I have employees?

"Max, do you think I have a secretary or something?"

"I don't know. You'd think they would have called you."

"Unless they were the one who conked me on the head. Or maybe they're excited that I haven't called them in to work? Maybe they're hiding." That seems like a natural thing to do. "I haven't figured out who I am, and now I have to figure out a business and how to run it."

Max looks at me pensively. "Maybe you could get an intern."

I laugh. That seems absurd.

I look up from under my lashes, helpless girl style. "After this afternoon you need a job," I point out.

He harrumphs, but I keep going. "And I just found out I have a multimillion-dollar dating empire." #slightexaggeration. "What do you say, would you work for me for a little while until you find a new lab or until I get my feet under me?"

Max starts laughing. Where the sun hits his face, his skin looks almost like copper and his eyes are bright and warm. He's beautiful. I should be putting him on the app, not hiring him.

"Umm, Mia, have you met me? I can do gene sequencing all day, but helping other people find love? You just witnessed the disaster of my latest relationship. I'm not the person you should turn to here. Not to mention I don't care about dating in general."

At the lab he'd been all self-righteous, but for just a flash, I can tell that his supposed indifference is a defense mechanism. He might understand the nervous system, but he doesn't understand women and he knows it. He just doesn't want *me* to know it.

"You don't have to set anyone up. You could just help me figure out the business end of things. Plus, this might be a good learning opportunity. Maybe figure out what makes women tick . . ."

"And what makes you think I don't already know? I can basically get any woman I want."

"But can you keep them? What was your longest relationship?"

His face falls. "I thought Fay was going to be 'the one.' We were together for a year before she dumped me."

"Do you know why?"

"Not really? I thought we were perfect. We were going to be a power couple of the academic world, maybe run a lab together and win a Nobel Prize."

"Maybe you got caught up in your fantasies more than in Fay herself?" I suggest.

He shakes his head. "Nope. We want the same things. We're both high achievers motivated by our search for the truth."

He needs my help as much as I need his. I say, "I'll pay you, and it sounds like you could use a romance internship more than another class about brains."

He laughs as if it's the funniest offer he's ever received. "No way, but that's sweet."

"I'm going to take that as a 'no, but I'll think about it.'"

While I wait for Max to change his mind—he totally will—I look down at my phone and see another Instagram notification. Ugh. I'm no longer getting the little happy shot of endorphins you're supposed to get from banners and red badges. Likes and comments last as long as the satisfaction I get from eating a Big Mac, after my insides are coated with french fry grease but before the regret sets in. (Mmm. I was definitely a meat eater at one point.)

It's a message from an official representative of Instagram:

Dear @Mia4Realz, Instagram looked into your concern and has concluded that no hacking has occurred. The post which you referred to was prescheduled by you on May 31, two weeks ago. Please let us know if you have any other concerns. If you need help posting on Instagram, please visit the Instagram help center at help.instagram.com.

This is so much worse than being hacked.

"Max, Instagram got back to me. You know that 'Announcement Coming Soon' post? It was prescheduled." I say it like I just lost my trial and have been convicted of something bad, like murder in the first degree or tax fraud.

After thinking for a second, he says, "Do you have any more scheduled posts? Maybe the actual announcement is in there too."

That's a great idea. My fingers know the way to the prescheduled posts, and I see one queued up to appear tomorrow at noon. Is this it?

"Anything?" Max asks.

It's hard to describe out loud what it is. It's like my pre-amnesia self is taunting my post-amnesia self. "It's a photo of me in a hot-air balloon that's about to take off." I'm with the same girl from the yacht. Apparently she and I had a fun day yachting and ballooning in cute outfits. My heart-shaped glasses and crop top are the height of hipster fashion. It's captioned: #GuessWhat? #GoldRushGirls.

Max blinks a couple times as he processes the photo.

"Don't ask me." I shrug. "Maybe I had too many hot-air-ballooning photos earlier and I was trying to spread them out?"

Max draws his eyebrows together as if he's deeply considering my hot-air balloon pic. "Do you think this is the actual announcement?"

I halfheartedly use the last chip to scoop up what's left of my taco. "I honestly have no idea, but there must be some reason why I scheduled this post." Was it advertising for Gold-Rush? Maybe I have an event at a hot-air balloon place coming up? I could almost push myself into an ice sculpture for writing the vaguest hashtag ever. #GuessWhat? Was that my idea of an announcement?

Maybe the girl with me is Crystal . . . Whoever she is, I didn't tag her, but we look like best friends.

"Max, I need help. I'm begging you."

He makes a funny groaning noise, like he's physically dragging a three-hundred-pound yes from deep within his soul. But when he pulls it out, it's perfect. "Yes, Mia. I'll do it, but let's work on the job title."

Hearing Max say yes is even better than finding out I own a company. I might actually be able to keep the business with his help. "Thank you, Max."

"You could call me a consultant."

"You'd rather be a consultant than an intern?"

"An optimization consultant maybe."

"Your job will be the same no matter what I call it."

"Words matter, Mia."

"How about vice president then?"

He nods as if that's acceptable.

"Vice president . . . of romance," I add, just to see the look on his face. He's so cute when he looks stern about dumb stuff.

"Mia," he admonishes me, his voice suddenly sounding like a sitcom dad's. "Vice president *period*."

"Are you sure? You could be vice president of anything. You could be the vice president of sex, even. As long as it relates to romance."

Max ignores me and looks serious. "What about a contract that covers our mutual obligations?"[24]

Mutual obligations. I know I've hired the right man.

The internet tells us how to draft a contract. I think it's a waste of time but if this is what makes him feel safe . . .

The top Google result tells me to title my document. I type:

GoldRush Employment Contract

Next step: identify the parties. Luckily I found out my last name a few minutes ago so I can make this thing legal. I type: Mia Wallace agrees to hire Max Charles . . .

Next: explain the job to be performed. "Ummmm . . ." I read the words aloud as I type them. "Max will help Mia understand her company and how to run it. This might include matchmaking, dating, accounting—" I stop and look up. "I don't know, what do you think?"

Max looks like he's rethinking his whole life, so I write:

Mia Wallace agrees to hire Max Charles to help with matchmaking and matchmaking support duties.

Sounding very disgruntled, he says, "That makes it sound

---

[24] Please note that I did not make a joke about mutual orgasm. You're welcome, Max.

like I'll be lighting candles and pouring wine."

"I'll add that in," I say, just to annoy him. "Let's move on to length of contract."

"Dear God. I don't know if I'm ready to commit to any length of time."

I make a *I hate to break this to you* face and say, "Maybe that was your problem with Fay."

"Oh my God. Just write a month. I'm sure it'll take at least that long to straighten out anything at the lab."

"We're almost done. Compensation . . . what do you need?"

He thinks for a minute. "I could use two grand for rent. Now that Eric fired me, I've got nothing."

I was expecting a smart-ass comeback, not a serious salary negotiation. "Make it four." That's probably pocket change for me. I show him the final version.

GoldRush Employment Contract

Mia Wallace agrees to hire Max Charles to help with matchmaking and matchmaking support duties, including candle lighting and wine pouring. At the end of one month, Mia will pay Max $4,000 USD.

Safe word: Jacques-o-late

He says, "That is not my safe word." Then he drops his head to his hands and starts shaking with laughter, the delirious kind that hits you when you're at the end of your rope.

"What's so funny?"

"I just negotiated an employment contract with a woman who learned her last name approximately five minutes ago. Are you even legally capable of signing anything?"

"They let me out of the hospital. That means I'm ready for business, Max." Then, more seriously, I say, "I have to be."

Max knows it, too. He sits up, throws back the rest of his horchata, and says, "Time for my employee orientation then."

"*Me* orient *you*?" I didn't know I had a business when I woke up this morning.

"Your phone," he says. "Let's check out GoldRush."

Max locates the app on my phone, which turns out to be an administrative version of the program with searchable profiles and access to accounting. After he changes my password, he downloads it onto his phone too. He lets out a low whistle. "Damn, Mia. You're a high roller."

"What do you mean?"

"Your GoldRush girls. You pay them five grand per date. I should have asked for more money. What kind of qualifications do these chicks have?"

"I think I described them as sophisticated and elite," I say, which is apparently an understatement.

"They must be pretty fucking special."

"Not as special as you, Max." I kiss him on the cheek. "Thank you."

CHAPTER

EIGHT

Before we manage to leave L'Empire Tacos, Instagram hits me up again, baiting me with another notification. My insides clench. What else am I about to discover about myself?

I see that I've been tagged in a post featuring a very, very, very attractive man in nothing but his underwear. His handle is @Jules_In_Briefs, which means he's both clever and unbearably hot. From the look on his face, he knows it. He's making bedroom eyes at the camera and doing something with his lips that makes me want more—pictures, that is.

Even though I know he's playing me, I let out an involuntary, girly sigh. When was the last time I had sex?

Then I notice the thought bubble photoshopped into the image: my profile pic, the one with me in a milk bath with glitter on my face, is pasted into the bubble. He's thinking of me!

I go positively giddy at the sight. How could I not? I'm

all smiley and flushed. Am I ovulating or is it just flattery? Possibly both.

"What are you smiling about?" Max asks. He inches forward, eager to see what has tickled my feminine fancy.

Of course I giggle and say, "Oh nothing." Max doesn't need to see this, but he sneaks a peek and his expression gets all confused and annoyed. "What the—?"

I have to admit, I get it. We just got off the phone with a Swiss billionaire who is totally in love with me, and now @Jules_In_Briefs is thinking about me on Instagram in his underwear. It's kind of a lot.

Max makes a disgusted face and says, "How many boyfriends do you have?"

"It looks like two more than you have girlfriends. I wonder if he's rich too?" I say, just for Max's benefit.

"He's not even a person, Mia. He's probably a bot. He's going to DM you and ask for your banking information and the last four digits of your social security number any minute now."

A second later, I receive a DM from @Jules_In_Briefs. I squeal.

Max glares at me. "What is it?"

In a higher-pitched voice than normal, I announce, "Jules . . . he just texted me. Whoever he is, Max, he knows me. I need to know what he knows."

Max sits up straighter. "Don't open it, Mia. This is serious. Whoever is talking to you is not that guy. It's probably some zitty teenager in his mom's garage trying to steal your money."

I smile at Max. There's no way I'm not talking to @Jules_In_Briefs.

"Whatever you do, don't click on any links."

Not that it's wrong to buy flattery from beautiful people/bots—we *are* in California—but I'm happy to find back-and-forth convos in the comment threads below my posts, implying that Jules and I have *some* sort of relationship. "I definitely know Jules. He's commented on my posts like a hundred times." I might be rounding up for Max's benefit. He's cute when he's all flustered and paying attention to me.

"Relationship with a bot," Max counters.

"You're just jealous."

Max continues to glower.

Another message pops up: Where you @ gurl?

I respond: Taco truck, wru?

Him: You forgot!

Forgot what??!! Deleted all my texts by accident!

He sends a screenshot of our earlier convo.

He had written: June 16. Meet me at 3 at Laguna Beach. To which I had responded: Koo, cu then. 😊🌊🌴

I look up at Max. I'm supposed to be in Laguna Beach right now in a bikini. I'm missing a date with @Jules_In_Briefs. I don't really know who he is, but I want to know more. I want to be there—RIGHT NOW!

I quickly write: OMG!! Leaving now! 🏃‍♀️ 😵

He responds: 👍🏃 On set, but we can still talk.

I don't know who Jules is to me, but I need to find out.

"Max, I have to run to Laguna. I'm supposed to be with Jules right now."

"Mia, are you insane? You can't go meet this guy. You don't even know who he is."

"I set the date before I lost my mind. I'm sure it's fine."

Looking unbelievably annoyed, he says, "He's probably a creep. You can't go alone."

"Um, no offense, but I think it would be weird if you came along. I mean, I'm an adult and I know him. He might be my gay bestie or a client."

"What about . . . JP?" Max asks, fumbling for any excuse.

"What about him? I still don't know what I have with JP, but clearly my pre-amnesia self thought it was okay for me to meet Jules, even while dating JP. I have to trust her."

Max looks huffy.

"I really don't want to go with you. I don't want to be weird and paternalistic, but you just woke up from a coma. If you insist on meeting a stranger who sent a photo of himself in his underwear, I'm going. I'm not going to be responsible for your death." He shakes his head. "I won't be able to live with the guilt when I see your murdered face on the news later."

"Fine. As long as you promise not to get in a pissing match with this dude." Just to push his buttons a little, I add, "No matter how jealous you get."

He looks annoyed at the suggestion. "I'm not *jealous*. I'm just worried."

"It's okay if you're jealous. I am sort of your girlfriend, or your boss, or both. However you want to play it."

Max looks beyond exasperated and I decide maybe I should stop messing with him, even though it's so much fun.

"What the hell is an Instagram model anyway?"

I can see from Max's expression that he doesn't get it and that the concept is making him mad. "Can anyone be an Instagram model? Like, all you have to do is take a picture and put it online, right?"

"Yes and no." He's obviously never thought about Instagram before.

"Could I be an Instagram model?" he asks.

I laugh. "You're like someone's grandpa."

"I mean, who decides that he's an underwear model? You can't just say that you're a genius or a model or a doctor. Someone else has to verify that. Like how a university can't be a university without accreditation."

I remember Brenda and Cindy talking when I first woke up. *Maybe you'll find out you're a movie star or a rocket scientist.* Nothing stopped them from dreaming big on my behalf. "When it comes down to it, all you have to do is tell the world who you are," I say. "That's why the internet is so powerful. Anyone can be anything."

Max arches a brow. "That's one way to look at it." He pulls out his phone, opens an app, and starts rapidly typing. "Well, looks like he's famous enough for a Wikipedia entry. Jules Spencer . . . born June 11, 1987 . . . got his start like most Instagrammers by taking a lot of selfies . . . starts each day by posting a pic in his underwear . . . has 30 million followers waiting to see his daily selfie . . . used this platform to launch his own line, JulesBrand, a monthly subscription service for boxer briefs . . . starring in a remake of *The Fast and the Furious* . . . and his personal life is a long string of high-profile breakups." He looks at me, a self-satisfied smile on his face. "There you have it."

"They're remaking *The Fast and the Furious*?" I ask, momentarily distracted. "I thought they were still putting out sequels?"

Max stares at me. "I bet you're setting him up on a date."

I flash a coy smile. "Or I'm going on a date with the next Paul Walker." Suddenly I know inside that I've watched the whole *Fast and Furious* franchise with my brother or my dad. I don't think I would watch them on my own but I've definitely seen them. It's my third day as New Mia. When is someone besides a hot guy going to come looking for me? Where are my parents, and why don't I have my mom's number?

Laguna is everything. It's beautiful, much like Long Beach, but without oil wells in the harbor or suspicious black puddles on the sand. The bus doesn't run this far down the PCH so there aren't too many tweakers and bums. It reeks of money, instead of weed and piss.

"I wonder why JP lives in Long Beach instead of here?" I say. Really, it would make more sense. This is where the money is.

Max, logical man that he is, says, "I'd rather live in Long Beach. There's good food, a lot to do, and it's more diverse, which makes it more interesting. Plus, Laguna is way the hell out."

I buy a pair of sunglasses and flip-flops to go with my magical yellow dress. If there's an event it isn't meant for, I can't imagine it. Max is wearing loafers that are undoubtedly filled with sand. Despite his brand-new job, which I think he should be thrilled about, his attitude is also still filled with sand. Max has been sandbagged by Jules.

Jules sends me a few Instagram messages with directions: Just look for the crew of photographers.

In my stars and stripes briefs.

Can't miss me.

I respond with a Coming honey!!!

Max rolls his eyes. "Fuck. I can't believe this is happening to me."

When I catch sight of Jules in his American flag underwear, a smile breaks out across my face. I try to smother it for Max's benefit, but I can't. This is too much fun. "Come on, Max. Have you ever been to a photo shoot?"

Hopefully Jules can drive me home and I can just send Max on his way. The sooner, the better.

"Jules!" I yell, waving like a woman stranded on a deserted island with Max, just about to be rescued by a crew of shirtless men.

"Mia! Baby!" he calls out, cool as fuck. He steps away from the crowd of people fussing over him and toward me. I would cue the entrance music but Jules already has live entertainment. A shirtless drummer playing bongos flips his dreads over his shoulders and leans into a syncopated beat as Jules walks toward me. His perfectly tanned skin is finely dusted with sand. When he wraps me in a hug, his sun-warmed skin against mine, I feel a little lightheaded. Proximity to beautiful, charismatic people has a narcotic effect on me, clearly.

"Look at you!" he says. "That yellow dress. Mmm. You look yummy."

While I wag my tail like an overexcited cocker spaniel, Max steps between us. "Hi, I'm Max."

"Oh." Jules looks between us. He gives me a little *you go girl* nod of approval and says, "Nice to meet you, Max. I'm Jules. Want a beer or a water or something? I've got a cooler on the set."

Max reaches for a beer on a nearby craft services table and grabs me a water. "You want one too?" he asks Jules.

"No. I don't drink." He gestures to his face. "Gotta stay hydrated for this glow."

"Yo, Jules," the photographer calls. "How about a shot of you with a surfboard?"

Jules nods. Then he drops to the ground, does a bunch of push-ups, and flips over for some sit-ups. "Gotta pump 'em up before the shot," he explains.

He trots off and strikes a pose next to the surfboard, dragging his waistband lower and staring off at the beach like the waves are calling him. I stare harder. Max just looks annoyed.

After half an hour of watching Jules flex and pose, I'm so relaxed. Does it even matter that I don't know who I am? Parents, job, friends, GoldRush . . . who freaking cares! One of the crew members brings over a beach chair and an umbrella. Jules tells someone else to make sure I have a refreshment, and I'm sipping San Pellegrino *limonata* through a straw. Max declines the chair and paces, looking tense. "What a waste of time," he mumbles. At this point in the day, his T-shirt slogan ("It's not your limbic system, it's mine") is probably right. I still don't know what the limbic system is, but it's definitely his because mine is perfect.

"I don't think Jules is going to kill me," I announce. "If you want to go home . . ."

"We still don't know why you're here. I'm staying."

When Jules is done being spritzed and pampered and has done all the required flexing, he drops into the empty chair next to me. "Let's get down to business. This date with Crystal . . ."

Ahhh. He's not my gay bestie. He's not my second boyfriend. He's one of my clients (yay me!) and he wants a date with *Crystal*, the woman who . . . hung up on me and is supposed to be dating Kobra? I decide to be vague. "Tell me what you're thinking . . ."

"I can't wait to meet her. She sounds"—he kisses his fingers and flares them out like a TV chef—"perfect."

For the second time that day, I wonder: does every man on the planet have a thing for Crystal? First Kobra, now Jules. This woman must be a porn star you can bring home to meet the family. "She is definitely perfect," I respond blandly. Must be.

"It's been a while since I've been in a good relationship."

"Tell me what you need from me," I say, all professional, almost like someone who knows where she lives, or her middle name.

He sits back. From the look on his face, he's getting into the spirit. "It needs to be splashy, something really impressive. A five-star restaurant, skydiving maybe. Have Crystal wear something fab, something that will work in the fanciest restaurant but is easily convertible to a walk on the beach." He looks at me like I know what I'm doing.

I open my Notes app and start tapping away like a professional.

"Oh, and let her know that we'll be doing a lot of Instagramming. I'll probably go live on the date at some point. She might want to stay away from bold patterns. Solids usually look best."

Only half joking, I say, "Are you going to wear clothes?" Does he ever wear clothes?

"Yes. Actually, I'll probably wear a blue suit. Crystal should wear something that complements nicely."

After I write down everything that Jules wants, none of which I have any clue how to provide, I say, "I can't wait to make this happen!"

"Sunday at 8. It's gonna be good."

I freeze. Did he just say Sunday? As in two days from now? There is literally no fucking way I can make that happen. "This is so exciting!" I say. "I better get going so I can finish some last-minute details." I look over my shoulder at Max, who has wandered back toward the craft services table and just popped open another beer. "Hey Max, are you ready to go?"

He stares at the freshly opened beer, takes a long glug, and chucks the half-full bottle into a trash can several feet away, a long arc of beer flying out and splashing a model nearby. He turns back to me. "Yup."

On the way back to the car, I start complaining. "I don't know how I'm ever going to give that man what he wants but I'm assuming he paid the going rate for this match."

"What's the rate again?"

"Thirty-five grand."

Max whistles. "Can you reschedule the date?"

"It has to be on Sunday because of his schedule. Something about flying to Fiji for another shoot."

"Do you know who Crystal is?"

I nod. "Kind of. She won't talk to me. Something happened before my accident."

"Hmm."

I remember my text convo with Kobra the other day. She might talk to *him*. The dude had a boat ride to Catalina planned for her. She must like him better than me, even with all of his biblical tattoos. He looks like the devil but he's probably just a typical macho asshole who talks shit and plays Xbox all day. He definitely doesn't look like one of my millionaire clients, although he could be some fucked-up trust-funder, the broadest catchall category of rich guy. I send out a Hail Mary text:

Did you ever get ahold of Crystal?

A few seconds later, he writes: No. Bitch playing hard to get. Thinks she cute.

Then:

Nvmd. She IS cute. Like Halle Berry wit bigger tits. What's her address? I wanna surprise her.

Gross! Kobra is starting to sound like a total creep. I don't know Crystal but I cringe on her behalf. Fuck Kobra.

I'll tell her you're looking for her.

Not. I dramatically shove my phone in my purse as if that will get Kobra out of my life.

"Max, for your first task as my employee, see if I have any profiles for guys named Kobra in my GoldRush app, will you? It's Kobra with a K, FYI."

"One sec . . . Kobra, Kobra, Kobra. Okay, found him. He's in international trade." He looks up from his phone. "Like what does that even mean? Does he work for the UN, or is he some shady importer-exporter who sends things back and forth to China?"

The thought of Kobra at the UN makes me laugh. I describe his full-body python tat.

"What else is there?"

"He's originally from Florida. For some reason he looks familiar . . . I think I know him from somewhere."

"Maybe you went to school together or something?"

I shrug. "Maybe."

Whoever he is, I would think Crystal would be excited about my matchmaking prowess. It seems like I'm giving her a shot with two millionaires. Even if Kobra is a tool, he's a *rich* tool. Plus, she has a five-thousand-dollar payday for the date with Kobra and is set for another paycheck for Sunday with Jules. That's ten grand for two nights! A Kardashian might even show up for that, which makes Crystal . . . I don't know, an heiress?

Max looks up from his phone. "What do you think? Will Kobra help us find Crystal?"

I shake my head. "I'm done with Kobra. I have a feeling something's off with that dude. I just wanted to figure out if he was a legitimate client or just stalking her. We can find Crystal without his help."

Max says, "You know, I'm starting to think Crystal might know a few things about you."

I laugh, but not in a good way. If Crystal is the only one who truly knows me, then that's not saying much. "Crystal hates my guts."

We're scrambling up a sand hill to get to the car, and Max holds out a hand to help me up. "I know you, Mia. I don't know how anyone could ever hate you."

I revise my earlier opinion. Max wasn't motivated to create a lie detector because he has a higher standard for the truth than others. Without the lie detector he doesn't have a clue. He can't see truth if it slaps him in the face. I could practically kiss him.

Before we leave Laguna, I want to make one more stop. I don't want to explain why, but I take a deep breath and spit it out. "Max, when I was at the art museum, a guy told me that

I fought with some chick at an opening because I was sleeping with her husband. It's probably not true, but I thought it might be worth checking out."

Max looks at me carefully. "Okay . . ."

"He lives in Laguna. We can just swing by real quick and, I don't know—"

"See if anyone at his house wants to kill you?"

"Exactly. It'll just be a quick stop to rule it out." I hope.

CHAPTER

NINE

Frederick Montcalm's house teeters on the tippy top of a mountain overlooking the PCH, a glass shoebox propped up on chopsticks. I can see it for three turns of the road before we arrive.

Max whistles. "Damn, Mia. This one is richer than the last."

"What can I say? I might be a slut." I'm making boyfriend jokes too easily at this point, but the potential affair with Frederick Montcalm disturbs me.

Max waves a hand dismissively. "You probably set this guy up with his wife. You're successful. People are going to talk about you."

I think he's trying to say "haters gonna hate."[25]

A beat later, I say, "I hope you're right. I'll be disappointed if I find out I'm a giant slut."

....

[25] Am I a T-Swift fan?

At the front gate, I square my shoulders, take a deep breath, and hit the button on the intercom box. "Is Frederick home? It's Mia." I could introduce Max, but I want to see if whoever answers says, "Mia, you bitch!" or "Come on in, sweetie."

Someone buzzes the gate open without commentary and I pull the Ferrari up to the turnaround. The housekeeper (of course there's a housekeeper) ushers us into the house and leads me to Frederick, who has a blanket covering his lap, a half-finished crossword puzzle clutched in his hand, and no hair. It's not male-pattern baldness, it's just that all of his systems have started failing due to age, including his hair. He's probably ninety.

There's no way I was having an affair with this man. Then I look around and realize maybe I was having an affair with his house. Did I pay for this view with an occasional blow job? I hug my chest as if to protect myself from the old pervert or maybe to restrain the demon inside me who would blow an old guy for a beautiful view. I look at Max with the fear of God in me and silently mouth, *Am I Anna Nicole?*

He gives me a genuine smile. *No.*

I certainly hope not. "Mr. Montcalm," I say. He's dozing and my voice brings him to.

He takes a minute to look around. "Hi, dear. You're home early."

Fuck. He recognizes me.

Max extends his hand. "Hi, sir, I'm Max Charles. Nice to meet you."

"Are you an artist too?"

Frederick thinks I'm an artist. Snapchat hearts practically spring from my brain spontaneously and encircle my head like a fairy princess wreath. This is my favorite misconception since waking up.

The room instills a zenlike calm in me, even considering the fact that I'm possibly meeting my ninety-year-old lover.

I exhale and decide to go for one hundred percent honesty. How else am I going to get to the bottom of everything? "I'm so sorry, Frederick. Do you know me? I'm having trouble remembering things."

He laughs. "You're so funny, sweetheart."

Fuck. I *am* having an affair with this geezer. I flash a panicked look at Max.

Frederick sets down his crossword puzzle. "What do you think of that latest painting from Jeric? I think it might be too obvious. I hate obvious themes."

I'm still staring at him. Am I an artist having an affair with this guy? I can't fit that in with everything else I've learned.

"Lauren, did you hear me?"

I don't respond. I just can't.

"Lauren?"

Max says, "Who do you think this woman is, Mr. Montcalm?"

Frederick looks at him, totally baffled. "My wife, of course."

Oh great. I've literally sought out an Alzheimer's patient to help me figure out who I am. #figures.

I glance at a framed picture of a middle-aged woman with

blond hair and a yoga body. That must be Lauren.

I point to the picture and whisper to Max, "There's the woman who must have tried to murder me." All of that inner peace must have exploded out of her in a fit of violent rage. I think that happens more often than people are willing to admit. It takes a lot of bottled-up rage to hold a side plank for a minute.

"So you have no clue who I am?" I repeat.

"Would you turn on the television, Lauren? I want to watch that show with all the cooking and the British accents." There's an edge to his voice now, like he's sick of Lauren not acting enough like Lauren.

I bet Lauren is out spending Frederick's money and talking to a lawyer about inheritance law in between yoga headstands.

While Max chats with Frederick about modern art and his wife, I decide to give myself a tour of the house I might have been gunning for. It's all contemporary California living, a sleek, sexy house with an open-concept floor plan for entertaining beautiful people. The side of the house facing the ocean is floor-to-ceiling glass that takes advantage of the view. Modern art pieces accent what little wall space there is. It's beautiful, but if you look straight down, it's almost as if you could tumble down the cliff the house is suspended above. I think it's a view that could cost you your life.[26]

On an expanse of white wall facing the ocean in the dining area, there's a painting that draws me in. It's all blues and

....

[26] And I've already determined that I'm not dramatic.

greens, the color of tropical water. A dark shape lurks below the surface. Not the typical hint of a shark. This looks like the outline of a woman with her dress billowing around her. She's drowning, I think. A placard below the painting identifies it as *Artist at Seashore* by Lauren Montcalm.

While I fixate on the drowning woman, my head starts to feel weird and I lean against the wall and slowly sink to the floor. When I shut my eyes against the pain in my head, I see Lauren. She's standing in front of the window overlooking the Pacific. The blue and green painting is in the background.

"Mia, what are you doing here?" She's upset with me.

"I need money."

"You need to stay away."

Lauren Montcalm . . . Why did I need money from her? Was it a payoff to walk away and leave her marriage undisturbed? Am I an extortionist trying to get as much money as possible from a nice lady who does yoga and paints pictures of drowning women that represent how she feels being married to a ninety-year-old man?

Am I a mean slut?

There's a martini shaker and a bottle of gin in the corner of the room. I might not know who I am but I know what to do with the shaker. I throw together a martini as if I've done it a million times, probably while entertaining all those billionaires drinking cocktails on *The Good Life*. Frederick pipes up from the corner. "Do I hear you making a drink, darling? Would you make me one, too?"

"Of course dear," I say like I'm in an old Hollywood movie, wearing my satin day dress. That seems to be Frederick's reality, at least based on the way he talks to Lauren.

Poor Lauren.

I carry three martinis on a silver tray to the cozy seating area Frederick seems to prefer. It's on the side of the house that faces the driveway and, in my opinion, preferable. "Frederick?" I say, handing him a glass. He takes it and says, "To us."

"To us," I echo as I lift my glass. Whoever the hell *us* is.

Max silently takes the third martini. I think he gets that it's better for me to play along with Frederick's delusion right now.

Frederick takes a few sips and starts to doze off again. Max wanders freely while I glance back at the picture of Lauren. I hate to say it but she looks like she can take me. I should probably exercise in addition to avoiding meat.

Max and I finish our martinis and leave them on the tray for the housekeeper, who's nowhere to be seen. Before we let ourselves out, I take a last glance at the Pacific, which is spread out before us looking like the $10,000-per-square-foot view that it is. I can't imagine trying to steal that man from his wife, but so far, betting against myself seems to be a winning strategy.

"Max, I remembered something. I've been to this house before."

"What happened?"

"Nothing," I lie. "I just saw Lauren in the house. She was mad at me, but I don't know why." I don't want to tell him I was asking for money.

"Hmm. Sometimes recovered memories aren't true. A lot of times, if someone suggests something, you can actually have a vision of that memory, but it's only because of the suggestion."

I nod.

"Just like when you think you remember events from your childhood that happened to a brother or sister because you've heard the story. That guy at the art museum might have unintentionally planted that memory."

"That sounds smart."

"You probably set up Frederick and Lauren or went to a party at their house, if anything."

I love how Max doesn't want to think the worst of me. It warms my heart. Thinking the best of myself is getting harder. I could easily believe that I was using so many people, that I was sleeping my way to the top, that I was associating with known criminals. And I haven't even told Max everything. I can't give up Max's good opinion. If I can only be the woman he thinks I am . . .

"You want to drive, Max?" What red-blooded American man doesn't want to drive a red Ferrari down a coastal highway? I owe him at least that.

He says, "Are you sure? It's JP's car," but he has an eager look on his face.

"I'm so sure."

———

Halfway down, Max pulls into a scenic overlook.

"I'm okay, Max. You don't need to pull over."

"I'm not worried about you. You might think you slept with that old guy, but there's no way you could have. I almost felt bad for him the way you were looking at him. I've never been rejected that hard before."

With a flip laugh, I say, "I bet you haven't." Any girl would think twice before rejecting Max. "Anyway, you're too optimistic." I would tell him about the extortion, but doing so would violate my policy of hiding the worst facts about me.

He gets out of the Ferrari and walks over to the gravel turnaround. There's a steep drop-off with no guardrail.

"We have too much to do, Max! We don't have time for scenic overlooks," I shout into the wind. I have to find Crystal, learn how to run a business, and figure out who assaulted me before Sunday. "Plus, are you sure you want to give up on your job completely?"

He gives me a *let's not talk about it* look. "I'm sitting my black ass down on this bench and looking at the ocean. There's always time for the ocean."

I give up and get out of the car, kicking the gravel with my toe in front of Max, who is defiantly relaxing.

"I like that house over there. That yellow one is bomb," he says. I recognize it for what it is, a prompt for me to chill and engage in the scenic view with him.

I nod. "Yeah, it looks good." They all look good. I can't bring myself to care about the stupid house, but I do care about Max, who, it strikes me, I know very little about. "Where are you from?" I ask. I can't believe I haven't asked him that yet, or anything else for that matter.

"Duluth, Minnesota."

"How does that work?" I ask, sitting next to him. "Isn't everyone in Duluth Swedish or something? It sounds like the whitest place on the planet."

He laughs. "It pretty much is. My parents are both math professors at the University of Minnesota. I was basically the only black kid wherever I went, at least until I got to college. It was a total culture shock."

"Professors. That sounds nice." I wonder what *my* parents do. Or if they're even still alive.

"It was nice. I grew up in a renovated old house in a residential neighborhood overlooking the lake. My childhood was all hockey, science fairs, hot chocolate after school."

"Overlooking the lake," I repeat. "Sounds pretty bougie to me." My cynicism about the view is melting away with Max, though. There's something psychologically healing about overlooking the world from a hilltop. "Why is a view so calming?" I ask.

"Because you can see your enemies coming. It's a biology thing."

He's right. If whoever pushed me into Cupid came running up the hill, I'd go in the other direction—or maybe stand my ground. Max is so smart.

"Duluth is the middle-class version of this. Lake Superior looks as big as an ocean, but it's gray and frozen half the year."

Suddenly I want to ask Max a million questions—Does he have siblings? What did he do on Friday nights when he was kid? Who did he take to the prom?—but my thoughts are interrupted by another notification from Instagram. I think it's going to be Jules but it's a message from someone called @JennyBeans11561.

Hi, saw your selfie at the museum. Super cute! 😍 🥰 Anyhoo, I worked the night of the party. Your GF is cray. 💯 She literally said, "If you ever come near me again, I'll kill you!"

My girlfriend? I'm just going to take this as confirmation that I definitely wasn't getting along with at least one woman at the party.

I respond, Thanks @JennyBeans11561! Let me know if you think of anything else. Love your profile photo! Xoxo.

Max isn't impressed when I read the message out loud to him. "I don't know if someone who goes by @JennyBeans11561 is a credible source."

"You can't judge people by their Insta handles. Yours is @BlackEinstein314," I scoff. I'm feeling defensive because I'm pretty sure I've been a @JennyBeans11561 at some point in my life.

"What's the matter with that? I'm proud of being black and smart. More black guys should be proud of that instead of bragging about street shit."

I hold my hands up. "OMG. We don't have to get all racial about this. I just think you sound like a total snob. That's all." I flash an overblown smile and he laughs.

"Coming from you?! All you do is take pictures of yourself."

"That's what everyone does, Max. Not taking pictures of yourself doesn't make you better than me."

"Ummm, it might."

I slap his arm and try to remember that line from the *MySelfie* exhibit about how selfies make the world more democratic . . .

"I just mean that you should take anything anyone says to you on Instagram with a grain of salt. It's not like she's testifying in court."

"But that's the beauty of Instagram, Max. You can be anyone you want online. There's a filter for any look you want to achieve, any mood you want to set."

Max gives me the side-eye. "I mean, that's nice if you only care about what's on the surface, but it's ultimately fake. Who cares if some chick in Florida likes your photos if your life actually sucks? I think people need to pay attention to what really matters."

I shake my head. "What are you, eighty?" I don't even know how he's surviving in this day and age.

"My point," he says, "is that you shouldn't trust everyone you meet online."

"Max." I look at him. "Not all of us need people to be hooked up to a brain scanner to understand if they're telling the truth."

He looks at me and starts laughing. "Oh, trust me—it helps. I'd take it with me everywhere if I could."

"You're going to have to make it a little sleeker, in that case. And really, do you always want to know if someone is telling the truth?" I stand and snap a few selfies with the ocean in the background, taking five shots at just the right angle until I have the perfect photo. After I filter it through Clarendon, which makes the blue of the ocean and my eyes pop, I show him the result. I look like I could be on the cover of any magazine. "Isn't this nicer than the reality that someone tried to kill me a few days ago and I have no memory of who I am?"

Max nods. "Yep, you look gorgeous—like a model, even. A beautiful girl in front of a beautiful view. But something's missing." He gets a sparkle in his eye and pats the bench next to him. "Come over here."

I start laughing. "Oh, I have an idea of what you think is missing."

He laughs, takes my phone from me, and slings his arm around my shoulder. He holds the camera in front of us, capturing the gravel turnaround in the background rather than the ocean. "There we go. Now *that's* a good picture."

I study the photo. Our heads are pressed close together. He has a cheesy grin, and I'm mid-laugh. We look happy.

"It captures exactly this moment and what I would want to remember."

"It *is* really cute. But if I were to redo it, I'd pose us in front of the ocean and filter it. And I'd make sure that you could see my whole dress and then maybe tag it #love or #firstdate or #myboo."

Max shakes his head. "It's perfect. Our expressions say it all."

What does he think our expressions say? "You're gonna have to hashtag it for me then."

He laughs. "Enjoy the mystery." He leaves his arm around my shoulder, and we look at the sunset for at least a minute before I pull out my phone again.

On our way back to Long Beach, I call Crystal. She doesn't answer. A small part of me is relieved to avoid the verbal harassment, not to mention a window into my past life I might not want to take a peek through. If it weren't for the $35,000 at stake and the fact that Jules is waiting for his foulmouthed dream girl, I would delete her from my contacts.

But I'm starting to think I should warn her about Kobra, or at least give her a heads-up. Maybe he's fine and just dying for another date with her, but . . . maybe he's as scary as he looks.

Crystal's voicemail message is intimate and cute: "It's me. Leave a message," she says like the only people who call her are her best friends.

I channel my inner BFF. "Crystal!! It's me. Mia. I got you a date with an amazing guy. It's on Sunday. Call me!" After I hang up, I text her the details. Date with Jules at 8 pm in two days. Sorry for late notice! He's super excited to see you!!!

Also, Kobra is looking for you . . .

I wait a beat and then decide to throw a Hail Mary and tell her the truth. Sorry for whatever happened between us. I had a head injury last week and my memories are a little fuzzy. Hope you're not still mad!

This is bad. Even without the head injury we're getting down to the wire. I charge $35,000 for a match, and Jules thinks he's meeting the woman of his dreams this weekend. I can only hope she'll decide to forgive me for whatever I did—and fast.

CHAPTER

TEN

As we head north on the PCH toward Long Beach, Max plays a neuroscience podcast called *The Naked Neuroscientists*—nerd alert. This particular episode about memory was obviously selected in my honor and Max looks like he would be taking notes if his hands were free, but all of the science talk makes me as sleepy as if I were drinking a glass of warm milk with cookies. Two minutes of mnemonics discussion and I'm out.

When the engine shuts off and the sudden silence wakes me up (how does that work?), all I want to do is go back to sleep or maybe drive back to Laguna with Max and admire the ocean view I was too busy to stop for an hour ago. Reality is too much. "Ugh." I rub the sleep from my eyes and groan. "I still have to find Crystal."

Max opens the door and gives me a hand out of the car. "We'll figure it out."

"Max, should you be worrying about your project, too?

I'm glad you're working for me, but I don't want you to lose your career, if you need to . . ." I trail off because it's not like I know what he should be doing.

"No. This is where I want to be." He offers me an arm to help me to the back door, either because I look too sleepy to walk or because he wants to be close.

I might not know my own mother, but I know I'm not a person to question a win-win situation. Thank you, Max.

As we pick our way through the lamplight to the back door, Max drops a bombshell. "Mia, I hate to say this but do you have anything else to wear? That dress, it's pretty, but . . ."

While he disarms the alarm system, I smell my pits. I still smell mostly like whatever designer perfume I put on pre–head injury, but there are some strong base notes that aren't quite floral.

"Don't get me wrong, it looks great. I think you got some coffee on it earlier, though, and I don't know what that is," he says, pointing to a smear of something along the hem, blood.[27]

He's right. I've been working this cocktail dress a little too hard. It's remarkably resilient fabric but it's not made out of yoga pants. "I don't have anything else."

"No problem. JP has a dry-cleaning service. They'll do it overnight. You just have to message them."

Wow—perks of being a billionaire. Crystal's giving me a headache, but the rest of this gig is pretty sweet.

....

[27] Men are so squeamish.

"Mind if I grab one of those for the night?" I ask, pointing at Max's mountain of T-shirts on the couch.

"Go for it."

Max's T-shirt features a picture of a guy dribbling a brain like a basketball and the slogan NEUROSCIENCE, GET IN THE GAME! "Do you play basketball?" I ask.

"Departmental team," he says.

All those nerdy lab geeks playing basketball. I clutch my heart at the vision of their awkward hooping.

I settle on the couch in Max's T-shirt, which smells like him—Old Spice deodorant, laundry soap, and a hint of something that must be pheromones because I want to bury my face in it.

Gotta snap out of it, though, and think about my "real" life.

I backtrack through Jules's files in my GoldRush app. According to his "ideal mate survey," he wants a woman between 5'9" and 5'11" who plays the harp, plus some other equally absurd qualifications. Was he joking?

Maybe there's a harp-playing Crystal lookalike on Craigslist? I think it's a long shot but my first search is a fucking B.I.N.G.O.

Beautiful princess lookalike for birthday parties! Elsa, Ariel, Snow White, Cinderella, Jasmine, Mulan, and Tiana.

"OMG Max, I figured it out." I explain my stroke of brilliance. "So all I have to do is decide which princess Jules is the most into."

One of the princesses even plays the harp. A birthday (or date, hopefully!) can include:

- Balloon art

- Caricatures

- Princess clowns

- Face painters

- Harpists

- Magicians

This could turn into quite the date. She could perform magic tricks and draw his picture if the sparks don't fly. Setting aside the matter of the princess clown, which now I can't help but imagine as someone's resume headliner, I focus on the harp player. "So the question is whether one of the princesses plays the harp or if some ugly dude accompanies them."

Max gives me a *duh* look. "All harp players are hot. It's an unwritten rule." He can tell I'm not convinced, so he brings Siri into it. "Okay Siri, show me pictures of harpists." He holds up the phone to show me the results and says, "See what I mean?"

He's right. All harpists look like Russian ballerina super-models. Even the male ones.

I'm ready to call it. Crystal is out and Elsa is in. I dial the number from Craigslist and one of the princesses, presumably, answers with a dramatic two-syllable "Hiiiii-eeee." I forgive her. She learned to talk by watching *Gossip Girl* as everyone of a certain generation did.

"Hi! I'm calling with a last-minute request."

"Ugh. We really can't do last minute. I mean, we're booked

out for, like, months," she says as if the princess clowns are Hollywood royalty. "Buuuut . . . we do have a cancellation this weekend, if you need it."

What a faker. They probably have no bookings at all. But I play along. "That's amazing!" And it sort of is. Now that I know about them, maybe I can just run my whole business with princess clowns. "So I would love to book one harp-playing princess for Sunday."

"Just one?" she asks. "We don't travel alone. For safety."

Jesus. "Well, this isn't for a child's birthday party. It's a party, just not a kid party."

"Umm," she says. "Are you asking for what I think you're asking for, because we don't do that. Ewww."

"It's just a last-minute thing. I set up a guy with a girl but she's not going to show up."

"I don't get it. Just tell him she's not showing. Why would you hire a birthday princess to go out with him? And for that matter, do you want the girl in costume . . . because that sounds extra freaky."

I let out a high-pitched laugh. "Of course not. It's just that I run a matchmaking service and I have a guy, a great catch by the way, waiting to go on a date with a girl who looks like a princess. He paid *a lot* of money."

After a few seconds of silence on the other end, she says, "I'm not a prostitute. I believe in God."

"It's sex worker," I correct her in a snobby tone. The indignant correction comes out of my mouth like I say it all the time. Do I? Also, God and prostitution are not mutually exclusive, but I don't think she wants to hear my opinion. I give it one last try. "I'm not asking you to do anything you don't want to do, just go on a date with a rich guy who will buy you dinner."

"I did not go to clown school to be a prostitute."

"I feel ya, girl. Me either." I take a deep breath and confess. "I'm an entrepreneur, too. I'm not pimping anyone. In fact, if he did anything you didn't want, I'd be the first to fuck him up."[28]

She doesn't respond to my generous offer, so I continue. "That's cool if you don't want to go on the date, but if you change your mind, you have my number. Look me up on Insta—@Mia4Realz. I own GoldRush."

When I hang up, I look at Max and say, "Doesn't prostitution sound like a natural consequence of clown school?"

"What?" He opens his mouth to say something else and repeats, "What? What did I miss?"

My eyes start to water. "Oh my God, what is the matter with me, Max?"

He puts his arm around me. "It's okay, Mia. Your brain is saturated. I think you took in more than you can handle today. I feel like I've lived at least five Fridays in the last sixteen hours."

The tears are flowing now. He's right. I've had enough and it's late. Also, am I a pimp? "I thought it would be so much easier than this. Just go back to where I took the pictures and

....

[28] I would be a great pimp, if I chose to go in that direction. But matchmakers aren't pimps, are they?

fill in the blanks, but it's all . . . I don't know . . . nothing makes sense. I was partying on a yacht that wasn't mine. I got knocked out at a party I wasn't invited to. Who am I? And where is the line between matchmaker and pimp? It's starting to feel blurry. Maybe Elsa was right."

"Don't worry." He gives me another squeeze. "You might be a pimp. I'm not ruling that out yet, but . . ." He catches my eye. "As your vice president, I'm advising you not to worry about your job description. You're out of sock-drawer money and you need to access your bank accounts. Get online and change your passwords."

I take a deep breath, square my shoulders, and shake off my existential crisis like a boss. "I'm so glad I hired a genius to help me," I say.

Max taps his fingers on the edge of the couch cushion. "Jules has never met Crystal, right?"

I nod.

"So your idea of finding a backup is good."

"I just need to deliver someone kind of like who he expects."[29]

"I'm pretty sure that you'll be able to find a woman willing to go on a date with an underwear model tomorrow night." He laughs. And when he phrases it that way, it does sound absurd.

"Oh, so you're good at finding dates?"

"Never had a problem," he says, with a look in my direc-

....

[29] "Kind of like a supermodel who plays the harp" is a definition with a large margin of error, I think.

tion that makes me believe him. I'd definitely sign up for some of what he's offering. "I don't know why that dude needs to hire out." He looks at me like I'm the expert and asks, "Why is that?"

Like I know! But before I say that, some guesses spring into my head from the ether, or my subconscious mind—one of the two. "I can see why they want my help. I mean, if you could buy yourself out of the online dating game, wouldn't you? I think some of these guys are just in it for the convenience. They probably think I know what I'm doing and will save them a bunch of bad dates, like I'll just provide them with their dream woman on the first try."

Max accepts that with a thoughtful nod.

"Also, there must be some narcissistic asses, guys with money who think they can just order a beautiful girl off a menu. I hope I charge those ones double."

He squeezes me shoulder before pulling his arm back. I can't help but notice that our relationship has been getting more . . . tactile. I like it, but the rapidly changing dynamic between us is a little too much for me to take in right now. I scroll through my home page on my phone and click on the Wells Fargo banking app. Thankfully my username is plugged in. I click "I forgot my password" because duh.

Obviously, I do not know the answers to the three security questions: mother's maiden name, town of birth, name of cat. Speaking of which: "What if I have a cat?" I ask Max, panic edging into my voice again. Somehow, I just know that I don't have a dog, which would require stability and consistency. No offense to me but . . . that seems like a long shot, especially if I have a boyfriend, a secret old boyfriend, plus a bunch of rich dudes looking for dates. Ugh. Who has that kind of time?

Max puts his hand over mine. "Don't worry. If you do, I'm sure a roommate is feeding it or something." With a confused look, he says, "Why don't you ask JP? He probably knows all of this stuff."

"I don't trust him yet," I say. "I don't know why, but I don't." That's not entirely true. The man apologized to me for something, and until I know what that is, I'm going to hold back a little—at least until we can meet in person.

I push thoughts of JP and my hypothetical cat aside and navigate to my Mail app. I see the email from Wells Fargo and click on "reset password." It navigates me to a webpage and asks me to create an alphanumeric code that I will promptly dump into the void of things I've forgotten, along with the rest of my life. At the end of the process, a dialog box pops up: Unable to reset password. Please contact a bank representative.

I go through the process again. The same message appears. "Do I actually have to go to the bank? That seems so 1999."

Max looks over my shoulder to read the message. "I think so."

I make a puking noise. That's how I feel about doing business in person. I'd rather get food poisoning. But it's too late to do anything about this tonight; the banks are long closed. "I guess I know where I'm going tomorrow morning."

CHAPTER

ELEVEN

Saturday morning and it's as if the failures of Friday have been washed away, some of them by dry cleaners. JP's fancy dry-cleaning service dropped off my yellow dress at the crack of dawn, or at least I assume they did. I wasn't awake then. Thank you for being rich and practical, JP! So glad I won't start today smelling like old horchata. California is showing off with low smog and lots of sun. It probably looks the same as yesterday, but the sleep filter is a miracle. My mood = Katy Perry's "California Gurls" featuring Snoop Dogg.

So hot I'll melt your popsicle, I make an entrance into the living room where Max is already neurosciencing and eating a bagel like the amazing man he is. His uniform today includes a pink T-shirt that says the MILLENNIAL FALCON, with a schematic of the *Millennium Falcon* drawn into the outline of an avocado, which makes me think of an avocado hurtling through space at warp speed.[30] I wonder if Max has paused from his quest for a Nobel Prize long enough to consider any of his T-shirts in depth. "So, Max, you were asking where those quinoa farms in outer space were going to be, right?"

He looks up, waiting for the answer, and I look deliberately at his T-shirt because that is the answer. "Max, where do you get your T-shirts?"

"Mostly at departmental functions."

As I suspected, he's not a shopper. These T-shirts just happen to him and he doesn't question it. Sort of like me. I am now one of his T-shirts. He doesn't know why I fit, but there's no denying that I sorta do.

"So I was thinking," he says, "let's start at the bank today."

"Let's," I answer.

———

We're pulling the Ferrari into a space on Linden near the bank when Kobra texts. Can I buy you a latte sexy?

What the—?

When? Why?

Yellow is your color. Meet at Cuppa.

Then, after a moment, he adds:

Now.

"This Kobra asshole is really starting to annoy me," I say to Max. But before I can tell him more of my thoughts on snake

....

[30] Band name idea: Interstellar Food Fight, just in case I find out I'm a drummer.

boy, I look over his shoulder and my blood runs cold. Max has just parked in front of Cuppa Cuppa, which is only a block from the bank—and of course I'm wearing my yellow dress, now stain free and smelling slightly of dry-cleaning solvents. How does Kobra know we're here?

I show Max the text.

"Kobra? Which one is he? I can't keep up with all of these assholes."

"Kobra with a K, the snake charmer compensating for his tiny dick, or at least I assume—how can you forget him?" I don't remind him that keeping up with all of those assholes is his brand-new job. "Remember? Crystal went out with him and never called him back."

"Learn to take rejection, asshole," Max says. "You gotta cut him loose from the roster and block his calls."

I'm waiting, the usual place, your regular drink.

The longer I sit with the weird string of texts, the more I get that sinking feeling in my gut. This isn't someone I can ignore. For whatever reason, Kobra knew I would come here. Did my phone send out some signal? Did I post something without knowing it again?

I show Max the text and he gets real quiet, probably thinking the same thing. "He's either following us or tracking you."

"Maybe I should call and tell the police that a creepy stalker is following me."

"Not a bad idea," he says.

"I don't want to call the police yet. I want to see his face and figure out what he wants. Right now, he knows more about me than I do—and I need to find out why." He's a piece of the puzzle, even if he's one I'll eventually want to throw out.

Max nods. "I'm cool with that. I don't think he's going to kill either of us in a coffee shop. And we need the caffeine."

"I know. And that maple latte was to die for."

With an expression that is 100 percent *Really?*, he says, "Maybe not the best choice of words given the situation." He opens the car door and hooks his arm through mine. "I'll be your bodyguard. Let's go meet this asshole."

"Do you think I should tell the barista, like maybe she could write down his real name and . . ."

"Unless she knows kung fu, I don't think you need to let her know. You already have lots of information about the guy from the GoldRush files. I mean, you had to have done some research to make sure he was actually a millionaire."

"Unless I'm an idiot." That seems likely at the moment.

"Definitely not an idiot," Max says, which makes me feel a little better. He's definitely not an idiot, so if he says I'm good, I'm good.

I take a deep breath and step onto the sidewalk. I can do this. I just have to pretend that I'm a badass. Actually, I don't have to fucking pretend. I *am* a badass. Who does this fucker think he is? I'm shaky but not from fear; I'm just mad as hell. "Let's get a coffee and find out what his deal is."

Max holds up his hands. "I wouldn't mess with you. Let him have it and I've got your back." He might be a neuroscientist who hasn't seen the outside of a lab since I hired him, but I believe him. Advisable or not, Max will defend me against all of my enemies.[31]

I don't say it out loud, but I know we're both thinking it—this is probably the guy who sent me to the hospital. Maybe art museum guy thought it was a woman, but Kobra has just moved to the top of my suspect list.

Once we're inside Cuppa Cuppa, I scan the shop. It's quiet, a few people with laptops are scattered around the room as far apart from each other as possible. The barista from Friday is behind the counter and she gives me a nod when she catches sight of me. "Hey!" She starts to ask if I want the regular before stopping herself to beckon me over conspiratorially. When I lean over the counter, she whispers, "I think someone might have already ordered for you."

"Really?"

"You know how you were asking me about your friends earlier?"

I nod.

"You've met the guy on the patio here before, once or twice. I remember the one time for sure because it was the same time you lost your cell phone."

"Ah. You found it in the bathroom, right?"

She nods.

I have a feeling that had something to do with Kobra. I don't know what, but it can't be a coincidence that I lost

....

[31] I should probably pay him more.

my phone when I was with him and now he's tracking me. Unless it is.

Before we step outside, I ask Max, "Am I just being a conspiracy nut, or . . ."

"Nope. People have evolved to believe in conspiracies because they exist. Natural selection favors people who avoid threats that might result in reproductive loss and harm, like conspiracies. Your ability to see potential conspiracies is evidence that your brain is perfect."

Is Max hitting on me? "Not as good as your brain, Max," I say in a semiseductive voice, then add with complete sincerity, "Thank God I hired a scientist."

"I'm a neuroscientist, Mia, not a Geek Squad guy, if you're thinking about the phone issue."

I point out the obvious. "A guy named Kobra who thinks he can charm snakes figured out how to hack my phone in a few minutes. I'm sure you can, too."

The back patio, which I didn't notice on our last visit, is a beautiful brick courtyard with bistro tables and big umbrellas. It feels very European, though the palm trees lining the square sort of ruin the vibe. I spot Kobra immediately, and he sees me too. He's wearing an unbuttoned shirt and his snake tattoo covers his whole torso. I feel sexually harassed just being in his presence.

"Hi, Kobra." I try to act as natural as a person can while saying hi to a guy named Kobra. I don't want this asshole to know that I don't remember anything before Tuesday, that I'm vulnerable. Even if he was the one who sent me to the hospital, he doesn't have to know he knocked all the brains out of me. #gameon.

Max dramatically pulls out a chair for me and I say, "Thank you."

"Of course."

I can't see Kobra's eyes through his shades. "Who's this? You bring security today? Or is he your new boyfriend?"

"None of your concern," Max says. His voice has a hard edge that I haven't heard before.

"I don't think Mr. French Billionaire would like that very much." Kobra gives me a nod of approval. "Nice dude, by the way. He's so smooth. I don't normally like Europeans, even the girls—I just can't do body hair. Can't charm my snake if your bush looks like it could talk back."

I cringe as he laughs at his own joke, if that's what it was. "Gross," I say.

"Tell me about it."

"I meant you."

He laughs. "Mmm. I always did like you. Feisty!"

"What do you want from me?" I ask. "How'd you know I was going to be here?"

"Good guess." He smiles, all superior.

What a snake. "Don't play with me," I say. "You messed with my phone."

He chuckles. "Of course I messed with your phone. I do that to everyone, sweetheart. It's just good business to keep tabs on some people."

I shake my head. "That's not how I do business. It's over."

"Well, if you don't like it, just turn it off. I activated Find My Friends." When I pull up the app, I see his name. It says my "friend" Kobra is following me. A stupid picture of him smiles back at me.

"See, it wasn't a secret."

I deactivate the app. "If you ever track me again, I'm calling the cops."

He chuckles like that's the best news he's heard all day. "I don't know how you keep your hands off her, man. She's *really* feisty."

I make a face like I'm about to barf and Max says, "Stop being an asshole."

"You gotta let girls know you're hot for them. That's how relationships work."

OMG. Kobra giving relationship advice. "Let's get on with it. Why did you want to meet?"

"You know why. Crystal."

Fucking Crystal! My head is going to explode. What is it with this chick?

"I paid to go out with her. I expected her to answer my calls after. Did I pay thirty-five grand for one date?"

"If you were acting like this, I understand why Crystal didn't take your calls after."

"Well, I want to see her again. As is, I'm not a satisfied customer."

"You are—no, *were*—a client, not a customer. You're not buying a woman. You're paying me to give you an opportunity to form a real connection. It appears that you already blew that. And I'm not surprised. Not to mention, why does it have to be her?" Not that I'll set this freak up with anyone, except the police.

"She's gorgeous, street-smart—everything I'm looking for in a woman. You matched me up perfectly."

Funny he should say that, given that I seem to be matching Crystal with everyone. "That's nice of you to say but I've fulfilled my part of the contract and so did Crystal."

He pulls out a Crown Royal bag and scoots it across the table to me. "I think you'll change your mind if you take a peek in there. You and Crystal split that up however you want. I want another date."

I pull the golden draw cord. Inside, I find wads of hundred-dollar bills, maybe two or three packs, which I happen to know hold ten grand apiece. That makes it at least twenty thousand dollars.[32]

While I'm gaping at the money, which looks like the real-life version of the money bag emoji, he looks toward the counter. "Did you see the pastries here? I'm dying for a slice of pie to go with this coffee."

He's about to flag down the barista and seems genuinely concerned about what kind of pie he might be able to find here. I cut him off. In as badass a voice as I can manage, I say, "If Crystal doesn't want to see you, she doesn't want to see you. You're done. I am no longer your matchmaker. You're fired."

....

[32] Maybe I used to work at a bank?

Instead of responding to me, he looks at Max. "You hitting that, dude?" He gestures to me. "I gotta say, I'm getting a little turned on. I hate the timid ones. If you want to go out instead of Crystal, I'll take it under consideration."

Ugh. I'm going to vomit.

"Word of advice, sugar," Kobra says. "You gotta know when your hoes are done. If Crystal's not pulling her weight, she's past her shelf life. You can't run her anymore."

"Eww! I'm not a pimp!" I throw the bag of money at his head. Hard. He ducks and it flies past him. "Asshole!" I scream. "No wonder Crystal won't call you back! You're. The. Worst!"

Kobra turns to see cash flying out of the bag. The other diners in the courtyard look on in total amazement, and a woman sipping a latte puts her mug down and looks like she might stand and make a run for the bag. Kobra sees her out of the corner of his eye and screams "You're a crazy bitch!" at me before running for the money.

Max grabs my shoulder and says, "Let's get out of here," in a voice that is 190 proof, only-Poland-makes-that-kinda-alcohol serious. I thought he was focused before, but all of his intensity has been distilled into laser-like focus on getting out of the coffee shop before the police come or Kobra decides to bite.[33] I agree.

....

[33] Or strangle us.

On the way to the bank Max is quiet. After a moment, he says, "Do you think there's any way that Crystal is dead?"

"She can't be . . ." I start to say. "I don't think so, anyway. She answered my call on Thursday afternoon and told me to leave her alone."

Max seems satisfied. "I'm sure she's fine, then."

"Probably. She might not mind if I was dead, though." Kobra was so awful. I can't believe I knew he was that bad before I sent Crystal on a date with him.

"He can probably be charming when he wants to be. Most assholes can."

"Can you believe he called me a pimp?"

"You're not a pimp."

"I know, right?"

Not a pimp. I'm just hooking girls up with sugar daddies. That's . . . maybe not like United Nations–approved charity work, but it's not pimping. I just have to get some better sugar daddies. Like Jules. Crystal will love him, if I can just find her.

CHAPTER

TWELVE

The Long Beach Wells Fargo is just a block or two over on Ocean Boulevard and has a stunning ocean view. In my head I hear a discordant buzzer and imagine crossing out *bank* with a big red X. There's something messed up about a bank taking up a spot where a casual restaurant with a dolphin theme could be. The more I think about it, the more strongly I feel about dolphin-friendly businesses getting prime water views. Someone who grew up by the ocean probably wouldn't even notice this or care. They'd be like "the ocean, who cares?" which makes me think I'm originally from the Midwest—someplace with a lot of corn and a dull, flat view. An ocean of corn isn't an ocean, after all.

"Did you do 4-H as a kid?" I ask Max as we head toward the bank, mostly because I'm wondering if I did.

He gives me a weird look. "Where did that come from?"

"Well, you're from Minnesota. I'm starting to think I might be, too. Or, you know, from some similarly dull place."

He guffaws. "Watch your mouth. *Prince* was from Minnesota. Minnesota is dope."

"I bet I was born somewhere right off the interstate, like in a pit stop on the way to somewhere else, destined never to arrive anywhere by virtue of my birth."

Max stares flatly at me. "And you say you aren't dramatic."

"So you don't think I'm from Minnesota, too?"

"I think you're from the Midwest and you came to California to become an actress but ended up doing other things."

Wow. That assessment was . . . a little too real. But it's probably true.

"Did you know that I was in a commercial?" he says.

"Stop it. You were not."

From his expression I know a good punch line is coming. "It was for a bacterial growth medium."

I laugh. "Sounds sexy."

"Basically every black kid in the sciences is an unpaid model. I'm the centerfold and cover model for every school I've ever been to."

I laugh. "You don't even need Instagram."

We enter the lobby and find it completely empty. Literally no one goes into a bank anymore. The only people who come here are olds who don't know how to digitally deposit checks. Most of the teller stations are closed but I see an Indian guy waving me over from the one open station. I walk up to him and see his nameplate: Kumar.

"Hi, Kumar!" I say brightly. "I need your help. I tried to reset my password for my account online but I got a message saying I need to come in."

He doesn't seem to be vibing with my cheeriness. "Driver's license or government-issued ID, please."

That's when it hits me. I woke up with: a rhinestone-studded clutch, a receipt for a Smartwater, a bobby pin, two keys, and my Pirate lipstick. Noticeably absent: money and credit cards. As the import of this dawns on me, I tell Kumar, "Um, I'm sorry. My purse was stolen. I'm actually here because of that."

He nods. "So you need replacement cards."

And then some.

Kumar, probably concerned about privacy at this point or maybe just manners, turns to Max. "And you are?"

Max holds out his hand like a good Midwestern boy. "I'm Max."

"Max is . . . Max works for me." The explanation rolls off my tongue like a clod of dirt off a shovel. It feels like a lie, probably because I feel more like his employee. I mean, I'm the twentysomething chick in a too-short dress. He's the neuroscientist. I'm the one with the earning power, though.

Kumar seems deeply uninterested in whatever's going on between me and Max. "I need to speak with my manager since you don't have ID. Please wait here."

Even though he's working with me, taking a guy to the bank feels worse than sleeping together too early.[34] Max feels

....

[34] Or maybe I just have issues with money?

it too. "I have to run out and make a phone call. Check on some experiments. You know."

"Coo" rolls off my tongue like I'm too cool to pronounce the whole word. I watch him walk away. Maybe it's because I've imprinted on him like a baby goose, but seeing him go makes my insides feel just a touch melty, like the best bite of a caramel roll. The caramel roll feeling lasts two seconds before I remember I have a boyfriend: JP. I'm pretty much living with JP. At least the old Mia was.

It's hard to care about a boyfriend I haven't met. Sure, I feel like I won an award being his girlfriend, given that he's so fancy and rich. But it's hard to believe that he paid to date me, like I'm the prize. Yet another puzzle. Maybe he just wanted to date a woman from a pit stop, like a novelty.

Either way, hanging out with Max is not cheating. I must hang out with all sorts of people who aren't my boyfriend all the time. I'm coo like that.

Kumar returns a minute later. "What's your birthdate and social security number? Can you verify those?"

"My birthday is . . ." I don't think it will help my cause to tell him I don't have a clue, so I pull up my Facebook page and click on "About Mia." I haven't filled in any of the info. Figures. I did input that I like *Keeping Up with the Kardashians* (which explains a lot) and #JulesBrand underwear. *Thanks a lot, old self.* Kumar seems to be noticing that it's taking me a long time to remember my birthday and I admit that I don't know the answer.

"Do you know your social security number?" he asks.

I shake my head. "No clue."

He sighs and runs his hands through his hair. "Technically, I shouldn't help you. I'm not supposed to talk with you unless you can answer at least some of these questions, but you've got nothing. You could literally be anyone off the street claiming to be Mia Wallace."

I nod, but the word *technically* gives me a spark of hope. I put on my friendliest "Help me, I'm just a girl" look. I'm due for a break. "If you just let me reset my password, I can get my whole life back on track."

"I would like to reset your password for you, but resetting your password is not the problem. The bank shut down your accounts permanently. You overdrafted and failed to pay."

I stare him. "That can't be right." I'm one of the top businesswomen under thirty in Long Beach according to that SoCal lifestyle website. "I'm running a successful business. It doesn't make sense."

Kumar looks more closely at the account details. "All I know is what I see here. It looks like you bounced a check for $5,000 to a place called . . . High Flying, a pretty big check to Delta Airlines, and another for $150 to an Italian restaurant." He frowns at the screen. "You also wrote a large check to . . ." He shakes his head in disbelief.

"What? What'd I do?"

"To JulesBrand. Do you know what that is? Is that a store or a . . . person or . . . ?"

"What?" JulesBrand, as in JulesBrand underwear? That makes less than zero sense . . . "How much is it for?"

"I've already said way too much . . ."

None of this makes sense. First of all, I'm a successful businesswoman. And I saw the prices I charge on GoldRush. There's no way I'm in the hole, no way I spent a substantial amount of money on men's underwear.

I start breathing a little too fast and sweating. Kumar looks concerned.

Someone definitely stole my shit. "I recently woke up in the hospital and didn't have any money or credit cards on me. This proves it. Someone stole my wallet."

"You were mugged?"

"I was *assaulted*." Basically.

"I'm so sorry. Do the police have any suspects?"

"I'm stopping by the police station next to check on progress in my case." He doesn't need to know that I haven't reported it yet. But now that I'm thinking about it, why wasn't that my first instinct?

"What do I do now?" I ask. "Can I get my money back? I mean, I can't do anything without money." I'm starting to regret throwing Kobra's bag of money into the courtyard right about now . . .

"I can report your card as stolen, but with that much money at stake, the bank won't simply return it. You'll have to bring a copy of your police report."

"Can you print out one of the statements so I can show it to the police? I probably have to show them what was stolen." I can just imagine the conversation without a bank statement:

"Ma'am, how much money was stolen and what unauthorized purchases were made?"

"Umm, like ten grand, I think, but I'm not sure?"

"What is the account number?"

"I don't know."

"So, let me summarize: you think you have a bank account and that someone spent all the money in it, but you're not sure."

"That's right."

"Hey, Mike, you hear this? This lady said she feels like she should have money and wants to report it."

At that moment, Max walks in smelling like a coffee shop and Old Spice. "Hey how's it going? Wrapping up here?"

"Totally. Let's roll." No point in dragging this out more.

"That's great news! You have an address and money and everything then?"

I shake my head. "I'm not sure about the address, but—"

Max's nerdy dad side comes out. "Kumar, could you tell us what address you have on file?"

"As soon as you come back with the police—"

"They have JP's address," I lie. Max doesn't need to know that I can't pay him. Maybe he's staying around for more than money, but maybe not. Regardless, I can't afford to lose him.

But Max isn't dumb. He can fill in the blanks. "Why do they need a police report?"

"Uh . . ." I can't tell him that I need a search warrant to look at the bank records so . . . "I'm going to report my assault. Can you believe I didn't do that earlier?"

He smacks himself in the forehead. "I guess I just assumed you had."

Max is the only thing I have going for me. I can't lose him. It's just a little lie. Or two or three little lies. I'll straighten it all out as soon as I file that police report. I'll have money and everything will be fine.

Still, I can't believe I just threw a bag of cash on the ground. God hates me.

CHAPTER

THIRTEEN

The closest police station is downtown in a big, official building, right across from the courthouse and a Starbucks. We park two blocks away. It looks nice but it smells like pee and the smell of weed is looouuud. As we approach the courthouse, there are more people who are obviously lawyers and fewer people who obviously peed on the side of a building in the last twenty-four hours.

I need some way to get rid of Max while I file this report. He doesn't need to know I'm broke. Maybe his first paycheck will be a little delayed, but I'll figure something out. Which means I need an errand . . .

"Max, while I'm filing this report, will you run an errand for me?"

I scramble for ideas. He's very thoughtful so I bet he'd be happy to pop on down to the drug store to get some headache medicine. The coffee shop is too close so it would only take a minute.

"Sure. Let's divide and conquer," he says.

Not sure where I'm going with it, I say, "We passed a library a few blocks back . . ."

"Genius. I bet a librarian will have some great ideas for how to research some of these issues."

Not. But Max is really cute so I'm like, "Great, you talk to a librarian and I'll talk to the cops. We'll compare notes after."

Librarian versus cop—he doesn't even notice that sounds funny. I wave and watch him walk down the street toward the library.

After taking a number and waiting for what feels like most of my life (and it really is a healthy percentage of my life, considering I was born only two days ago), the last woman I want to see comes out. She has an "I don't have time for your bullshit" look on her face before I even open my mouth. I don't think I have the right vibe for her. Her first name is Denise and her last name hard to pronounce, so I know what I'm going to call her.

"Follow me," Officer Denise says, pointing to a chair across from her desk. She leans back and takes a sip from a Styrofoam cup of coffee and says, "What seems to be the problem?"

I explain everything—waking up in the hospital, the memory loss, the bloody cape I tossed, the eyewitness account of me being pushed into an ice sculpture, my possible disagreement with Lauren Montcalm, and lastly, the fact that my accounts have been completely drained and closed.

"So we have a possible assault and . . . I'm sorry about the money, but I can't do anything about your debts."

"No, that's just it. I think someone stole it."

"Why do you think that?"

"I woke up in the hospital with no wallet, no ID, no money."

"How much do you think was stolen?"

"I don't know. All of it. I don't know how much I had to begin with, but I charge a ton for matchmaking so I think I was flush."

It sounds bad when I say it out loud in a police station. Most things probably sound bad in a police station. The truth sounds the way your face looks under the unforgiving lights of a truck-stop bathroom. She jots down a few notes on a yellow legal pad and asks, "Do you know anyone who might have a problem with you? Do you have any enemies?"

God. Enemies—that sounds so gangster. "Like I said, I have a few guesses. Right now my biggest lead is Lauren Montcalm."

"Wait a minute. Are you talking about the artist Lauren Montcalm?" she asks.

"Yes! I had a recovered memory that I asked her for money."

"A recovered memory?"

I nod. "The doctor said they would come back to me in flashes, like visions."

She recoils at the word *visions.* "Oh boy. Anything else?"

I pull up Kobra's Instagram profile and explain my issues with him.

"He's a major problem," she says.

"Wait, you know him? Who is he?"

"He's a major meth dealer in the area. We've never been able to get charges to stick, but he's definitely dealing."

No surprise there, except I wonder how I hooked up with him in the first place. "Is he dangerous?"

"You don't get to the top of the heap in the drug world through pacifism."

I nod vigorously. I bet Kobra lied to me about being an international trader when I vetted him for the app.

"What about this boyfriend?" Denise says *boyfriend* in a tone that is anything but innocent until proven guilty.

"He's in Switzerland." Why does everyone have to assume it was JP?

"Was he in Switzerland the night you were injured?"

"I don't know."

"Speaking of your boyfriend, why can't he help you find your residence?"

"Again, he's in Switzerland."

"Don't you talk? Doesn't he have a phone?"

I take a deep breath and shrug. "I don't know. I just . . ."

"You don't trust him, do you?"

I look down at the desk. "Of course I trust him," I lie. I mean, I sort of trust him. "I really don't think that he hit me over the head." JP is all I've got going for me, except Max.

She's doing that thing that cops do where they let you keep talking until you share some information that they can use against you. I correct myself: I'm here so she can help me, not so she can use something against me.

"If anything, I'm worried he's going to dump me. I mean, I'm a burden right now. I don't know who I am. I have no access to money. And JP's a catch. Like I said, I think some chick who wanted him for herself might have pushed me."

She nods thoughtfully. "I got it. I need to look into him, though. If we find that a crime took place, domestic partners are the most common assailants in cases involving injuries like yours."

"It wasn't him."

"But you don't remember the injury. Am I right?"

I nod.

"How long has he been out of town?"

"I don't know."

"Does he have access to your bank accounts?"

"I don't think so."

She clearly thinks he clocked me and skipped town, but I'm sure he didn't. "We'll let you know if we find anything," she says, and hands me a business card so I can give her a call if I remember anything else.[35] This is my cue to walk out, and it is clear that I was hoping for something she isn't going to give.

....

[35] Ha!

"I just need to file that assault report and get my money back."

"Gotcha."

But does she? I don't need her distracted by JP and Kobra, even if he is a kingpin. I just need my money and I'm sure I can fix it all myself.

━━━━━━━━

Max is already waiting for me when I leave the police station. As we walk back down the pee-filled streets to the car, he says, "I think I would have rather talked to a cop than a librarian. Jesus."

"What happened?"

"God. I think that poor woman forgot the reasons she went into library science to begin with. It seems like she's just a bouncer for the homeless. And bitter. I've never seen so much attitude, and I'm a black man."

With a laugh, I say, "I'm sorry." I really am.

"How did it go for you? Did the police figure anything out?"

"Not yet. She has some ideas." I wish she was less interested in JP and more interested in finding my money.

A sick feeling overwhelms me when I think of telling Max that I'm broke. What if he leaves? What if JP really is the bad guy in my life? I'm not ready to face any of that, especially if I don't need to. "She's very interested in JP as a suspect. I don't know, though. Casting suspicion everywhere just feels like unnecessary drama."

Max blurts out a laugh. "Mia, that's what the police do. They investigate suspects."

He's right. Plus, I have a business to run while the police do their job. And I have an idea. While waiting for Officer Denise, I couldn't help but notice the chick next to me in the waiting room scanning Craigslist for casting calls. I announce, "I think we should go to a casting call. There will be tons of out-of-work chicks desperate for an opportunity, or at least a free meal."[36]

I wait for him to congratulate me on my genius. Instead he looks skeptical. "You want to solicit a date from all the women in line?" he says, thinking through the strategy out loud. "That sounds . . . awkward."

"True, but it's pure genius."

"Let's table that idea for now." Table it until I forget it, is what he's hoping, I think. Given my condition, this isn't a bad play on his part.

Meanwhile, I need to pop into a grocery store while he changes his mind. "Let's stop by Vons. I need ibuprofen and water." After yesterday's all-day investigation and this morning's escapades, I've got a tension headache the size of California.

We get into the car and I tell him what I've learned about Kobra.

"We had coffee with a drug lord this morning?" He stops to reflect for a moment. "That might be why Crystal isn't talking to you."

....

[36] Brilliant, right?

Come to think of it, that makes sense.

"You know, I've made it until the age of twenty-nine as a black man without getting into trouble. And here you are, a pretty white girl, and you can't seem to stay away from it."

He has a point. The only question is: how much trouble am I really in?

Max navigates us smoothly to a nearby Vons and then offers me his arm as we walk up to the storefront. I don't know if I'm just desperate and vulnerable or if I'm falling for him. His arm feels warm, solid, and muscled. "Max." I look up at him all, let's be honest, desperate and vulnerable, but also overcome. This man has been here for me like no one else and he doesn't even know me. I want to tell him he looks handsome and reach up on my toes and kiss him. I want him to wrap his arms around me tight. Instead, I say, "Thank you."

Outside Vons is a homeless guy, and I recognize him immediately; he's the guy from the beach on Friday. "Yo, Mia," he says.

"Wassup, Don?" His name rolls off my tongue without thinking.

Max stops and does a double take. Then he looks directly at the guy. "You know Mia?"

"I told you I volunteer at a local soup kitchen," I say, all self-satisfied and smug. "Don remembers me." I must have been one of the kindest volunteers.

The guy laughs like that's the funniest thing he's ever heard. "Um, no. I *work* for you." Then he adds, "And you ate at the shelter with me at least once, back in the day."

"Sorry . . . what?" *What* does not capture how confused I am.

I *ate* at the homeless shelter? How real does my life have to get?

Max laughs. "I work for Mia too." He holds out his hand and says, "I'm Max, I'm helping her with . . . day-to-day operations."

The guy nods.

"I also chauffeur now and then."

Don brightens. "Really? God I'd love driving that Ferrari. You wouldn't even have to pay me. Glad you do, Mia, but damn that's a fine machine."

Just in case Don knows me better than I suspect, I ask him if he knows any other pertinent details, like, for instance, where I live. I kind of hope he says no, even though I want him to say yes. One way or the other, I'm not as highbrow as I thought. You can only be so much of a snob if you're homeless.

Don's memory of me doesn't extend that far. "I just know you have a thing for Jacques-o-late," he says. This actually makes Max rolls his eyes.

"Whaaat?" I say, all sarcastic. In a teasing voice, I add, "Once you go Jacques-o-late, you know."

Don laughs, and Max makes a noise like he's holding in a comeback that's about to burst out.

After I verify that I still have Don's number and give him another five bucks, we head into Vons. Max grabs a cart and then changes his mind and gets one of those half-size carts.

I can tell he's processing the conversation outside. Either that or he's way too concerned about grocery carts. I act casual and look at a stand filled with Republic of California T-shirts. "Maybe I should get one—"

"Mia, this worries me. I think you might have been running with a . . . dangerous crowd before."

"Max, you can't say that just because I hired someone who's struggling with homelessness. That's how you make the world a better place, by offering people who are down on their luck a second chance."

"Um. True. But . . ." He stops pushing the cart in the middle of the aisle and looks into my eyes. "You're currently vulnerable, and for whatever reason you're making connections with—"

"Don't worry. It's not like I'm hanging out with them. And any shady characters I *have* been hanging out with are being investigated by the police right now, remember?"

He seems satisfied with that. After I grab some headache meds, we meander into the deli area. I peruse the deli counter sushi and stare so hard at the little plastic trays of California rolls with ginger that isn't the right color and thumbprint-size dollops of wasabi, as if I think they're about to tell me a secret and . . . they do.

I suddenly flash back to the art museum. It's not like I'm watching a movie, but I can see glimpses of the accident. I see sushi rolls arranged in an elaborate design. I'm eyeing the California rolls and some with the orange caviar stuff on top. I'm picking up a few and balancing a wineglass when I hear a commotion just outside the building.

"Bitch!"

I look up from the sushi table toward the door, along with a whole room of people dressed like they're going to the Grammys. I don't want to miss whatever is about to go down. I feel a little thrill, like I'm about to watch an after-school fight. Whoever yelled isn't in sight so I add some wasabi to my plate, thinking I still have time before the fight breaks out. I pick up my drink and start walking somewhere with a better view of the drama. I spot a nice place close to an ice sculpture of Cupid.

"I know you're here, bitch!" the voice yells. I look around for the angry woman, ready to watch the catfight that is clearly coming.

"MIA, where are you, bitch?"

Mia? She's looking for me! Still clutching my drink and plate, I scan the crowd. From the sound of her voice, I'm thinking of ducking into the bathroom.

It's exactly like an after-school fight. All the ritzy philanthropists and art lovers in Long Beach are forming a circle to watch. "Excuse me, but would you hold my wine?" I ask the person next to me. I don't want to spill it when the fight starts.

I toss my hair like a pony as my attacker enters the circle. It isn't a woman, though. It's JP.

I gasp in horror and lean against the deli counter to catch my breath.

"Ma'am!"

I blink and look again. No table of raw oysters on a bed of ice. No artfully arranged rolls of sushi. I'm back at Vons where the sushi is prepackaged and ready to go.

The guy behind the deli counter repeats himself. "Ma'am? Do you need something? Are you okay?"

I answer without looking at him. I'm looking for Max. "Sorry, I'm fine."

"So you don't want the three-roll combo?"

"No thanks. Sorry!"

I spot Max. He's in front of the Naked juices thinking way too hard about something. "Max!"

"What is it?" he asks. "Did something happen?" He sets down a Green Machine juice.

"I just remembered something. A woman was calling me a bitch and talking about her man, but then she disappeared and JP was standing there, but he was angry. I don't know . . . it was confusing."

"Just sit down for a minute. You'll probably start having more of these, especially when you talk about the events. It sounds like your mind is putting pieces together but still working out what should go where."

He steers me toward the front of the store and we sit in the in-store Starbucks. I drink a whole bottle of water and swallow some meds while Max waits patiently. I'm reeling from the vision, not to mention the headache. Thank God Max is here. Knowing that I'm not going through this alone is everything to me right now. I reach out for his hand and he gives mine a supportive squeeze in return. Tears of gratitude start to well in my eyes. I can't believe I have this man to help me through this.

For his part, I think he might just be waiting out my recovery, which is confirmed when he says, "That double bacon sandwich looks good."

I can't help but laugh at the whole *Men Are from Mars, Women Are from Venus* aspect of this moment. Either way, I appreciate the support. A moment later, I let go of his hand because I'm totally buying this Martian a double bacon sandwich.[37]

I'm not sure if he notices that I'm sort of crying in line while I get him a sandwich or if he's just pretending not to because—tears, I get it. No judgment either way. Do I do tears? I doubt it.

When I hand him the sandwich, he must notice that I look a little off. I mean, I am crying in a grocery store where we're buying headache medicine because of my traumatic head injury and we just left the police station where I belatedly reported an assault.

"Are you okay?" he asks.

"I'm fine," I say with a smile that probably looks as fake as it feels.

Max unwraps his sandwich and says, "Great. Do you still want to go to that casting call?"[38]

"Do we have a choice?"

"I still think it's a dumb idea, for the record."

....

[37] More like letting JP buy him a sandwich if we're doing proper accounting, which obviously isn't my thing.

[38] And the verdict is in: he's a 100 percent typical heterosexual male. Still cute, though.

I don't mention that it's not my first choice either. Barely holding back tears at Vons says that loud and clear, but whatevs. I decide to be as fine as I told Max I was. "It's the only idea was have. Let's go make some wannabe actress's day and cast her as Crystal."

CHAPTER

FOURTEEN

Max cuts the engine when we get to the audition. It's in a big old warehouse not far from downtown. The parking lot is surrounded with green plastic fencing that reminds me of the stuff strawberry baskets are made from. FOR RENT/FOR SALE and PARK HERE FOR $249 A MONTH signs are posted on the side of the building. It looks like they're trying to make a buck off of literally anything. Like, don't stand in front of this building or they might hawk you right along with a parking space. One girl, probably a wannabe actress, hops out of an Uber and heads toward the building. She's the only thing keeping it from looking totally abandoned.

"So how should we do this?" I ask Max. Up until we got here I hadn't thought through the details. "But more important: can you do it?" I would like nothing more than to take a nap in the parking lot of this nearly abandoned warehouse right now.

"No way in hell. This is the dumbest idea we've had yet." Max looks like he means it. I can tell there's no way he's getting out of this car.

"You are such a shitty employee." I probably shouldn't feel bad about not being able to pay him. He barely does anything.

While I look at my reflection in the rearview mirror to slap on another coat of Pirate by Chanel and smooth flyaway hairs, Max takes a moment to grandstand.

"I'm offended as a black man that you don't see the problem with this."

"Umm, I mean . . . I just want to take a nap."

"Mia, do you seriously think I can walk into a casting call and try to recruit some girls to go on a date? It's pretty sketchy just coming from a white girl. Coming from a big black guy—at the very least I'm getting kicked out. I wouldn't put it past someone to call the cops. They'd probably think I'm some kind of pimp."

"Whatever. I'm already doing it. You can stop your whining now."

He scoffs. "I'm just telling you how it is."

I've stopped listening to Max. He's right about the awkwardness of the whole thing. No matter which one of us walks in there, it's going to be suspicious. "You're right. It's gonna seem like I have an angle."

"You do have an angle."

"I think I'm going to pretend that I have a crisis and—"

He cuts me off. "Good luck and text me if the cops come." Why do I feel like these should be our parting words every time?

As I approach the warehouse, I see a line of beautiful women, all between the ages of twenty and thirty, standing outside. It shouldn't be hard to find one of them who would like to go on a date with a millionaire. All I have to do is not come off as a total freak.

I sneak into the line. I just want to be in the highest density of potential dates. "No cuts," one chick says.

"Oh, sorry."

She glares and I head to the back of the line. A redheaded girl next to me looks like she could go on a date with Jules, i.e., she's the right age and probably looks good in her underwear. All around me, people are doing vocal exercises and pantomiming actions while reading lines from a script. Redhead is not.

"What's this audition for?" I ask her.

"Umm . . . I can never keep track." Glancing at a sheet, she says, "It's like a *Grey's Anatomy* kind of show. Some hospital soap opera."

"And what are we all auditioning for?"

"Did you just walk in off the street?" she asks.

"I just do so many of these," I say.

"I feel ya. This one is for Pretty Girl Number 2."

"Can I see the lines?" Way to shoot for the stars, ladies! Pretty Girl Number 2! Shouldn't we be going for Number 1 at least? Or maybe a role with a name?

Redhead looks at me like I'm crazy. "The lines aren't that important." She hands me a sheet. Pretty Girl Number 2 has to scream and run. She also has to yell, "*Oh my God!! Help!*"

I don't know what these girls are practicing for. I have a much bigger challenge ahead. I shudder as if to shake off the reality that I'm living, shut my eyes, and visualize the scene I'm trying to create. When I open my eyes, I'm fully in character.

I start scrolling on my phone like everyone else in line.

After an appropriate amount of time, I gasp. "FUCK," I say, like someone has just taken a melon baller and scooped a chunk of my heart out with it. I stomp my foot. Then, like I'm trying to pull myself together, I stand up straight, shoulders back, and shut my eyes. I'm wrapping up my emotions tightly.

A few girls look in my direction before they start talking again. I completely ignore them.

I'm not done yet, though. I hang my head and start crying a little, gently weeping. Redhead can't ignore me anymore. "What is it?" she says.

"It's just . . . It's so silly. I'm embarrassed."

"I'm sure it's not silly. What is it?"

"I was supposed to have a date tomorrow night with Jules Spencer." I look up to see if she knows him. "You know, the famous underwear guy?"

From the look on her face, I can tell she knows him.

"I can't go. My boss just texted and said I have to work. I need that job."

"Ohmygod. That's like hashtag the *worst*."

That's like hashtag the dumbest sentence I've ever heard, but I nod. I shut my eyes like I'm trying to hold back tears. I let one leak out. It's easy. All I have to do is think about my life. I wonder how many of these other bitches can cry on demand. "A blind date with a millionaire—I mean, how often does that kind of opportunity come along?"

Redhead rests her hand on my forearm and looks appropriately upset for me. "I'm so sorry. Sometimes it just seems that no matter how hard you try, you can't get ahead in life."

"I don't know if this is weird, but do you want to go? I mean, it's a blind date. It should go to someone."

Redhead's hand flies to her heart. "For real?"

I shut my eyes like I'm on my deathbed and willing her my only child. "Someone should go. Better you than one of these other bitches."

I tell her the time that she should meet Jules tomorrow and start to fill her in the details. I can't lie. I'm starting to enjoy myself.

"Where is this place?" she asks. "What should I wear?"

A guy in glasses and schlubby clothes wanders over slowly, like he has all the time in the world, and interrupts Redhead's questions. He starts clapping for me. "Congratulations, miss. Why don't you come me with me?"

"Um . . . who are you?"

"I'm the director, and you just won a spot at the front of the line. Probably the role, even."

"Why?" There's no way I'm going with him. Talk about snake oil salesmen—he definitely looks like one.

"I saw your performance in line. It was brilliant."

I glare at him.

"I think you have just the right energy. Your whole vibe." He does a weird thing with his hands, like he's feeling my aura. Fucking Hollywood loon. "And you dressed for the part," he says. "All these other girls are just trying to look cute, but you're . . . gritty." He says *gritty* with a growl. "Are those staples?"

With the reminder, I run my fingers along the hard metal ridges. Dr. Patel said they had to stay in for ten days. It hasn't even been a full four yet.

He gives me an admiring look. "You're just who we need. I just want you to read for the camera and we need to see how you look without that dress on."

I look at Redhead to see if she heard him. "Did you hear that? He wants me to undress! I don't know if you got the memo, dude, but that kind of Harvey Weinstein bullshit is over." I look at the crowd of second-string pretty girls for some support. "Amirite, ladies?"

I'm not getting any support, though.

"Miss," the director says, "do you know what kind of movie you're auditioning for?"

"Pretty Girl Number 2, medical drama."

"That's true. It's set at a hospital, but once we get in scene all the clothes come off and the script isn't that important. Ya feel me?"

"Fuuuuck me."

"Exactly."

"But you didn't say that in the informational material." I read Redhead's sheet. It sounded like *Grey's Anatomy.*

He shrugs. "Whatever. It's a job."

"It's exploitative." I look at the line of women. "Do you all know this is an audition for a porno?"

Some of them look surprised. No one looks *that* surprised, though.

"That's messed up, dude. You know these women are desperate for a job and will do anything once you dangle a few false promises." I look to the line of women. "Who's walking out with me?"

"Jesus fucking Christ. I'm going to have to ask you to leave now. I'm trying to make a movie."

I scoff. I can't believe he thinks I'm the problem. "For real? Is it even legal to make a porn?"

He nods. "It's a highly regulated industry. Do I need to call the cops?"

"Maybe. Someone needs to stand up for these women." When I realize he's serious, I backtrack. "Sorry, I'm going." I look at Redhead and stage-whisper, "Do you still want that date?"

"Uh, no thanks."

Dammit. "I'm not crazy. I just want better for us."

She averts her eyes as if she's scared of me.

All I want is one woman to pretend to be Crystal for a night. How fucking hard can it be? This guy has women lined up to get naked on screen and do who knows what. So I throw a Hail Mary. Projecting like I'm on stage, which I'm apparently great at, I say, "I'm leaving, but I want to offer one of you women a job. I run a matchmaking service and I need someone to go on a date with a rich man tomorrow night. It's a great deal."

A woman who's close enough to have heard everything says, "Lady, that sounds way scarier than what he's offering."

"It's just the way I phrased it," I say. "I set up millionaires with regular people. I've been written up in *SoCal* magazine. I just need one pretty girl and any of you would qualify. For me, you'd be Pretty Girl Number 1."

The director has his phone out. "I have a situation here."

"Got it, I'm leaving!" Maybe one of the wannabe actresses will meet me in the parking lot. As quick as I can in my heels, I walk to the Ferrari and open the passenger door.

"That was quick," he says. "Does that mean it worked?"

I shake my head. "Definitely not. The cops might be coming."

Max looks over to see if I'm telling the truth. "You're kidding, right?"

"One hundred percent serious." I'm shaking a little. How many interactions with the police can I have in one day?

"Roger that." He starts the car and high-tails it out of there.

On our way out, a police cruiser turns into the lot. I groan and sink lower into my seat. "I'm an idiot."

"No, you're not an idiot."

"You told me not to do that."

"True. And I turned out to be right, but you gave it a shot. If you were a scientist, I'd probably think you were doing a lot of harebrained experiments, but you take a lot of risks. You'd be the one to make the big breakthroughs."

Max has silenced me with his sincerity. That is the nicest

compliment ever, especially coming from him. Normally I would prefer a comment about how great my ass looks, but from Max all I want to hear from now on is, "If you were a scientist . . ."

"Thanks, Max."

"All of us suffer from confirmation bias, only recognizing ideas that support our existing beliefs. Just hanging out with you, I'm starting to recognize my biases. It's a good learning experience for me."

"That's what this internship is all about," I say with a ridiculous smile. "I assume you think I'm hot, too?"[39]

He chokes on a laugh. "Duh." He looks at me in a very familiar way. "Super hot. And this is a vice presidency, not an internship."

"Whatever you want to call it, Max," I say, and pat his arm. "Now that we have that cleared up, I have one more idea. It didn't work at the casting call, but I think pretty much any girl at Starbucks could be Crystal. And there's a Starbucks just ahead."

We're at a stoplight. He looks over at me skeptically and says, "Go on." I can tell he's trying hard to listen without shooting me down immediately.

"How about we walk in and yell out, 'Hey ladies, anyone here wanna go on a date with Jules Spencer, the underwear model?'"

....

[39] If he wants a learning experience, I'm gonna let him know how he's actually supposed to compliment a lady.

He laughs.

"I'm serious."

"So am I. I'm not doing that."

"I thought you said I should be a scientist."

"I take it back."

I'm about to argue my point when my phone pings. "MAX!" I scream way too loudly given that we're inside a car. "Cue the hallelujah chorus!"

"What? Did that Craigslist Elsa text you?"

"Even better. It's Crystal."

Pick me up from work. 6 pm. Tomorrow.

I almost tell her to take a long walk off a short pier, but I hold back. She's the one who I matched with clients when I had resources and my wits about me.

Awesome. Text me address.

Back at JP's, I tell Max I'm off to lie down. I'm officially out of energy.

"Thank God. I was worried about you. You know that you can die from lack of sleep."

"I don't think it's that bad."

"Trust me. You need more sleep than you realize right now."

"The sun hasn't even set yet. I just need a little nap."

I schlep down the hall and plop into the center of JP's giant bed. It would take up the whole room, if the master suite wasn't luxury sized.

Max knocks on the doorframe. "Mind if I tell you one thing before you go to sleep?"

"As long as I don't have to sit up. And it's just a nap." I pat the bed next to me and say, "We can have a meeting here. You can even turn on Netflix if you want."

Max sits on the edge of the bed. "I'm glad you got some good news with Crystal . . . because I have some bad news."

I stare at him wordlessly.

"So, it's not really bad news. It' more like 'Joke's on us' news. When I was waiting for you at the casting call, I went through some of your GoldRush material and found out something about Jules."

I can't imagine what he's going to say.

"So you know how we're doing all of this because Jules paid you thirty-five grand?"

My eyes are wide now. "Uh-huh."

"Well, he didn't pay you anything." He lets that information sink in for a second before continuing. "You paid him $100,000 to use GoldRush. He just has to post a few times using #GoldRush. And he agreed to take Crystal to several locations where he will be photographed by paparazzi."

I sit bolt upright in the bed. "WHAT? Am I insane?"

"I thought so at first, but maybe not. He's an influencer, so you're paying him to influence people, I guess." He puts his palms up and gives me a half smile. "This is all new to me."

I pull the covers over my face. "I almost got arrested looking for a Crystal replacement today. I could have given him anyone. I could have gone."

"Joke's on us."

"I guess it doesn't matter. I really needed to find Crystal. If we were in Oz, I think she'd be the Wizard."

"But at least you're so crazy rich that you can blow one hundred grand on wild bets like paying Jules for an Instagram post. Must be nice."

I laugh like it's funny. It's definitely not, considering that I actually have no money. I keep that to myself. If I don't go into a Netflix coma right now, I'm going to explode.

Instead of leaving, Max turns on the TV and leans back to watch with me. "I'm just going to watch until I fall asleep," I say. I think about turning on *Grey's Anatomy*—the casting call made me all nostalgic for it—but then I have a flash of awareness. Max is with me and he's not planning on sleeping through the show. "What do you want to watch?"

"Um, I might just read."

"Okay, I'm picking something out for you then." It's like a fun little gift-giving challenge. I settle on a documentary called *The Beginning and the End of the Universe*.

I don't know if it's what he would have picked, but he smiles contentedly and rubs my arm in acknowledgment of . . . my TV choice, or maybe more. Before I drift off, the narrator's monotone voice says, "It's a good rule of thumb that, in science, the simplest questions are often the hardest to answer."

If that isn't the truth.

"Wake me up in an hour, will you?"

He nods. "This bed is the size of the *Titanic*—and so much

nicer than the couch." He spreads so far out that we're not even touching anymore. Damn. "Just think, if Kate Winslet's life raft had been this big . . . she could have saved herself and Leo."

Right now the bed feels like a life raft. It's for me and Max. We're sheltered from the world for just a little while. I scoot closer and lean against him. "Don't say anything. I just want to fall asleep with you."

His eyes are darker than usual, and I can tell he's looking at my lips, but he makes a joke. "That's what all the girls say."

"I know that's a lie." Max isn't the guy you want to just fall asleep next to. "Wake me up in an hour," I repeat as I let my eyes drift shut.

CHAPTER

FIFTEEN

Waking up is worse than coming out of a coma—and I should know. I'm in my bed fully clothed and the TV is still on. A screensaver is flashing between pictures of waterfalls and scenic grasslands and the Great Wall. Max isn't in bed anymore, but there's a big rumpled spot in the blanket where he was.

I look down at my phone. It's Sunday. My own personal The Bachelor is flying back from Switzerland today, probably with my red rose in his teeth, and I just spent the night in his bed with his house sitter. I think. I press my nose to the sheets and detect a faint piney smell. I know it's just deodorant but it's weirdly intimate.

I'm still staring at the doomsday proclamation that it is Sunday, the day of the date that will determine the fate of my business, when Facebook notifies me that it's Emily Carol's birthday. I write happy birthday! 🍰 just in case she's my best friend. While I stare at the happy birthday message, Emily starts to respond and my heart rate goes wild. Emily knows me! But her response evaporates. It's as if I'm truly alone in the universe, except for Max.

"Maaaax!" I call. "Where are you?" There's no point prying myself out of bed unless I know he's ready to distract me from myself, or "help me confront my problems," as he'll probably say.

"Whaaaaat?" he calls from the other room.

"I need assistance."

"For what?"

"Facing reality."

Max walks into the bedroom. "Um, you're paying me to assist you in your business, not guide you through an existential crisis."

I laugh. "Like you're really invested in matchmaking. You're just getting a paycheck while you're having your own crisis, if we're being honest."

"No, I really just need to pay the bills, actually. I've got everything handled."

I laugh. His ex-girlfriend just sabotaged his life's work and now he's hiding from everything at JP's house with me. "You're definitely good at crises. Your methodical, scientific approach is calming."

"Most of the time, women just like my body."

"Well, that's nice too." It *is* a nice body. The man is genetically gifted. As I stare at Max, admiring the muscles outlined under his nerdy T-shirt, I remember that JP is on his way home. In a few hours my life will . . . be back to normal? But what is normal? I don't think it's a relevant concept for me anymore.

I groan like everything hurts and mutter something and make a noise like I might vomit. "Ohmygod, what am I gonna do about that date?" Then I start in with the involuntary groaning again. The waves are pushing me toward failure's rocky coastline and I'm just about to go down. #TheGoodLife feels like an ironic statement on my prow.

"You're set," he said. "I gotcha covered, babe."

I love the way he just called me babe, even if he didn't mean it. I bet it just rolled off his tongue. I know I shouldn't be, but I'm all heart eyes about it.

"I got a Groupon for the date tonight."

A Groupon? As if I can send a trendy millionaire to some Groupon date at Dave & Buster's. No one wants to go to Dave & Buster's. I might as well send them to Chuck E. Cheese. "Max—" I start to say. It's like he doesn't understand anything. "Rich people want exclusivity."

"I know it's not ideal, but on short notice with no money? We've got limited options."

"I'm scared to ask what it's for."

"I got a $100 voucher at a Brazilian steakhouse for $60, plus a couples massage." He shrugs. "Sounds like a sweet date to me."

Max is a simple creature. He sees the world in binaries: true versus false, right versus wrong, black versus white, eating out versus eating in, fine or not fine. He's adorable and wrong and clearly not qualified to facilitate a romance. I pat his head like he's a golden retriever.

"I just don't think there's any way to use a Groupon. What am I going to do, ask Jules to show it to the waiter so that he gets a discount when he pays? And is the place even Instagrammable?"

He nods. "I was thinking we could just have Crystal do that part. She can be in on it, right? And if we're lucky, he won't know what Groupon is."

"I don't know, Max. It doesn't sound like it'll work."

Jules is trendy. The only way he'd go for the Groupon is if I said the steakhouse had the best lighting for selfies, or if he was really into irony. Maybe I can make Max's plan work. Coffee first, though.

We head downstairs and Max passes me a cup of freshly brewed coffee over the large kitchen island. I take a stool across from him.

"You look better today," he says. "Not that you didn't look great yesterday. Just more rested."

"I feel better except for the panic, dread, and anxiety."

"It'll be fine."

They're just words, but when he says them, I perk up.

"If you don't like the Groupon idea, I have something else up my sleeve."

I give him a *go on* look while I reach for the box of Sugar in the Raw on the counter and stir some into my coffee.

"So, if you drive down the Pacific Coast Highway past Laguna, there's this little cove. I went there once and it was filled with these glowing jellyfish. It was incredible."

My jaw drops. Now that sounds unique and romantic. "Why didn't you lead with that?"

"I can't really remember where it is."

Never mind. Groupon it is. We can't spend all day driving around looking for some jellyfish he saw once on the coast of California because, as we've already determined, we have zero time. Jellyfish probably aren't even in season. Or maybe they're always in season. At any rate, no to the jellyfish.

"I'll take you to see the jellyfish someday."

"That sounds lovely, Max." And it does, no matter how improbable.

"I'm going to the lab this morning if you want to come," he says. "I want to check out the software and see if there's anything I can do to salvage it. I don't think Fay would have wrecked it completely."

And he's come to his senses! I was always on Max's side, but it's nice when the person you vowed to support isn't watching his dreams go up in flames just to stand by a principle.[40]

"I think she just wanted to make a point," I say encouragingly.

"Well, I got her message loud and clear," Max seethes.

I look at him adoringly. I'm sure he has no clue what drove Fay away.

———

On the way to the lab, Max continues to fixate on Fay. "I'm so over the breakup. That's old news, but I don't get it. We were working together. Why did she throw everything away, not to

....

[40] Principles—not something I'd go down for.

mention make a mess for me to clean up?"

"Maybe you never really knew her." That's obviously the answer. He can't admit it, though. Based on his Instagram handle alone, I can tell that Max thinks he knows everything. In some ways he does. Brain injuries and logic games—Max is your man. Give him a crying woman in a grocery claiming to be fine, he's like, "cool, you wanna hit Best Buy next?" He's a genius intellectually and a basic bro emotionally, but it could be worse. It seems like I'm the opposite, so no big—he can do my homework and I can do his.

"I just can't believe she would drop everything after so much personal investment. If we accomplished our goals, we could have published our findings in the top journals, gotten a patent, great jobs—the works."

"I guess she decided she didn't want that?" But that sounds wrong even to me.

Max just shakes his head. "She won't even answer my calls. I got a few texts from mutual friends in the neuro department who say she's leaving the field altogether. Who does that? Who just walks away from their life?"

My gut twists. I'm not sure yet, but I think I might be exactly that kind of person.

We walk into the office building past the rows of conference posters. Max is so used to how fancy and cool this place is that he doesn't even notice it anymore. He's nervous, though. He's not bad, but I can feel the negative energy pulsing off him.

"Your boss is probably going to be thrilled to see you," I say. "It would suck to lose two smart people in one week."

With a nod he acknowledges the truth of that. "I don't like dragging this personal mess to work. It's embarrassing."

"Just fix it. Next week the personal mess will be old news." Pretty sure I know this from experience. "Show me around the lab again," I tell him. "I feel smart just being here. I love it."

He smiles, genuinely happy that I'm showing interest in his non-matchmaking work. It strikes me that I'm probably part of his scandal now. When I look around the building, I can't help but notice that none of the other scientists have brought chicks wearing four-day-old cocktail dresses to work with them. It's only Bring Your Skanky Ho to Work Day for Max. I don't consider myself to be skanky, but we're in a science lab so I'm measuring skankiness like Einstein, using relativity. Fay is the only Newtonian skank.[41] To his credit, Max ushers me in like I'm a princess, like he wouldn't want to roll any other way.

We make our way to the lab and Max shows me some scans from the brains of uniquely gifted people. I stand close to him and prop myself up on the high stool next to him. "It was so super smart of me to hire a science genius," I say. It's the kind of stool that's handy for sitting next to a high counter and doing lab work, but it's equally useful for showing off your legs. I take advantage of the latter and cross my legs all sexy-like.

Max looks at my legs and then slowly looks up at me, his eyes a shade darker than before. This thing building between us is definitely a thing. I know how I feel and I don't think

----

[41] Maybe I'm a scientist too?

I'm reading Max wrong. His eyelids are a little heavier than a moment before, his breath just a little shallower.

His gaze lingers on my mouth and I know what he's imagining. I'm thinking the same thing. We both know it, and that knowledge charges the air. It's a fact we can no longer ignore. It's right there between us: I want him and he wants me. He moves a touch closer until he's pressed up against my thigh. His hand rests there lightly, and my whole body tenses with anticipation. I close my eyes, breathe deeply, and savor the feeling. I want more. I want his hands on me. I want his mouth on me.

He leans in. With our lips just inches apart, he hesitates—but only for a fraction of a second. He closes the distance and lets his lips rest on mine for just long enough to savor the feeling of closeness. We're not supposed to be doing this but that makes the kiss even more delicious. He takes my lower lip like he's been craving me for days. I open my mouth for more when—

"Oh my God!" someone screams from the door. For a split second I almost care about his job.

Max pulls away, his hands still on me. "Oops."

Whoever it is flees, leaving us to ourselves again. I open my legs and he slides between them and angles his head down. We let ourselves make out for real for a minute. I haven't been kissed like this in forever. Even if my brain can't remember anything, my body can—and it's been a been a long time since it has responded this way.

Still, I pull away. "Max, we can't do this. Your job . . ."

He shrugs. "I'm more interested in you right now. Plus, Fay already lit my reputation on fire."

"And we're literally on our way to pick up JP."

Max breathes heavily, still reeling from the kiss. "I don't know JP, and there's a chance he tried to kill you."

"I think you're jumping to conclusions. You said it yourself that I can't trust my own memories right now."

He exhales loudly. "Maybe, but there's something off about him. About you and him. Why did it take him so long to reach out to you after your accident? I don't trust him, Mia."

I can't deal with Max's logic right now. I need JP to be a good guy—to be *my* guy.

Max has his PhD, but all I have is JP.

JP looks better on paper. Actually, no one has ever looked better on paper. He's a billionaire chocolatier. Just thinking the name Jacques-o-late makes me feel like I've been kissed, by fortune if not by a man. He's been endorsed by the ABC Network, which wanted him to be the bachelor on *The Bachelor*. And let's face it, I'm paying Max to hang out with me. I'm not sure if what I'm feeling for him is real, or if I'm so vulnerable, needy, and scared of loneliness that I can't see straight.

I stand up, putting some distance between us. "I'm going to get a soda."

I walk to the vending machine in the hallway. When my Diet Pepsi gets stuck, I kick the shit out of it. I hear the lab door open and footsteps running toward me. "Hey, let me help you with that," Max says gently. He tips the machine a little and my soda comes loose.

He holds the can out to me like a rose. Like he's chosen me.

Suddenly, I'm overwhelmed. What am I doing? I need to uncomplicate my life—not make it messier and more dramatic.

"You keep it," I say. "I'll wait for you in the car while you finish up in the lab." I walk away but can feel Max's eyes burning through me.

———

An hour later, we're driving south on the 701 back to JP's house. The silence between us is pregnant, just like I would be if I lived out my complete fantasy with Max because God knows that I don't have a birth control plan. Maybe I have an IUD? It's just as likely that I'm on the pill and have forgotten to take it for four days. That'll make a good *Bustle* article, at least.

I'm on my third Diet Pepsi. I'm not even thirsty but I need to keep my mouth busy—and I've already checked all of my social media platforms twenty-five times.

I run my finger along the stitches in the leather seat one at a time. The stitching is perfect, probably hand-done in Italy.

"I shouldn't have kissed you," Max says quietly.

"It's 2020, Max. We kissed each other." The kiss was definitely wrong, but it was also the only thing that felt right since I came out of the coma. Talk about a cliché.

"You have JP."

"I have JP," I echo.

"I guess my question is . . . do you want to *know* JP?"

I breathe deeply and shut my eyes. So much has happened in the last few days. "I just can't even think at all. Would it be okay if we just chill for a minute?"

He sighs. "Sure, but I hope you understand that I don't want to be your backup guy."

So much for chill.

I look at him, studying his eyes as they study the road. "Max, if I didn't have this boyfriend who I don't remember, I would be all over you without any hesitation."

"Exactly my point," Max says. "Think about what you want."

I turn to settle back in my seat. What Max doesn't know is that I don't have the luxury of pursuing what I want. JP is rich and could solve all of my financial problems. I'm ashamed to even think this, but there it is. I don't want to just use him for his money, but I can't help but see how easy life would be if I were with him.

Speak of the devil—my phone pings and I see a text from JP.

Hey Hunnybunny. See you in a couple of hours!

Hunnybunny—has he met me? Sugary endearments fit me like an XL hoodie from Old Navy.

Put on that lacy black dress. Taking you to Mr. Chow's for dinner and drinks. I have something very important to ask you. xoxo

Based on photos in my Instagram feed, we've been dating for at least six months. I have a toothbrush at his house. He calls me Hunnybunny. In that first text convo he said something about a present even more sparkly than my personality.[42]

JP is definitely going to propose.

Max notices the change in my expression. "Is everything okay?"

"Yeah, it's nothing."

"I just met you three days ago, Mia, but obviously there's something between us. What happens is up to you, but like I said, I don't want to be your backup guy. I definitely don't want to stand around and hold your purse while you test-drive JP to see if he's better than me."

I slump and look at my lap. He's throwing the decision back at me, which makes sense, but I'm so overwhelmed by JP's text that my brain goes into self-preservation mode.

"I hear you. For now, I just need to figure out how to get through today. JP made reservations at Mr. Chow's, which I'm thinking we can use for Crystal and Jules. It's much fancier, and we can save the Groupon for later."

Max looks at me seriously. "I don't know if we can just sweep everything aside, Mia. I'm worried about you. I think that cop had a point." His face hardens. "I know JP is handsome and rich and seems nice, but let me ask you again: are you sure he wasn't the one who put you in the hospital? In cases like this, it's usually the boyfriend."

If I could slump even further into my seat, I would. "I don't think so." Still, I can't help but flash back to our first

....

[42] Side question: has he met me?

text conversation, post-amnesia: *Is everything ok? U still mad?*
Clearly we had some kind of argument. And I doubt he's referring to the art museum fight. That was a full-on assault, not
an argument. It couldn't have been JP.

Max isn't buying it. "I don't think you should be alone
with him until you make sure he isn't the one who did it."

Now I'm starting to get a little pissed off. I don't need
supervised visits with my boyfriend. Let's face it, only a total
psychopath would knock me out, run to Switzerland, and
then act as if nothing happened. JP might be a rich douche,
but I don't get psychopath vibes from him. He has a chocolate
company, for fuck's sake. He's on the same level as Santa Claus.

I give Max a sweet smile and say, "Sure."

He sees right through me. "I'm serious, Mia. Someone
really hurt you, maybe even tried to kill you. You can't brush
that off."

For the moment, that's exactly what I'm going to do.

CHAPTER

SIXTEEN

Since I'm meeting JP for the first time, it makes sense to dress up a little. I take a shower, but there's only so much I can do about my wardrobe given that I have one outfit. How have I not solved this yet? I've been out of my coma for several days and I still have nothing else to wear. I guess I've had better things to do . . . like figure out who I am.

Looking in the mirror, I realize it doesn't matter who I was. Currently, I'm a ho in a five-day-old cocktail dress. It's my only option besides something from JP's closet. If that doesn't say something about my circumstances, nothing does. Even though the dress has been recently dry cleaned, I give the lining a few squirts of Febreze, so it doesn't stain the satin, and put on an extra-thick coat of Pirate lipstick.

"Do you want me to come?"

"To pick up *my boyfriend?*" Is Max insane?

"I meant it when I said you shouldn't be alone with him."

"Max, you can't come to the airport to pick up JP with me. That's just not going to work." I don't mention that his house-sitting services won't be needed anymore either. That should be obvious.

"Mia, you might not realize it, but you could be in danger."

"Max, I told you. I remember who pushed me into the ice sculpture. It was a woman. I'm sure of it."

He sighs and shakes his head. "Recovered memories aren't always accurate. And right now, you're just believing it because it's convenient. If you believe it, you get to have a fairy-tale, happily-ever-after ending with a billionaire Prince Charming. But maybe he's not the right one for you."

I pause to let him fill a suggestion for who might be the right one, but he's quiet.

I kiss Max on the cheek. "Can I borrow a few bucks? My new credit card hasn't come in the mail yet." I don't want to lie, but what else can I do? I have to fill up the Ferrari after two straight days of driving it all over LA. A little voice in my head says, *Tell the truth* but I tell it to shut the F up.

"Umm, aren't *you* supposed to be paying *me*?" Max points out.

"As soon as I get access to my money. I promise." Assuming I don't go to jail. "Max, I know this whole situation is weird, but I really appreciate you standing by me. Are you going to stick around for a little while longer?" I put on a dramatically oversize sun hat from the front closet while I wait for him to respond.

"You're stuck with me. Someone needs to have your back. Besides, I have to be here when JP gets back. Remember, you're not the only person I'm working for here."

I give him another peck on the cheek. "You're the best intern ever, Max. I'll see you when I get back."

"No, I'm vice president," he says lamely.[43]

<hr />

On the way to the airport, I get gas. Because I only have cash like it's 1999, I walk into the station.

God, I want a fucking slushie.

Just as I think that, I know the impulse is true and honest. I love slushies! I grab one. If JP loves me, maybe he loves slushies too.

I count out a few dollars and change for the slushie, slap it down on the counter, and head back to the car.

The Ferrari looks like I've been living out of it. Fast food bags with muddy footprints on them are shoved into the corners of the footwells, and the previously pristine cup holders are starting to fill with the debris of life: straw wrappers, change, and crumbs. It even smells like Friday's tacos. When I stepped into it a couple of days ago, it looked like I just drove it off the lot. Is JP a neat freak or does he have an army of people sweeping up taco lettuce and coffee cups behind him?

Traffic isn't bad for LA, surprisingly. I drive past billboards for all the important shit, like new Netflix specials. A giant billboard of JulesBrand underwear dominates the view just past the Carson exit. Jules stares over the 405 toward Compton like he has a secret.

....

[43] Ugh. Come on, Max.

If my investment in him doesn't pan out fast, I'm going to jail. That's my secret. Well, one of them.

Does JP know this? How much of my life have I shared with this man?

I follow the directions to Terminal 7 and pull up behind a line of Ubers, which reminds me that I probably should have made JP take an Uber. Why did I volunteer to drive to the airport? Because that's what you do for the man of your dreams, I remind myself.

I tap out a quick text. I'm here. Baggage claim 7.

I haven't felt this nervous since two days ago when I turned the key to the door of the pink house on Ocean Boulevard. I'm about to meet the person I chose: a guy with a too-clean car, a perfect house, and a square jaw. I feel like I'm floating above the world, watching my life unfold. My hands are on the wheel, my foot is on the gas, and I can hear myself breathing too fast. The AC blows too cold on my face and I open the window.

Immediately, the sounds of car horns honking angrily in an enclosed space and the smell of exhaust assaults me. I can hear people yelling at each other to get out of the way. A cop motions for me to move along and I manage to push the gas pedal down and drive a couple of car lengths ahead.

I can't get Max's voice out of my head. Am I really picking up a man who might've smashed my skull in less than a week ago? Both Max and the cop I talked to thought JP was the prime suspect. But my memories of that night tell me he isn't the one. Sure he showed up in that memory, but it seems like some angry chick did it. But WTF do I know? Do I only pay attention to things that validate my theories and opinions? That's basically what Max accused me of doing. That's probably how people live fairy-tale lives, though—they only see the good things. Fairy tales only exist if you keep your rose-colored glasses on, like in that movie with Amy Adams, which, come to think of it, was all about confirmation bias.

Shut up, Mia. My mind is racing in every direction now.

I don't think I'm hyperventilating but I don't feel good. I lay my forehead against the steering wheel and shut my eyes. Someone behind me honks but I don't even lift my head. If I don't move, I can't get into more trouble. Just stay put, Mia. Don't move.

I hear a knock on the passenger-side window. If it's that goddamn cop, I'm going to tell him to move the car for me. I need help. But when I look up, I see JP.

JP.

When he sees my face, his smile changes to genuine concern. "Mia, are you okay? What's the matter?" His voice sounds far away, and I can see his mouth moving, but I can't understand anything. What am I even doing?

I've been wearing the same dress for days and I'm wearing a hat to cover the staples in my head. JP wants to kill me or marry me, and I just made out with Max in a science lab.

JP hurries around the car to my door and opens it, grabbing my hand and pulling me out. I stand as tears well up in my eyes. My legs feel like jelly. I open my mouth to talk but

I'm just breathing. I can't say anything and I can tell that I'm making a hideous face. I'm in the throes of a light panic attack.

"Oh my God, what happened to you?"

He puts his arm around me to prop me up and basically drags me to the passenger side. I'm done. I know it. I don't know what I've been doing, but I can't do it anymore. He opens the door and helps me into the low-slung seat. I lean my head back and shut my eyes tight. This is the weirdest introduction to the man who is going to propose to me, assuming I understood his text correctly.

While I shut my eyes, too freaked out to confront the first person from my real life, JP quickly loads his luggage in the trunk and runs to the driver's side.

"Mia, are you okay?"

I nod. There aren't many places to pull over and rest on the way out of the airport, but he takes the first exit and turns into a parking lot.

"Mia, you're not okay. What happened?"

"I'm sorry," I say, "I started feeling so . . . sick all of a sudden."

He takes a long breath and rubs my back. "Have you eaten anything?"

I can't remember if I've eaten anything. He looks around, sees the slushie, and picks it up. He reads the 7-Eleven logo like it's written in a foreign language. "Did you buy this?" he asks.

I start breathing harder. The slushie was the only thing I knew to be true so far today, but JP seems shocked to see it in the cup holder.

He repeats, "Did you buy this?'

I nod.

He peels off the plastic top and inspects the contents. The slushie is unnaturally blue and starting to melt. He takes a sip and makes a smacking noise like he's tasting a slushie for the first time in his life.

With a nod, he says, "You need the sugar. Take this."

I'm crushed that he doesn't know what a slushie is. He's never met me the real me. I know it as deeply as I know that I love slushies. I take the drink, though, because he's right. The slushie will help.

I stare forward and suck the blue-raspberry flavor down, racing to the bottom faster than I'm doing in real life. When I'm three-quarters of the way done, I feel okay again. I'm breathing normally and I'm not sweating. "I'm so sorry," I say. "I don't know what happened." I mean, I sort of do, but I'm not going to tell him. A tear leaks out of the corner of my eye and I wipe it away with the hem of my dress.

"It's okay, sweetie. Let's just get you home."

"I'm sorry," I whisper.

After ten or so minutes of normalcy, JP says, "You're not pregnant, are you?"

A laugh burbles out of me, loose and messy. The idea is absurd.

"No," I answer with the confidence of someone who was recently hospitalized.

"Are you sure?"

"I really doubt it."

He nods. "Low blood sugar can hit you hard. Maybe you should have your thyroid checked."

I nod. "Good tip." I look at his face, and my panic has subsided enough that I can see how blue his eyes are. He looks like he's been filtered and photoshopped into the driver's seat of a Ferrari, but he's sitting next to me. He's worried about my thyroid. What planet am I living on?

I blink and JP's eyes are just as improbably blue as they were before. His hair is just as jet-black.

"I think you were right about my blood sugar. I think I skipped breakfast."

"All coffee and no calories, if I know you." He leans over the center console. Before he kisses me, he pauses to let our breath mingle and let the heat build and sizzle for the briefest of moments. When he closes the gap, pressing his lips to mine, I let my eyelids close and drift off to wherever this kiss is going to take me. Suddenly all I want is for him to fuck me senseless. I want to forget everything. I want to forget that I've forgotten everything important, and I want it now.

I can feel him smile through the kiss and he says, "Down, girl" in the kind of voice that tells me he's feeling it too.

When he pulls away, a semi rushes past and the wind rocks the car just slightly. "We have to get home first at least."

He turns on the radio and I lean back against the black leather bucket chair.

JP didn't bash my head in. I just know it. He's caring and thoughtful and sexy as fuck. Pre-amnesia Mia was smart and chose him. Her choices should trump everything that I've done in the last few days.[44]

I don't think Max is going to like him.

As we pull back onto the freeway, Jules stares down from his spot on the billboard overlooking the 405. *See ya soon, buddy.* Suddenly everything seems a little more possible.

"So how was Switzerland?" I ask, suddenly remembering that I'm not the only person in the world.

"Amazing. There's so much history there. Everything just feels so much more . . . real."

I almost laugh.

"Next time you should come with me, if you're not too busy with work."

I nod enthusiastically, picturing myself sliding into a chalet on skis in body-con ski pants and a fluffy jacket trimmed with fur. I know enough about myself to know that I don't give a shit about bunnies. I'd happily sip a chocolate martini wearing at least two dead animals and then let JP fuck me with his big dick. I assume he has a big dick. I mean, everything else about him is perfect. I need to get fucked hard, no gentle lovemaking that I might be able to remember my name through. I want to feel nothing but a technicolor orgasm, over and over.

Drugs would be fine, too. I wonder if I do drugs?[45]

....

[44] I think . . .

[45] Should I be worried that I want to forget my life so badly when all I've been doing is trying to remember?

"So how did the trip to Sonoma with Mackenzie go? Did you check out that little cottage you had your eye on by the vineyard?"

I look at JP like he's crazy. A house by a vineyard? Is that really what I was into? And who the hell is Mackenzie?

"Umm, it was a no-go. The . . . bones weren't good." JP nods like I just said something reasonable. Thank you to whatever HGTV show I watched in my former life.

JP revs the engine and shoots into the left lane to pass someone without signaling. I find this kind of sexy, even though I don't have health insurance or money to pay my medical bills if I break my whole body in a car accident.

"It's good to be home." He looks over at me meaningfully. "So, Mr. Chow's tonight?"

"I would." I smile weakly at him. "But I have a work thing tonight. Can I take a rain check?"

Looking a little deflated, he lets out a small "Oh."

I need to pick up Crystal and get her ready for her date with Jules—and at this point, I'm going to have to hustle.

"You rest up," I say. "I bet you're super jet-lagged."

I am about to say, *I'll see you when I get home* but I realize he might not expect that. I only have a couple of things at his house, which must mean I'm not living there full time.

"You want to come to my place tonight?" I ask instead. It's risky but he's my best chance of figuring out where I live.

"What?" He looks at me with complete disregard for traffic, like he's in an old movie and the passing cars are on a green screen.

"Careful!" I yell, feeling every staple in my head.

"I'm so sorry, Mia, I just never expected you to invite me over."

I stare at him, dumbfounded. He's never been over to my place?

He grabs my thigh and squeezes. "I'm so glad that you're finally ready to share your life with me, though."

My heart sinks. JP doesn't know me any better than I know myself . . . but whose fault is that?

CHAPTER

SEVENTEEN

As we pull up to JP's pink house on Ocean, the world gets fuzzy and I feel all floaty and disconnected. Another memory is coming. I can feel it.

We're in the Ferrari. It's drizzling outside and rain is splattering on the windshield. I'm wearing the same yellow dress and holding an invitation. It's for the opening of the MySelfie *exhibit.*

JP is in the driver's seat but he hasn't shifted the car into gear. His expression is irate. "Who does that sort of thing?" He's practically yelling.

"I had to, JP. Do you know what my life was like? Do you know how my boss treated me? I had to get out of there." My voice is firm. "I did what I had to do."

"I don't care. There are rules in society. You broke the law, but more than that . . . you're just messed up." He looks me square in the eye. "You're a fucking head case. And you used me."

"I didn't know you. I met you after I took all of the GoldRush material."

"I don't know, Mia. I'll go to this opening with you and then I need to get out of here for a few days. I'm going to Switzerland. To clear my head."

At that, I step out of the car and slam the passenger door shut. JP rolls down the window and tells me to calm down and that he'll still drive me, but I'm already pulling Uber up on my phone. My destination: the Long Beach Museum of Art.

I snap back to reality.

"It's good to be home," JP says, completely calm. We're in exactly the same position in the car as when we argued. He seems fine now, like he forgave me for whatever horrible, messed-up thing I did, but I study him carefully. If we just had a huge fight less than a week ago, and if he called me a head case, why is he potentially proposing to me? Something isn't right here—and his calm demeanor is throwing me off. Is JP the kind of guy who can go from 0 to 100 and back again? I still don't want to believe that he attacked me, but I can't take him off the board yet.

"I hope you don't mind that I've been staying here. My place is being repainted," I lie again. I don't know why I didn't think of that before. It completely explains almost everything.

"Sure, it's no problem. I know you've been renovating your house for quite some time. I assume that's why I haven't been invited over until now," he teases.

Ah. Apparently I've gone to this well a few times.

As we get out of the car, my sense of dread increases.

I don't want to hang out with JP and Max together. When my phone rings, I don't even mind that it's the cops. Officer Denise is preferable.

"Meet me at the bank," she says. "I got a warrant to look at your bank statements."

"Right now? I'm kind of busy."

"Right now." Officer Denise is taking this assault and robbery very seriously. I'm not so sure I want to find out anything else, though. My haters gonna hate mantra is starting to feel a little thin.

"JP, I'm so sorry but I have to run. I'm having a money problem—major fraud on my account—and the bank is calling me in to answer some questions for their investigation."

"Okay, I'll settle in and see you in a few." He looks disappointed but I bet he's dying for a shower and a nap.

"And then don't forget I have that GoldRush thing, so I'll just be stopping by for a moment to get ready. You won't even see me—I'll be in and out like that." I snap my fingers.

He nods. "Handle your business and I'll see you tonight." He kisses me on both cheeks, European style, and I step back into the Ferrari. JP doesn't even blink; he must be used to me borrowing his car. I wave as I pull out of the garage. I look totally carefree but my heart is racing.

———

At the bank, Kumar is waiting for me. "Good morning. Would you like some coffee?" he asks.

Coffee? It's almost like I'm here for fun. "Yes, thank you," I say.

"Would your fiancé like one as well? I assume he's coming, too?"

I give him a funny look before I realize he's talking about Max. "No, he won't be coming." I assume he's having an awkward moment with JP and brooding about the kiss. In that way, this little visit to the bank is a blessing—if you count one disaster as a good distraction from another disaster.

Kumar smiles sadly and says, "That might be good," which I take to mean that my financial statements aren't going to make me look like a desirable marriage prospect.

Kumar leads me to a desk where Denise is waiting for me, and he prints out my statements like it's 2006 or something. He hands the pages to Denise first and she frowns hard.

"What is it?" I ask. I take a sip of my coffee. It doesn't make me feel any better.

Denise breaks out a pair of reading glasses. "I want to make sure I'm seeing this right." With a glance over the top of her cheaters, she says, "Mia, do you have any idea what kind of cash flow you normally deal with?"

"No. All I know are the prices listed on my website. They're high." Understatement of the year.

"It looks like you gave away all of your money two weeks ago. Combined with the assault . . ." She looks up at me. "I don't want to jump to conclusions, but . . ." From the look on her face, I can tell she already has.

She probably thinks Jules stole all my money and tried to kill me. "It wasn't Jules. I paid him a hundred grand for two Instagram posts. I have the documentation to prove it."

That information doesn't seem to compute for her. After the longest time she just says, "Okay. How about these other charges?"

She points to a $5,000 charge to High Flying and another $2,000 to Prada.[46] "Those are business investments," I say lightly.

By now, Denise probably thinks I hit *myself* in the head.

"Denise . . ." I say.

"Yes?"

"When you fingerprinted me yesterday, did you find out anything about me? My address, for instance?"

"You still don't know where you live?"

I shake my head. "I'm staying at my boyfriend's house."

She raises her eyebrows. "So you trust him?"

"He might be the more trustworthy one between the two of us."

This almost gets a laugh out of Denise.

"I would like to know where I live, though." So far I've only seen myself in relation to JP, Max, and now Jules the underwear model. At this point am I really figuring out who I am, or am I just figuring out what kind of girlfriend I am— who JP and Max *think* I am? Should I even care? Who the hell are they, even? I'm so fucking confused.

....

[46] At least I'm getting a lot of use out of the dress.

"Come with me to the station," she says. "I pulled your record yesterday."

"Are we done here?" I ask in surprise.

"I've seen all I need to see," she says with another arched eyebrow.

Denise doesn't drive a real cop car, which is a slight disappointment. No lights on top or cage in the back. It's not even an unmarked Dodge Charger or anything sexy. It's tan and nondescript. If it were a guy, he'd be named Mike Nelson and I would be surprised to remember I went to school with him every time I scanned the yearbook. This is the car equivalent of *oh yeah, that guy.* Then again, I wouldn't have remembered my own name if Siri hadn't told me, so nothing against Mike.

At any rate, it's a lame car and I bet Denise wishes she'd been something cooler than a cop. Look at me. I have no money or memories prior to the last few days, but at least I'm driving a Ferrari.

Once we're in the car, she looks at me very seriously, like a mom about to have a conversation with her daughter about herpes or consent—definitely something sex related. Those are ninety percent of serious conversations with daughters, which is fucked up, right? Shouldn't we talk about self-actualization or what to do if you wake up without your memory?

"Miss Wallace, do you have any family or friends to rely on?"

"Not that I know of."

"Do you feel safe where you're staying? Have you been seeing the man you gave all your money to?"

"I feel safe. And I know who I gave the money to. It's all legit, and I'm pretty sure he didn't coerce it out of me." I pause, afraid to ask the one question that's been lingering all day. "Did you find out something about JP that I should know?"

"Nothing," she says. "He has a clean record."

I can tell she's thinking about saying something else, but she bites her tongue. Before we know it, we're at the police station, five minutes away from Wells Fargo, just long enough for one almost-conversation about herpes, or about how women shouldn't define themselves through the men they're with, et cetera, et cetera. But we all have to define ourselves in relation to something, and let's be honest—a hot guy with a Ferrari isn't a bad point of definition.

"Follow me," Denise says, charging ahead to her desk so she can hand me another pile of clues about my life. "I've got a list of known addresses and your criminal record. I made a copy for you."

"Criminal record?" I didn't see that coming, though the minute she says it, it seems obvious.

"Yes. It's mostly juvenile. Shoplifting and then one arrest a few years ago."

"I'm a criminal," I say flatly. That's who I am. I should have known that I wasn't a supermodel princess ballerina with a yacht.

"You were arrested. That does not make you a criminal." Nice of her to say. "What was I arrested for recently?"

"Theft. And you have some outstanding unpaid tickets." I take the papers. "Thanks, I really appreciate it."

"Good luck. I'll let you know if I find out anything about your assault." She gives me a hard look. "Mia, now that we know that no one stole your money—well, at least it doesn't look like it—it's important to consider the consequences."

"That I just spent that much money? Why would I have done that?"

She shakes her head. "I don't know, but that hot-air balloon ride and the Prada dress purchases amount to felony check fraud."

I have no words for this. I just start shaking my head. "I'm sure I didn't mean to do that. I must've expected some money to come in and was hospitalized before I could take care of it."

Denise sits back and crosses her arms over her chest. "If no one stole that money from you, then you stole the money from the bank. Even if Wells Fargo doesn't prosecute, we will."

I lean back in my chair. I'm breathing too fast.

This can't be happening to me.

All I wanted to do was retrace my steps to find my old life. To figure out who all the faces and places were on my Instagram account so I could figure out who *I* was. I never expected all this sleuthing to lead me here, to a copy of my criminal record and the threat of prosecution

"There's no intent requirement for check fraud, Mia. You might want to get a lawyer."

I look at her in complete bafflement. She, of all people, knows I can't afford a lawyer.

I nod wordlessly, turn around, and walk out of the station.

Unsure of what to do, where to go, or who to talk to, I go

to Starbucks and buy a latte I can't afford. Actually, if we're being honest about it, I buy a latte with money I borrowed from Max because I ran out of the money I stole from JP. Is this what I've always done? Is this how I operate?

I carry my kind-of-stolen latte to a table on the patio and try to calm down. The stresses are piling up.

Felony check fraud. An impending marriage proposal.

Worst of all, I can't even share it with the only person I trust—not without risking our not-really-a-relationship relationship.

CHAPTER

EIGHTEEN

Now that I've had my daily visit to the police station, I hustle back to JP's to get ready and pick up Crystal. I'm definitely late at this point, which means I'll have to be in and out of there quickly—the one blessing of the day. Hopefully Max is still there because I have no idea where he lives—and I can't pull off this date night alone.

I walk through the front door and see JP sitting at the kitchen island with Max, beers in hand.

This is literally my nightmare.

"Heeyyy guys," I say, tiptoeing forward. "JP, I thought you'd be asleep by now?"

He smiles broadly—and a little drunkenly. How many beers has he had? More important, how many has Max had? Enough to tell him all of my dirty secrets? I shoot Max a death glare, just in case he deserves it.

"Max was just telling me about his research. Fascinating stuff. He's quite an impressive person."

Max holds up his bottle as if to toast me.

"Yes, yes, I'm sure he is." I eye Max, still waiting to find out how much he's said about me.

"How much time did you two spend together?" JP asks, noticing the glimmer of tension between us.

"Ummm . . ." I say.

"We just had a few kitchen conversations," Max says.

So he hasn't been talking trash to my boyfriend after all. I retract the death glare.

"Well, it's so good to see you again, Max," I say. "JP, you really should get some rest. I'm just going to freshen up. I have a date to arrange tonight and have to be on my way."

Max takes the hint. "If it's not too much trouble, would you mind dropping me off on your way? I'm a little woozy from the booze, and now that JP is back, I'm all done with my house-sitting duties."

"Sure! No problem!" I say a little too excitedly. JP looks at me weirdly. "Why don't you pack while I freshen up? Be back in a jiff!"

A jiff? Max is looking at me like I'm a lunatic.

"Bye!" I dart out of the room, my blood pressure rising for the hundredth time today.

———

Fifteen minutes later, I slide into the driver's seat with a fresh coat of Pirate on my lips as Max settles into the passenger seat. The second he shuts the door, I whisper-scream, "You had beers with my boyfriend?! Are you trying to make things more dramatic for me? Because I'm literally at my limit here."

"I know, I know, I'm so sorry. But what was I supposed to do? Refuse to have a drink with the guy? He offered me a Stella and I had no reason not to take it."

I wave my hand. "Fine, fine. Did you say anything about me?"

He scoffs. "Believe it or not, I have other things to talk about besides you. I just told him about my work."

"Ahh, so you were trying to put him to sleep. Good strategy."

Max glares at me. "You're lucky I find you so attractive."

"Whatever. Do you have any cash?" I see a Starbucks on the corner and need another fix. Max reaches into his wallet and grudgingly hands me a ten-dollar bill, mumbling about how I'm supposed to be paying him and not the other way around.

I pull up to the drive-through speaker and shout, "Two venti white chocolate mochas!" Max looks visibly ill at the idea but I say, "You're fine. Shut up and drink your coffee."

I plug the address Crystal gave me into the car's GPS. It tells me to turn on Atlantic. Pretty soon we're driving by Tam's, the fast-food burger place, and a bunch of oil wells. "Wait, is this place in Signal Hill?" I ask. Signal Hill is sort of ritzy, but it's also right between Long Beach and Compton. Max manipulates the screen to study the map and says, "It looks like we're headed to the far side of the neighborhood."

We drive past all the mansions and stately homes and turn right on Long Beach Boulevard. The neighborhood doesn't feel like the kind of place where a harp-playing, sophisticated woman would hang out. Pretty soon, we drive right out of the ragged end of Long Beach and straight into Compton. "Ummm . . ." I say.

Max looks confused. "Do you think you got the wrong address?"

I think back to GoldRush's ad copy. Sophisticated and elite California beauties. Something about how they're California's most important resource.

There are plenty of beauties walking the streets of Compton, but the website was definitely misleading. I miss a turn and take the next left down a side street. There's enough discarded furniture in the street to tell the story of something, like inadequate trash removal or . . . something less than elite. I drive over the LA River, a giant concrete aqueduct. A guy walks along the bank, watering his horses like it's the Wild West. "What the—? Is that a burro?"

Max nods. "I think so."

"Where are we?"

"I don't think Compton is that bad anymore. It's not like a giant gang fight, at least. Not like in *Straight Outta Compton* or whatever."

I look at the black Midwestern nerd sitting next to me. "Uh-huh. Sure."

There do seem to be a lot of cute kids playing on the sidewalks with their moms. Still, it's not Santa Barbara. "I think we took a wrong turn somewhere."

"Maybe she's volunteering or visiting relatives?" Max says.

I shrug. I literally have no clue. On the GPS I can see the blue dot of our final destination. "It's says we're close . . ." Minutes later, I look up to see a Walmart Supercenter.

Now I'm even more confused. "Do you think she meant Long Beach Boulevard West but we went east or something?" Walmart doesn't seem right.

I pull out my phone and text Crystal. Are you at Walmart? Duh. I get off in 15.

What the fuck?

At this point I realize everything about the GoldRush copy is total bullshit, but I decide to test the waters anyway. I don't have room for you and the harp.

WTF?

"Um, Max. I don't think Crystal plays the harp."

"Really," he says, his voice 100 percent sarcasm.

"That's probably the only criterion she doesn't meet, though. I mean, how the hell was I going to find a harp-playing philanthropist who was a dead ringer for Sleeping Beauty?" Talk about impossible. "She's probably super pretty and into social justice or . . . IDK."

Max raises his eyebrows. "Let's go meet her."

The Compton Walmart is a plain old Walmart, but it does feel a little extra Walmarty. I could pretty much walk out of the place with any young woman there, and she'd be ready for a date. Long nails, tight dresses, good hair. Lots of girls are dressed to go somewhere other than Walmart. Hell, I'm in a cocktail dress.

I'm not sure where Crystal works but I figure any girl I hire isn't stocking shelves or operating a forklift in the back. I scan the registers and find Crystal finishing up at checkout #7. I can see why Kobra compared her to Halle Berry. She's got a popping figure and a cute pixie cut but, more important for my immediate purposes, she's the only twentysomething in the place dressed in full-on sweats. She must have something else to wear in her employee locker. I catch a snippet of her conversation with the customer she's helping. "Girl, she ain't got no money."

Tell me about it, Crystal.

"Crystal?" I greet her as she turns the light off on #7.

Her customer service tone vanishes in a second. She angles her head and the look she gives me is pure *I can't even with you.*

"Crystal . . ."

She holds her hand up. Whatever I did to her, she has no intention of hurrying for me. "Let me close out this register. I'll be right with you."

"Okay. I'll just wait over there." Max and I head to the cafeteria area and grab a table while Crystal takes her sweet time doing whatever it is she's doing.

She walks over, pacing herself like a queen. "Thing is," she says, "I don't have anyone to watch Kai tonight."

"You have kids?" It comes out like, *you have herpes?* And how could she not have a babysitter yet? This date has been on the books since way before I lost my mind.

"What's the matter with you? You know Kai."

"My memory is a little fuzzy," I say.

"Oh." I think that's the first time it hits her that I have a real injury. I think about explaining the whole thing, but what's the point? We have other things to worry about.

I level with her. "Crystal, do you understand the stakes here?"

"What do you mean?"

"This is a date with a millionaire. He has flown his ass to LA just to see you. He wants to take you to a fancy dinner and get to know you." I gesture to her surroundings, my implication obvious—she can do better than this. "This is a powerful guy."

She shrugs. "Whatever. Same bullshit, different restaurant."

I take a deep breath. "This is a good opportunity. He has money and it doesn't look like you do."

"Umm, that's what you said the last time."

Kobra.

"Kobra has money," I say, more to myself than to Crystal.

"He's a straight-up criminal."

"Did something happen on that date?"

She nods. "Let me tell you about that fool. He took me to some warehouse by the pier. He has a tricked-out loft inside. It's sketch as hell and full of drugs. When we showed, he was throwing some party with his homies. Booze, drugs, girls. You get it."

I nod. Sounds romantic.

"I don't want anything to do with that. I signed up for this to get out of that lifestyle. Enough motherfuckers like that around here."

"Understandable. Sorry about that."

"I was cool, just gonna ride it out and have a few free drinks. But dude was showing off big time."

I just let her keep talking.

"They're all high and he's like, 'Wanna see my snake?' I was like, 'Hell no, brother, this ain't that kind of date.' He laughed like it was the funniest thing ever and he brought me downstairs. He had all these snakes and shit, like zoo animals. One was this pure white python with yellow stripes. I wouldn't wanna see it through glass. Pure killer. No soul."

"Oh my God." This is shocking but somehow not. What else would an asshole with millions who fancies himself a snake charmer buy?

"Next thing I know, he lets the snake out. It slithers out and he does some sort of 'snake charming' shit, which was, like, nothing. That snake didn't give a damn about him. Him and his buddies laughed like a bunch of idiots and forgot about it. I asked for a ride home and he was like, 'Later, baby.'"

"What an idiot."

"You're telling me." She shakes her head, her eyes still big and her expression grim. "An hour later, the python wrapped itself around one of the other guys—Pedro, I think. Pedro was high as fuck, pretty much passed out. The snake just wrapped itself around him. I started screaming and yelling and some of the homies all freaked out. Kobra tried to get the snake off him with some sort of magic."

She shook her head.

"Did Pedro live?"

"I don't think so. I didn't wait to find out. I ran out of there. It ain't a good neighborhood late at night, but . . . I didn't trust that motherfucker."

No wonder Kobra was looking for her.

She stops talking and the sounds of Walmart fill the void, including a woman yelling at her kid that he can't have more candy. The whole scene feels surreal.

"I'm sorry."

"You should be. I thought you knew these guys."

"I'm sorry. I don't know what to say. But, I swear, you'll love Jules. He's not a drug dealer, and his business is legitimate."

Crystal looks like she's teetering on the edge, and then my phone pings with a text. Bitch, you owe me.

Could Kobra sense that we were talking about him? I look wildly around the Walmart, completely paranoid.

Owe you what?

Crystal and Max stare at me. I look at them evenly and smile. "Are we ready to go?"

CHAPTER

NINETEEN

We are not ready to go. I guess I'm not surprised that Crystal doesn't trust me to set her up on another date given what a disaster the last one was. She's lying back in a patio chair in the gardening section like she doesn't want to get out of it. Like she just needs a damn break. Don't we all. As soon as I get Crystal out the door, *I'm* going to take a break. At least a little one.

"I spent the afternoon with Jules yesterday and he's super nice. And handsome." I shake my head despondently. "I'm so sorry I set you up with Kobra. I don't know how that happened."

"No shit, girl. I knew he was a dealer the minute I laid eyes on that fool. And not even anyone with style. A redneck meth dealer." She shakes her head dramatically and murmurs, "Uh-uh."

I don't dispute that point. Bad move, former self.

I look meaningfully at her outfit. "Do you have anything else to wear?"

"You got a problem with how I look?"

"No. But you're going out with a wealthy man who's going to Instagram your whole date."

She looks up at me from her slouched position, 100 percent *who gives a fuck*.

"Don't worry. He's just going to look cute in his underwear for you."

"Oh my God." Crystal takes a deep breath. "At least I'll get a free meal out of it."

Crystal has the biggest fucking chip on her shoulder in the history of chips on shoulders. Maybe another date wasn't the best way to make her feel better about the last one.

I'm about ready to ask the girl in aisle 5 if she wants to go on a date with Jules Spencer, the underwear mogul, when Crystal manages to drag her ass out of the patio chair. "I'm gonna go splash some water on my face."

I don't know if she's doing that to prepare for the date or to recover from talking to me.

"I need to make a phone call," Max says from behind a potted palm. I'd almost forgotten he was there. "Chan from the lab keeps calling. I think he might have figured something out."

I think Walmart just reminded him that he wants to be a scientist, but I wave him off. "See you in a minute."

I hurry after Crystal and see her disappear into the women's restroom. I push through the door and knock some kid in the head. "OMG. I'm so sorry!" The little girl bounces back and then runs out of the restroom, unperturbed. I feel a pang of jealousy. Damn kids and their bouncy, resilient brains.

Crystal is washing her hands when I walk in. I see her face reflected in the mirror and she looks bone tired. Not, like, didn't get enough sleep tired, but tired in a way only other women can understand. When I peel off her layers of frustration and rage, I realize that she's me. She's everyone: trying to decide whether to give up or keep fighting.

If I can do it, so can Crystal. And vice versa. We're gonna girl-power our way to the end of this day. I can see in her face that she knows she doesn't have a choice, and as she looks back at me through the mirror, she can see that I don't have one either.

"Crystal, I don't know how I screwed up before. I'm so sorry for Kobra. I never should have set you up with him. I don't know how that happened. But I learned from that mistake. Jules is a good guy. Really."

She sags over the sink. "I'm just so fucking tired of working doubles, taking care of kids, being late on bills." She looks up through her false eyelashes. I notice for the first time that they have little crystals on them. "You're paying me this time, right?"

Am I? I don't have a clue. "What was our arrangement?"

"You're supposed to pay me five grand for each date but you haven't been delivering those checks lately. And I'm sick of trying to impress millionaires. They don't like me, and I don't like them."

Damn it.

"I can't trick them into thinking I'm something that I'm not. I know that's what we talked about, but it's not working. I'm just me. That's all I can be."

What is this, an after-school special? "We're adults, Crystal. We can be anything we want. That's what makeup is for. And filters. And lying on resumes. And online degrees. It's 2020. We can all be anything we want to be."

She hardens a little at my *we're adults* comment, so I take a deep breath. "Crystal," I say her name like a teacher trying to reach out to that one student with all the potential who won't listen. "It's so easy. All you have to do is try a tiny bit harder. Put on a classy dress, stand up straight, and let them know that you deserve everything." I gesture to the dirty Walmart bathroom, the wet floor with paper towels stuck to it, the overflowing trash can. "Look, I don't know much, but I know you deserve more than this. Convince them that you can be one of them, that you *are* one of them. Don't give up."

A beat or two later, Crystal takes a deep breath. "You gotta pay me, though."

I nod. "I promise that I'll pay you. We just have to make it through tonight."

When she exhales, I'm pretty sure she's done fighting me and I say, "Let me just get you a new dress. If you're going out with a millionaire, you've gotta look like a million bucks." I brighten a little. Everyone loves a makeover. Crystal should be psyched about this.[47]

....

[47] If anyone needs a makeover, it's me.

We head over to the women's clothing section. Our cart barely fits between the rows of clothes, and the hangers scrape the metal rack as I flip through medium-size sundresses.

I text Max. Where are you? Can I borrow your credit card? If she's going to Mr. Chow's, a new dress isn't optional.

He texts: You don't have any money, do you?

I do, but . . . Can I just borrow money one more time? $100 would do it. $50 even.

Last time.

"Ooh, what do you think about this one?" It's body-con and bright pink. It'd be a show-stopper, at least until it shrinks in the wash and fades. Walmart clothes are basically one-use items, according to NPR, which apparently I listen to when I'm not shoplifting.

"Is *he* dressing up for me?" she asks.

"Of course he is." At least he will be wearing his very best underwear. "You know who he is, right?" I ask.

"I was joking," she says.

I pull up Jules's Instagram. I see that he's already posting about the date and hashtagging GoldRush. I feel like I'm careening past the pit of total failure on two wheels, burning rubber and trying to make a full turnaround.

"He posted a few stories about his date prep." I show her a video of Jules deciding between a pair of purple underwear and green underwear, captioned Hot date tonight on the West Coast. #GoldRush. "How cute is that?"

She leans back and folds her arms over her chest. "For real?"

I don't show her the next post. Jules is mugging for the camera making the only face he knows how to make: sexy. It's captioned, Can't wait to meet my angel. She plays the harp.

Crystal still doesn't look excited but she agrees to try on a simple, classy sundress and some strappy sandals that will look nice the first couple of times she wears them, until the shiny fake patent leather peels off. I fill the cart with anything I can imagine someone wearing on the red carpet—jewelry that isn't emoji-based, sexy heels, a few more dresses.

"Just change into whatever you want to wear and we'll pay on the way out." My whole life is riding on this date. I will buy any crap that gives this date a fighting chance. Well, Max will.

I don't ask if she has an employee discount. It might give away the fact that I don't have $5,000 to pay her. Not that I'm going to stiff her, but no one is getting paid until I have some money.

While she's changing, Jules posts again. This time it's a screenshot of him making a duck face and a snap of Crystal that I must have sent him. It's Crystal when she's not at Walmart, and she looks pretty damn good. She's all pouty lips, smoky eyes, and a little black dress.

Crystal walks out of the dressing room looking 100 percent more like her picture. She's a total knockout, like Walmart should definitely hire her to do all of their ads immediately. That's when I know I'm a genius. Jules would be fucking lucky to go out with this woman. "Can I snap a pic of you?" I ask. Time to start hyping up the date from my end. I mean, that's what this is all about, right?

I post a photo and tag Jules.

"I don't know. I don't like this dress," she says.

"It looks awesome."

"I just feel weird. Kai has a cold. I'm supposed to work at the club tomorrow. What the fuck am I even doing?"

"You can do this, Crystal."

From the look she gives me, I know that all of her thoughts have coalesced. Her inarticulate feelings of despair and apathy have hardened into some kind of resolve. *Dear God, please make Crystal go on this date. Sorry if I've been a bitch my whole life. Sorry about Kobra. But please! I NEED THIS.*

Crystal gives me a weird look. "Have you ever asked yourself why *you're* doing this, Mia?"

I give her a panic-stricken look. I'm losing her. What am I going to do? While I watch her walk back to the dressing room, JP texts me.

When are you gonna be home? I miss you! 😍

Miss you too! Home soon.

K. I'll wait up.

Maybe don't. 🙁

Crystal walks out of the dressing room in her work outfit, her hands on her hips. "I'll go. But I'm going like this. Take it or leave it."

I shut my eyes against reality for a second. Crystal doesn't understand. All I need to do is get through this date. If it goes well and Jules hypes GoldRush and I snag just a few more customers, I'll be back in the money. I will be able to pay everything off.[48] My life is riding on this. If she shows up in this out-fit, I'm financially doomed—and potentially going to prison.

It's time to come clean. "I paid Jules one hundred grand to go on this date and post about it," I say.

Crystal's eyes go crazy big. With her eyeliner and all the fake lashes she looks like a cartoon. "What?"

"You heard me."

"What the fuck is wrong with you?"

"Honestly, you're not wrong to ask that. I can't go into it now but I spent every last dime on this and I'll never get out of this hole without your help."

She laughs. "So how are you paying me?"

Fuck. I shouldn't have told her. "I don't have any money left, but as soon as I do, I'll make it up to you."

I run my hands through my hair. She's going to use this to get more out of me. To wring me dry.[49]

"Well, my price just went up. If you want me to put on the dress it'll be ten grand. For five grand, you're getting a single mama in sweatpants and a Walmart apron. "

I shake my head. "I'll take you in the uniform. I'll wait by the front door while you get your things."

I hope Jules has a sense of humor. I shoot a quick text to Max. Where are you?

Went to get the car.

....

[48] Looks like I'm a gambler.

[49] Bummer for me but hats off to Crystal. R.E.S.P.E.C.T.

Thank God for Max.

When Crystal emerges from the locker room, her purse is the size of a diaper bag. In fact, it *is* a diaper bag—an old one, all dirty on the bottom from being set down on the floor. And she looks tired and angry. This is going to go really well.

"So, about my Kai," she says. "We need to pick him up. Then can you drop him by my mom's?"

I sigh. I'm completely out of leverage. "Yeah. Let's just get to the car."

———

We end up picking Crystal's kid up from a friend's house, a third-floor walkup not far from Walmart. I watch her haul the kid down a flight of stairs in a giant car seat that bangs against her leg with every stair she descends. A diaper bag slung over her shoulder provides a counterbalance to the car seat that looks too big to carry. Plus the apron. Nothing about this scene is Instagrammable.

She plugs him into the back seat of the Ferrari, which looks as wrong as it sounds, and says, "Let's roll."

The date was supposed to start thirty minutes ago and we still have to get to her mom's to drop off the baby. Kai is cute, but he's a baby, and by baby, I mean small human-shaped obstacle to goal achievement and financial stability. No offense, kid.[50]

....

[50] Not a natural mother.

Halfway down Long Beach Boulevard, Kai starts crying. Crystal looks at Max and says, "Do something. Shake a toy, talk to him. Don't just sit there."

Max looks about as good with kids as I am.

"Hello, Kai. My name is Max."

Kai keeps crying. Max shrugs and pulls out his phone.

"Max, what are you doing?" I say. "Stop looking at your phone and hand it to the baby!"

Crystal gives me an approving nod. "Listen to your girl."

I look at my phone. Jules has posted a picture of himself looking sad and waiting for his princess.

On her way! Car trouble, I text.

Pin me location. Coming.

As soon as we get to Crystal's mom's, I drop a pin. I'm too tired for pretense and Jules is on the payroll anyway. Come get her!

After passing off baby Kai and the diaper bag for the night, the three of us sit on the curb like teenagers with nothing to do and nowhere to be. Crystal kicks her feet out and tips her head back.

Jules rolls up in a stretch limousine like it's prom night.

I'm in an '80s movie and Crystal is playing the part of Molly Ringwald. Max and I are her misfit friends. He's the nerd and I'm . . . the one going through an identity crisis, whichever friend that is.

Jules hops out of the back looking just as good as the guy at the end of every John Hughes movie. Perfectly imperfect. He's not wearing a tux but he's in something better and cooler—something Instagrammable.

Crystal, despite herself, glows. How could she not? She just got off her double shift at Walmart. Her mom is watching her kid and Jules is a real-life rom-com hero.

Her exhaustion evaporates, or, rather, her hopelessness. This is just what she needs: someone to take her out and treat her like a queen for a night. I sigh with relief because at this moment I know that Jules is up to the task.

She smooths her hair back and slides on some lip gloss in a hurry. Bet she's regretting wearing her Walmart outfit. I try not to gloat. Jules walks over and gives her a hand to help her off the curb.

At this moment, I know why I went into matchmaking. They're so beautiful together. He doesn't even flinch at her Walmart apron or the fact that she doesn't meet all of his specifications. Thank God he's not an idiot. Crystal smiles at me and whispers, "Okay, you did good this time."

She turns to him. "I'm sorry, I just got off work," she explains.

Jules says, "That's cool. Me too."

"You have a reservation for two at Mr. Chow's. Give them JP's name, Jules!"

Jules waves at me without taking his eyes off of Crystal.

They drive off, leaving Max and me on the curb in descending twilight. Finally, something went right. I might not have woken up to a pristine fairy tale, but I think I just gave one to Crystal. I hope.

CHAPTER

TWENTY

With Crystal accounted for and on a date with Jules, Max and I just sit on the curb and embrace the emptiness because what else is there? I can't remember. It's that moment after you've finished bingeing a show and you can't remember who you are or why anything matters. I feel like I've been looking for Crystal my entire life.

"I think it's time for me to go home," Max says.

At those words my heart starts beating out of control. "What do you mean?" Max can't leave me. Not now.

"I haven't changed my mind, Mia. You can't keep me on hold while you decide whether or not to be with JP."

Why not? That seems reasonable to me.

"And you lied to me."

Fuck. How many times am I going to hear that today?! "I don't even know who I was before, Max. I know I lied. I don't know why, but that's not who I am now."

He's wearing an expression of disbelief, the look of someone who's heard too many excuses. "What happened at the bank? Did someone steal from you, or are you just broke?"

"I can explain," I say.

"Does this explanation end with you paying me for my services? Or Crystal, for that matter?"

"I just have to figure out my financial situation. It's all messed up and . . ."

He shakes his head. "Mia, you don't get it. I would have helped you for free. I really like you, but you lied to me."

My shoulders slump. I've fought as hard as I could today but I don't have anything left in me.

"You're the same as the person you were before you woke up. You might not remember her, but you're making the same decisions. It's who you are."

A liar, a scam artist—that's all Max thinks I am. He's the person who I trust the most, the first person I want to text with any news. If he doesn't trust me . . . I don't know what I'll do.

"I was scared you'd leave me if I told you the truth," I say.

His face fills with sadness. "Looks like neither of us can trust the other."

"Don't say that . . ." I put my head between my knees like someone who's about to faint. Actually, I *am* feeling faint. Dizzy, even.

He shakes his head. "You can't possibly be with someone you've been lying to."

Is he talking about himself or JP?

"And I think we both know you don't have five stars from the Better Business Bureau."

I lift my head. "Max, that's enough. Can't you see that I'm flailing here? You want me to assume responsibility for mistakes I don't even remember making, solve problems that run deeper than I even understand, and be a saint while doing it. So what if I cut corners? So what if I didn't tell you the awful truth about me? I'm doing the best I can here."

Max looks at me with concern. "Mia, I don't care that you're a hustler. I'm more worried that you're in over your head. Yesterday we met a drug kingpin and you threw all his money straight at his head. Who knows what that asshole might do?"

"I know he's a lowlife, but so am I."

Max gives me a look. "You're not a lowlife."

"Yes I am. But I can handle myself. I know I can."

He sighs. "Okay. Fine."

I sit up straight. "Wait, what?"

"Maybe you can handle yourself. There's only one way for you to find out. Go home to JP. Figure out what to do with GoldRush. I'm here if you need me but . . . I have to head back to my own life now." He stands, dusting off the seat of his pants. "I can take an Uber."

"No, let me take you home. I have the Ferrari." It might be awkward but I owe him this much. And I'm too wrung out to cry.

———

Max asks me to drop him off at the lab instead of his house. "Chan isolated the problem with the lie-detecting software. I can fix it and start the process of getting the lab up and running again."

"Does that mean you can get your job back?"

"If we can fix everything she did, then yes. Chan thinks it's doable."

"Awesome," I say, but I don't mean it. I'm not ready to let Max go back to the lab. I'm not ready to let him go at all. I don't want to go our separate ways, and back to the life I had.

"Let me come to the lab with you. I want to see how the brain scanner works." It's pathetic. He's trying to get rid of me and I'm just begging for scraps.

"Um, you don't need to come with me."

"No, I'm invested. I want to know that everything is going to turn out okay." I paste on a smile.

He's still thinking.

"I really want to see how it works. I've been waiting since that first time I walked into your lab."

He relents by the time we arrive. "Come on up." I don't think he means it but I'm too desperate not to take the invitation. Leaving Max and going home to JP and the life I've been looking for is the scariest thing I can think of doing. When Max and I step off the elevator onto the third floor, a bunch of his labmates are already there. There are a lot of forced "Hey Max!" greetings and awkward averted eyes. Something definitely went down.

A bro-y dude saunters up to Max. "Hey man. She got you good, didn't she?"

Max narrows his eyes. "What did she do to it?"

Bro-scientist raises his hands defensively. "You better go find out for yourself. She didn't just fuck with the software, she made some serious points about . . . your relationship." He laughs uncomfortably. "I mean, it's clever AF. If I didn't know you, I'd probably high-five her. You're not gonna like it."

Purposefully, like a soldier marching into battle, Max walks down the hall to the room with the brain scanner and the computers. On the wall, there's a schedule of who is using the brain scanner. It's all Max and Fay up until he became my intern. He writes his name down in all the available slots on Monday and my irrational sense of abandonment increases.

One of the bro-scientists sidles up to me. "I don't think Max introduced us," he says.

"Mia." I hold my hand out.

"Are you and Max a thing?"

"Ask Max," I say. Professionally, Max might be struggling a little, but his bro-scientist and scandal points are going through the roof. He's trying to salvage his career from breakup drama with me in tow. I smile dismissively at the bro-scientist and use the reflection from a framed poster of Einstein to apply more Pirate to my lips. A quote is superimposed over Einstein's picture: *Imagination is more important than knowledge.*[51]

....

[51] Let's hope.

When Max is done with the calendar, I follow him into the fMRI room. The helmet of truth is just sitting there taunting me. I can feel it coming. Someone is going to have to wear the damn thing, and here I am like one of the girls on *The Price Is Right*—wearing a fancy dress and ready to demonstrate the product.

This is probably not the work crisis I should have tagged along to witness.

"So how does this work?" I say. *Please don't make me test it. Please don't make me test it.* I'm the only person in the room and he needs someone to take it for a test drive.

"Well, maybe you can help me test out this thing . . ."

What did I tell you.

He sets me down in a chair in the center of the room and puts the wearable brain scanner on me. I'd rather be putting on some lingerie to get his attention instead of a twenty-pound metal helmet.

"You should be able to move freely while you're in the helmet," he says.

"Maybe if you're a linebacker. You should make this thing smaller."

"Next version."

When I put the helmet on, inspiration hits. "Max, are you testing this thing? Is it on?"

"Let me just ask you a few questions to make sure it's working right, and then we'll try to trigger the bugs Chan identified."

He looks down at a sheet of paper and then up at me. "None of my test questions are going to work on you."

Duh. I don't know my address and I still have to look up my birthday on Facebook.

"I'll just freestyle," I say. "My name is Mia Wallace and I don't remember my life before last Tuesday. I own a business and have a boyfriend who I've met once on the way home from the airport." It sounds even more pathetic when I say it out loud in a laboratory while wearing a brain scanner.

"Looks good," he says.

I frown. "What's good about that?"

"I just mean that's all coming up as truthful. Keep going."

"Well, you accused me of being a liar."

He looks up, his expression worried. He knows I'm going to take this somewhere he doesn't want it to go.

"That's true," I confirm. "I lied to you."

"Mia, stop. It's okay."

"Number one: I found out at the bank that I'm broke. I spent money I don't have and am in serious debt. Number two: I'm wanted for check fraud. I was too embarrassed to tell you. I probably told a thousand little lies to back up those bigger ones, but those are the main lies."

"Mia, you don't need to do this."

Oh, but I do. "I'm not a habitual liar, though. I really like you and I didn't want you to think less of me."

I stop and look up. "How did that come out? Does it look true?"

He nods, which is amazing. I was 70 percent sure it would fail.

"I know, Mia. You're not a bad person, but I don't think I can trust you."

"Max, maybe I feel this way for messed-up psychological reasons, but whatever—I can't worry about where my feelings come from. I just experience them."

From the look on his face, he's preparing for a crash.

I step on the accelerator. If we're going to crash, so be it. "I love you," I say, loud and clear.

He looks at the brain scanner results and says, "Um, no you don't."

"What?" I'm genuinely shocked.

"No, the imaging says that you definitely do not love me."

"This machine is bullshit then. You can't tell me how I feel."

Chan, who is totally not paying attention to the drama, wanders into the room and hands me a list. "Just read these lines," he says to me. Looking toward Max, he says, "Watch the scanner while she reads. Fay programmed these statements to come up as automatically false."

I stand and say, "Chan, you read them. I'm out of here."

"No!" Chan looks pained when I suggest this, but I'm out. I put myself on the line and Max not only didn't respond—he told me I was wrong. I still don't think I'm intrinsically dramatic, but that has to be the worst "I love you" ever.

"Mia, wait," Max says.

"It's okay. I just need to be alone right now. I'll text you later."

In the parking lot, I sit behind the wheel of the Ferrari and say a silent prayer of thanks for the heavily tinted windows so I can have a good, private cry. I turn on the breakup music and sob.

I don't know what I want—Max just proved it with science. Crystal texts a Thanks to me, and I start crying even harder. I want to tell Max about it, but not after that fiasco in the lab. I could tell JP, but I don't even know who he is. Why would I text somebody I just met with news about Crystal and Jules? It doesn't feel right.

Of course, that's my own damn fault. JP has been there for me the whole time. It's not his fault that he was on vacation when I decided to have a head injury. I look at his last few texts—it's nothing but messages that he misses me and wants me to come home.

The irony hits me. I'm avoiding him out of fear that he might want to declare his love for me. This entire emotional affair with Max is probably just a subconscious act of self-sabotage. I'm scared of letting someone love me and so I am avoiding it.

Time to stop being such a chicken shit, Mia. I text JP: On my way! Autocorrect provides the exclamation point. As I start the engine and drive to the only home I know, I try to match that enthusiasm, for the man who wants me and for the life that I actually have.

When I pull up to JP's, I sit and listen to the Ferrari click for a good long while. It was a hot day. Hot car. The lights inside the pink house are on and JP is waiting inside for me. The life I had planned for myself is waiting inside for me. Throw pillows and vacations to Switzerland.

I could be Mrs. Howard. Mrs. Jacques-Pierre Howard, the queen of Jacques-o-late. I start laughing, the kind of hysterical laughter that's basically crying.

I pick up my sparkly clutch and will myself all the way to the door. It's still #homesweethome. Pink house with pink door and a flowerpot.[52] Such a beautiful facade.

Do I knock or just storm in and throw my stuff on the floor? This morning I would have thrown my purse on the couch, flopped over the edge and put my feet on the coffee table. But JP doesn't seem like a feet on the coffee table, eating cereal in bed kind of guy.

Max ate cereal in bed with me.[53] My eyes start to water at the thought, which is dumb. Eating cereal in bed is gross, and we shouldn't have done it either. Max and I are both gross. We are . . . perfect for each other. I decide to knock while opening

....

[52] I almost threw away life with a French chocolatier who lives in a pink house. A PINK HOUSE FILLED WITH CHOCOLATE. Somebody slap me.

[53] Frosted Flakes, straight out of the box, right before we watched that dumb show about the universe, and it was perfect.

the door like a nurse entering a hospital room. I belong here, but I'm not in charge.

"Hi!" I call out.

There's takeout on the kitchen island and I can hear the TV from the bedroom. I head there and see JP on top of the covers, half propped up against the headboard. At the sound of my footsteps, he blinks back to life. "Mia . . ."

I sit on the bed next to him. "Sorry to wake you up."

He scoots over and puts his head in my lap, which might be normal for people who are dating, but for me it's strange. We just met. If only I'd trusted him and told him about the memory loss.

"Rub my back, would you?"

His skin is hot to the touch from sleeping. His body is undeniably beautiful, muscles and smooth skin under my hands. He's Jacques-o-late, though, not chocolate. Does that make him a substitute for the real thing, for Max? Is he seitan, the vegetarian wheat meat?[54]

"Mmm," he says. "I tried waiting up, but jet lag. How was your work thing?"

I'm in an ad for The Good Life.

"I'm sorry I took forever. I had trouble getting one of my clients to her date." I remember the flashback from earlier. "Do you still want me to give up my business?"

He sighs. "I want you to sell it and make lots of money, and then have some beautiful babies with me." He looks at

---

[54] Shut up, Mia!

me suggestively. "Speaking of which . . ."

Is that what I want too? Was I going to dissolve Gold-Rush? Investing $100,000 in Jules wouldn't make sense if that were true.

"Mmhmmm," he whispers into my neck between kisses. He slides his hand up underneath my dress along my bare thigh. "I missed you."

On the one hand, that feels really good, but on the other, I wish he'd buy me a drink first. "Can we take it a little slower?" I ask.

He groans. "Reading you loud and clear. Let's make this last." He flips me back on the bed and slides my panties down.

I guess he thinks "take it slower" means more foreplay. Who can blame him? He's practically my fiancé. We've been apart for almost a week and we fought right before he left. He's probably been looking forward to the make-up sex for days. I should probably want to tear his clothes off too. Girls who don't know him probably want to tear his clothes off.

His hand on my leg feels good. Sort of. Then his head is between my legs, which is really nice of him. JP seems to be very generous. Ohmygod.

He looks up. "Relax, *cherie*."

I can't. I can't shut my brain off. A sexy billionaire who wants to marry me is going down on me—that should be a good thing. I close my eyes tighter and try to power down my stupid brain. *Relax, Mia—a billionaire is on your clit. Just enjoy it.*

This isn't a big deal. We must do it all the time. This is probably the gazillionth time that I've had sex with this man, but it feels like having sex with a stranger.

I should probably just tell him I have a headache, but I don't want to fuck up a second relationship in the span of an hour. "Is there some lube around here?" I ask. "I'm sorry. I'm just really dehydrated."

He slowly undoes the side zipper on my dress and pulls it over my arched hips and down my legs. "I forgot how beautiful you are."

"Funny you should say that."

He trails kisses from my stomach up to my breasts and somewhere in the middle of everything my brain goes blank. I'm floating on a cloud and I don't know if I'm in the moment or remembering some past moment. Either way JP comes hard and doesn't notice that I don't. I guess JP isn't that perfect. Do men ever notice?

He has some sort of wet wipe in the nightstand for cleanup. He hands me one and I wipe between my thighs.

With my head on his chest, his breathing goes even and there I am with a beautiful stranger who loves me. But here I am crying. Real love should feel better than this. I reach over him for the remote. Maybe something silly will take my mind off of everything that has happened today.

I turn on a rerun of *Keeping Up with the Kardashians*. Kim and Khloé are on their way to the police station. Kris is yelling at Kim to stop taking selfies because "Your sister is going to jail."

I giggle in spite of myself. Kim is so vain but I love her. And Khloé is such a ho bag but I love her too. Here I am tucked into the crook of a handsome man's arm. He's just made love to me and wants to propose, and the only people who feel like family are the Kardashians. They're like my sisters except they forgot to give me a K name.

And really, if anyone could relate to what's happened to me, it would be the Kardashians. *Girl, you wouldn't believe it, but JP just proposed and we made love, but I can't remember him and I think I really love Max even though I just met him too. Oh, and I might go to jail for check fraud.* If anyone would get that, it would be them. I wish I could meet them for cocktails and tell them all about it.

I wish I had a sister who would take selfies in the back seat while my mom was driving me to the station to turn myself in for check fraud. I need a girlfriend to talk this over with. Max is great, but I need to talk about him too.

Now I'm full-on crying.

JP wakes up, probably concerned about an impending flood, and looks at me. "Are you okay?"

I laugh half-heartedly. "The Kardashians." I smile weakly. "This show makes me cry." He looks confused. "I think I'm overtired or getting my period or something."

"Aww. Poor baby." He hugs me tighter and kisses the top of my head. It's sweet and comforting.

He's consoling me for all the wrong reasons. I should probably tell him I'm crying because of him, but . . . I can do that in the morning.

Before I fall asleep, I check Jules's Instagram. He's posted a photo of him and Crystal on a moonlit beach. They look beautiful. I see #GoldRush at the end of the caption.

CHAPTER

TWENTY-ONE

I wake up to the sound of my phone buzzing. It's Crystal.
Can I have a ride?

I doubt that I'm normally this excited to give someone
a ride at six in the morning, but today . . . I look at JP. He's
passed out naked next to me. Sexy, naked billionaire with
a French accent, and I'm a red-blooded American girl—I
shouldn't be so excited to run out of here like someone is
chasing me, but here I am.

I slide out of the covers carefully, trying not to fan him
or disturb him in any way. Poor JP. He mentioned waffles
and coffee in the morning, like that's something we'd do. It
sounds nice.

I'm lying to everyone, JP more than anyone, and I'm tired
of it. In the hall bathroom, I freshen up and text Crystal. Send
me the address. Omw.

JP gets one too: Back in an hour. Crystal needs a rescue.

Crystal actually sounds fine. I'm the one who needs a rescue, but no need to get into it.

Before I get on the freeway, I remember the Kardashians last night, how all these women love and support each other, even while they're being epically dumb. Maybe I could have that kind of relationship with someone. Maybe even Crystal. I pull the Ferrari up in front of Cuppa Cuppa and walk to the register.

"Hey, Mia!" the barista calls out. "The regular?" Little sparks of joy light up my being for a fraction of a second. I belong here.

"Actually, make it two of them to go."

"Is the second coffee for that cute guy?"

"I wish," I say, sighing into the words with full angst. "He's mad at me." I shake my head. "I've been sort of a jerk."

She makes some sort of sympathetic cooing noise. "I'm sorry."

"And I don't know. What do you think, can you fall in love with someone after three days?" I think I'm unloading a little too much on her, but someone has to help me.

"Umm, I don't know. I don't think I believe in love at first sight." We're both quiet for a minute, and then she adds, probably to make me feel better, "Maybe because it's never happened to me."

"I'm probably confused," I say.

"You're not talking about that tattoo guy, are you?"

I laugh. "No. I definitely don't love him. The other one."

"Phew. He was a little scary."

Now there's an understatement. "That's what happens when you forget to feed the snake, Pedro" echoes through my mind. As if it was Pedro's own fault for dying. She doesn't need to know all of that, though, so I steer the conversation elsewhere. "How are you doing?" I ask, and I suddenly realize I haven't uttered those words many times this week. I've been in crisis mode, but that's probably not going to help the whole isolation problem.

She tells me some things about her life and I realize that she's becoming my friend. Holy shit. It's like I'm turning my life around already. I could give this woman a hug.

"What's your name?" I ask. "I see you all the time. I should know your name at least."

"Roberta."

At least one of my relationships has improved since the head injury. And things are a little better with Crystal. She's texting again and might have even had a good time with Jules. He liked her at least. Jules posted a selfie this morning at the airport. Miss her already. #Babe #GoldRush #JulesBrand #Dating #TrueLove

By the time I see it, 1,245 people have liked it. There are tons of comments, mostly asking if he scored and if she gives good head. Men are idiots, especially on the internet. Anonymity is the enemy of civility.

Turns out Crystal needs a ride because Jules had to leave for Fiji at the crack of dawn (#roughlife)—he offered to take her with him but she isn't the type who can leave in an instant. She could have taken an Uber, but I owe her $5,000.

The minute she's in the Ferrari, she starts talking as if we're in the middle of a conversation. "I have rent due and I need to pay the sitter and . . . that's why we started this whole business—so we could pay for things and make our lives better. I never should have cut my hours at Rush. Walmart can't even come close."

"What's Rush?"

She leans back and looks at me. "You serious, girl?" When I nod solemnly, she says, "You don't remember a thing, do you?"

"You could say that."

She rolls her eyes. "Figures. You always have to be the center of attention. I hate you sometimes."

"We're best friends, aren't we?"

She says, "Bitch, you crazy," and gives me a look to match. "You don't have a best friend."

I want to change that. I think I want a best friend in life this go-round, or at least someone to drive to the police station with me. Maybe I'm being optimistic, but I still think Crystal is an option. "I'm sorry. I don't know how I'm going to do it yet, but I'm going to figure out the money."

"I really need it now. Can you borrow some from JP?"

Not if we break up . . .

"Did he give you this car?" she asks, making a not-so-subtle point.

"Umm. I'm borrowing it." Come to think of it, I didn't ask to borrow it.

She looks at me skeptically. "Is it worth it with JP?"

"Don't know. I just met him yesterday for all I know."

"So you were for real about the memory loss thing?"

I nod. "How did we meet?" I ask.

"Um, work."

"Walmart?"

"No. The strip club. We've been through a few of them together."

A strip club! I shoot my hand over my mouth. In a loud whisper, I say, "I was a stripper?" I'm like the old lady next door, totally shocked by strippers, except I'm the fucking stripper. I don't know why I'm surprised. Facts have been pointing this way for a while.

"No. You only wish you were stripping. Hostesses make shit."

I'm starting to feel lightheaded. "Is that how I got into this?"

"Uh-huh. We were like, 'Wouldn't it be great if some rich fucker came in here and he wasn't an asshole and we could get married and live happily ever after?'"

Makes sense.

"And you were like, 'Let's make it happen.'" A sad look crosses her face. "I loved you for that, you know."

So we *were* friends! I knew it.

"Are all the GoldRush girls strippers?" I recall the advertising language—California's most sophisticated and elite women. I totally billed these women as actresses on the cusp of winning Oscars.

"Exotic dancers," she corrects, and then laughs. "And some other randoms."

"So I'm just a hostess?"

"You also do the books for the club."

"And now I'm a freaking scam artist."

"Or a social activist. You hooked us up."

Sort of. I hooked her up with a drug dealer who killed a guy in front of her—accidentally, but still. Jules, though—maybe he made up for it, if anything can make up for that. "Tell me about Jules," I say.

Crystal smiles a faraway smile like she's reliving last night.

"He didn't mind the Walmart apron? Did you tell him you have a kid?"

"I kept it one hundred," she says. "Told him the truth, that I was just in it for a free meal and to pay off a favor to you." While she's talking she digs through her purse for makeup and starts doing her face up in the flip-down mirror.

"Dude couldn't stop laughing. Like he thought I was joking. He livestreamed the whole thing."

Wow, that is way more publicity than I paid for. He was only required to do two Insta posts. A hundred grand is starting to seem like a deal.

"While you're explaining my life to me, do you know where I live?"

She stops putting on her lipstick and looks at me with a shocked expression and only half her mouth painted. "OMG girl. You really don't know shit, do you?"

"Do you?" I ask.

"I don't know where you're crashing now, but you have some stuff at the office."

My jaw drops. I have an office! My own space. "Will you help me find it before I drop you off?"

"When I say 'office,' I don't mean 'office,' if you catch my drift."

"Sure, whatever. Take me there."

I turn up the music and start belting out some tunes. I'm going to my office, baby! This is the best news I've had since finding out I'm a mogul.

"Don't get too excited, girl. It's not that great. And I need to pick up Kai from my mom so we need to hurry." Maybe that's why she's doing her makeup and hair in the car.

"Do you want to get him on the way?"

She gives me a weird look. "I'm not bringing my baby there!"

An office not fit for children—that's interesting. "Just tell me how to get there."

She shakes her head. "Take a left at the next light."

"It's one way. Do you mean the next one?" Between going through her purse to look for something, texting Jules (at least I think that's what she's doing), and giving me directions, she spills her coffee all over the place.

"OMG. This isn't my car!"

"I thought you were locking this mofo down."

"Really?"

She shrugs. "You mentioned something about getting engaged."

"We'll see. I'm not who I was last week." Right now, I want to return the Ferrari to JP and move in with Crystal, wherever she lives. I feel such a kinship with her. Not to mention Kai seems sort of like he might know me. Like he knows I suck at giving him bottles and stuff, but he's used to seeing me. "You were just teasing me before. We're besties, right?"

"Bitch puhlease," she says.

The way she says it, I know we're besties. "Do we talk a lot?"

"Ugh, just drive."

When we pull up to my office, I gasp in excitement. "Is that it?" We're in front of a low-lying building. It's not fancy, but it's big. If I own all that space, I'm not going to complain. It looks like a relic from the '70s with a flashy marquee that spells out GOLDRUSH in yellow lightbulbs. I own an entire building. I thought it was going to be a classy little office next to a nail salon, not a full-on club with its own parking lot.

Sophisticated and elite dancers! Studied dance at the Royal Ballet! Former beauty queens! Best of California! And then . . . *All nude!*

Everything on the marquee is pretty much what I have on my matchmaking app, except . . . the all-nude part. "Um, what's with the all-nude thing. Is this my building?"

Crystal laughs. "Oh my God. You know *nothing*, girl."

"I've been telling you that." I notice that the building has no windows. "I don't get it. This looks like a strip club."

"That's because it *is* a strip club."

Posters on the side of the building show the same girls from the GoldRush app. *Tatiana the Russian ballerina. Real tits!* On my app she's described as a Russian ballerina looking for a soulmate. No mention of her tits.

Brandi, Miss Orange County 2016, is also on my app, except that in her headshot she's wearing a dress instead of titty tassels.

And there's Crystal.

"It all started when management asked you to make a website for the place and then decided not to pay you."

"Assholes," I mutter.

Crystal explains it all to me. All of the GoldRush girls were sick of our jobs, sick of getting groped by customers and management, sick of working as independent contractors with zero paid time off, no benefits, and long hours. "Stripping is sexy and all, but the job sucks," she adds.

"So I decided to get us all sugar daddies?"

She nods.

The GoldRush matchmaking app is just the GoldRush strip club with a makeover. "You just glossed us up online."

I look at the club. I didn't even change any of the marketing. "Does the club know?"

"They didn't until a couple of weeks ago when that article came out about you being one of the hottest young entrepreneurs in SoCal." She laughs. "That was pretty fucking funny."

Crystal seems to be softening toward me a bit. "Sorry I snapped at you about Kobra. That wasn't your fault."

She holds a big metal door with chipped paint open for me and ushers me in. "Welcome back."

Like a lot of strip clubs, GoldRush probably looks better at night. A strip club in the day is like a living room decorated for Christmas in February—completely wrong. Maybe it looks sexy when the lights are low, the music is pulsing, and a girl is booty-popping on the runway. At the moment, it's Christmas in February. Someone's kid is running up and down the stripper walk and fooling around on the pole.

"I thought you said this place wasn't for kids."

She shrugs. "Not my kid, I should say."

As I walk through, a big greasy-looking dude shouts, "Where the fuck you been, Mia?"

Crystal says, "Cut her some slack, Jake. She got beat up."

Somehow that sounds sadder in the dull light of a strip club at eight a.m., the sun filtering through a few small dingy windows, while I stand next to a Budweiser sign and a poster advertising happy hour lap dances. Of course I got beat up. Getting knocked around is just an expected part of my life. I want to run away, back to a couple of days ago, when I thought I was a hot young Millennial on the verge of finding her condo on Ocean Boulevard, flirting with a cute scientist.

Ten seconds into this life, and I'm pretty much done. I'm going back to Ocean Boulevard. I'm going to be one of the hottest entrepreneurs in SoCal if it kills me. A little voice in my head says, *Maybe that's what happened last time.*

"For real, Mia, you need me to beat him up?" he offers.

"As soon as I figure out who did it, you can totally beat him up."

"So where's my office?" I ask Crystal.

Jake laughs at my use of the word *office*. I saw that coming.

My office is just a storage room in the back of the club. A desk with a computer on it is tucked among boxes, papers, and costumes.

"I think some of your stuff is in here," Crystal says.

"Where do I live?" I ask.

She shrugs. "I think you slept here some nights. JP's sometimes. I know you had a place with Jesse for a while, but I'm not sure if you still do. I think you moved out when her boyfriend moved in. That was just last month." I peek inside the boxes, which appear to be filled with the contents of my life.[55] It seems like I might live in the back of GoldRush.

I sift through the boxes until Crystal says, "I have to get back to Kai. Will you drop me off?"

"Sure. And I better get back to JP's." Looking around, I can't help but think that his proposal will be the quickest way out of here.

"You and JP—I just can't, still." She starts fanning her face to keep from laugh-crying.

"Why? What about him?"

....

55 Clothes, shampoo, makeup, a couple of wigs, a leather jacket. I'm not surprising myself with any medical textbooks or volumes of poetry.

"How much do you remember about JP?"

"Nothing. I only know what I read online."

She laughs. "Oh, girl. JP owns GoldRush."

CHAPTER

TWENTY-TWO

"What?" JP can't own this place. He's the king of chocolate! He donates to charities and good causes and . . .

Crystal stares at me. "Mia, for someone so smart, you are so dumb. Men like JP don't just own a business. They have a portfolio of investments. You didn't think he made a billion dollars off of chocolate, did you?"

I look at her, mouth agape. "Actually, I did."

She laughs.

And why shouldn't she? It's comical. I was sheltering him from my reality when he was the secret money behind my abusive employer, GoldRush. I had everything so wrong. So, so wrong. I look around the room, trying to reimagine it with JP walking the floors. "Does he sit here every night in a shiny suit in his very own corner booth?"

"Nuh-uh. Never seen him here. Dude owns a lot of businesses, but his full-time focus is the chocolate company. He has minions who run these side hustles. He doesn't even know about us. That's how you scammed him."

So that means I worked for him in a roundabout way, stole his business name and all of its advertising material, and now I'm dating him? I guess it makes sense that we were fighting in that flashback, especially if the club told him what I was up to. I can barely wrap my mind around it, so I say it out loud and slow. "Let me get this straight. He signed up for the matchmaking app and paid $35,000 to date me," I say, "when he was already paying me to do books in this club?"

She puts her hands in the air like I'm Beyoncé belting out the lyrics to "Formation" and strutting. "You're a genius. Straight up!"

I didn't even take this dude to Red Lobster. Of course, if I'm following Beyoncé's advice, he hasn't earned that yet. Maaaaaybe later.

I look around at the club. It is literally a billionaire's forgotten pocket change. He was in Switzerland skiing while everyone here worked two jobs and couldn't afford to pay for childcare or get their cavities filled.[56]

"Girl, you worked for that rock you're about to get. Don't let him get away with some chippy little thing."

I feel lightheaded. Suddenly, I flash back to a conversation I had with Max.

"You have no capacity for making decisions, especially big

---

[56] Not that I know for sure, but it looks like most of the money is going to hair and nails.

decisions," he'd said. "Whatever you do, take it easy. Don't do anything you can't undo."

I recall being offended at that statement.

"People base their decisions off their lived experience, their memories. You don't have any right now," he had said.

"If you haven't noticed, I remember a lot of things," I had responded.

"That's true. You remember everything about everyone else. For instance, if someone proposed to one of the Kardashians, you'd be the first person I'd ask. You probably are more aware of their lived experiences and patterns of decision-making than they are."

Max really is smart.

"One of the most vital purposes of memory is to guide decision-making," he'd said. "It's like they say—learn from history, or it'll repeat itself."

What do I do?

JP picks this moment to text. I told him I'd be home in an hour, which was almost two hours ago. I have not been the best girlfriend to this man, in so many ways.

He texts: Alone again . . . WRU?

On my way!

———

JP's been waiting at home for me for hours while I've been tooling around LA in his Ferrari, again. I'm being such a jerk, but I laugh at the absurdity of my housebound billionaire. If he wanted to, he could probably have the dealership drop off another Ferrari this morning, a newer model even. Still, I'm a jerk.

I'm sort of impressed with myself for sticking it to the man so hard. I mean, that was one hell of a raise: a $35,000 bonus for one date, plus a billionaire fiancé, and my own company. Props, old me!

But mostly I feel sick. Actually sick. My stomach is all acid and bile, and I'm sweating all over the Ferrari. My thighs are pretty much stuck to the seats. JP really is an innocent babe in the woods who I've tricked into marrying me, not that he's proposed yet. I love the beautiful house and JP seems swell, but I'm not sure I can do it, not without remembering everything I lived through to make me this messed up and angry. And was JP really the one I was mad at? He's the innocent one, too sweet for his own good. If there's such a thing as an innocent billionaire . . .

He texts me: I brought you chocolates. There's a special kind for drizzling . . . I know where I want to put it.

We need to talk.

Good, I want to talk too.

I wonder if he is 100 percent over the argument I remembered in my vision. Now that I know what I did, that is obviously what the argument was over. And all of his accusations were right. I was definitely messed up and I 100 percent used him. And going to Switzerland to sleep it off sounds pretty reasonable. Since arriving home, he hasn't mentioned it once, as if he's over it and nothing will change—drizzling chocolate and a surprise sparkly present waiting at home. My stomach tightens at the thought. I hope he waits a little while.

On my way into the house my phone rings. I recognize the number as the Long Beach PD. It's probably Denise saying that she's coming to arrest me. JP could make that go away, but I can too. I hit the ignore button.

I find JP sitting on one of the stools in the kitchen, a silk robe open over some pajama pants. "Morning, *cherie*," he says, kissing me on the cheek. "I'm so glad you're back. Where were you?"

I mumble something about Crystal. I don't mention the police station or impending criminal charges.

JP looks like an ad for luxury living on Sunday mornings. Speaking of which, "You know that yacht, *The Good Life*? Do you know who it belongs to?"

"I was thinking of buying it," he says. "You like it so much. All those pictures." His expression is filled with meaning. "It could be an engage—"

"Do you want coffee?" I cut him off hard. I'm not ready. "We really need to talk. There are some things I haven't told you." So many things.

"More?" he jokes. "I had to go to Geneva to recover from your last reveal."

"Yes," I say. I assume he's referring to the fight in the car on the way to the art museum. In my recovered memory he called me a criminal, I assume because I stole all of GoldRush's taglines—as if the comically fancy stripper descriptions were unique. No one goes to GoldRush because it has a Russian ballerina. They go there for boobs and liquor. No one cares if the boobs belong to a ballerina.

When I don't laugh at his joke, he turns serious. "You've been acting so strange since I got back. What's going on?"

I take a deep breath and sit on the stool next to him. I pick up a fresh bagel from a basket and put it back down again. It's time to pull on my big-girl panties. There's no reason not to tell him anymore. "JP, I probably should have told you—"

"What?" He looks concerned.

I give him the unembellished story. All of it.

"Why . . . why didn't you tell me?" He looks hurt and confused. "I thought we were together. Partners. I'm the person you should run to when things get bad."

I look at my lap for a few seconds and shut my eyes. He's right.

"I didn't want to lose you." I don't tell him the second reason—that I didn't trust him.

"As if I would leave you because you were injured!" He puts his hand over mine. "I would have flown back immediately."

This is killing me. JP is saying everything right when all I want him to do is screw up and make it easy for me to storm off in a huff. "But what about GoldRush?"

He looks at me calmly. "Well, I was surprised when my lawyer suggested that I sign off on a lawsuit against my girl-friend for stealing intellectual property from a business I didn't even know I owned."

"I bet."

He takes my hands and looks deep into my eyes in a way that makes me uncomfortable. Maybe I would feel better if I returned his feelings. "But I still want to marry you."

JP is insane.

"Why?"

"Because I love you."

"JP, that is so sweet, but I don't even know you. And . . . look what I did to you."

He shrugs. "I didn't even know I owned GoldRush. I don't care that you stole its stupid tagline and name. Have it. If that is the price of love, then so be it. You can have the entire strip club."

"Ummm. Well . . ." I think this is the first time anyone has offered to give me a strip club. "Can I get that in writing?"

He blurts out a laugh. "Really?"

"Kind of?"

"You really don't remember me, do you?" He looks like he's finally starting to get it.

"Nope. I don't remember anything."

For the first time, he looks hurt. "You can definitely have the club. It's an embarrassment. So low class. I don't want anything to do with it. Come to think of it, I don't want you to have it either. Why don't you do something less . . . sleazy."

Now I'm offended. "I worked in that strip club, JP. For years." I'm just guessing at how long, but "for years" sounds good. "And my friends still work there." At least until I can get them out.

"I know this, and I want to marry you anyway."

"Know what?"

"That you come from a low place and have low friends."

I bristle. "They're low because they don't have opportunities and your strip club exploits them and doesn't pay fair wages. You didn't give them paid time off or benefits—nothing. How are they supposed to raise themselves up working at a place like that? You can pretend that you have nothing to do with what they're going through, but you own the club. They work there. You are exploiting those women and paying them shit."

He didn't see that coming. I'm starting to feel the familiar burn of anger. I know I've felt this before. This is how I ended up here. Pure anger fueled me all the way from that strip club to this kitchen island.

"I can't be responsible for how all of my investments conduct their affairs. I have too many to keep track of, and they're run independently, with their own management teams."

"Maybe you *should* keep track of them. At least be more careful about what you invest in. If you own a business, you should make sure the employees get paid. Not to mention, why do you own a strip club anyway? Buy a hospital. Invest in clean water. If you have a billion dollars, you should make the world a better place."

"I am trying." I can tell that his patience is wearing thin. "You know what I'm doing for the rainforest at Jacques-o-late."

"That's nice, but it feels like a marketing gimmick. It's about image," I spit out. I don't know where it's coming from, but I can feel more anger rising up. This is about more than my experiences at GoldRush.

"This is not how I saw this marriage proposal going," he says. "You wanted to get married so badly."

"I had a major head injury, JP. I don't even know if I'm that person anymore. I think I just need some space for a while. I need to figure out who I am—who I *really* am." I stand and head for the door. It's clearly time for me to go.

JP follows me to the door. "I understand. Sort of. I think it might be best if you just take a nap, though."

I don't think he realizes the extent of my existential crisis. Maybe he's never had one.

When I walk out the door of the pink house on Ocean Boulevard, I can feel it—I'm shutting the door on the person I was before, the person I was for my entire life until last Tuesday. I don't even know her completely yet, but I'm saying good-bye. The old Mia was going to get married and become Mrs. Jacques-Pierre Howard. She would have lived in that beautiful house with her fast car. JP was buying her The Good Life.[57]

That girl is not me. JP seems really nice, perfect even, but I need to be on my own for a minute. I don't know if the head injury altered my brain, if the new perspective opened my eyes, or if I've just gone mad—but here I am.

A girl in a cocktail dress with no money.

I just turned down the life I always wanted.

I have a company that isn't really mine because I stole it.

....

[57] JP is going to have to revise his slogan. Once you go Jacques-o-late, sometimes you do go back.

But my eyes are open. I know what I'm doing, which is better than when I restarted my life on Thursday, completely blind. This time, I know what I'm facing and what I walked away from. I walked away from an easy solution to all of my problems. JP could have solved everything for me with a few swipes of a credit card, but I don't want that. This is my life and I'm going to do my best to make it right this time. I'll probably fuck up because it's me, but I'm going to try.

CHAPTER

TWENTY-THREE

When I look in my clutch, I realize that I don't even have enough money for bus fare. I walk to Cuppa Cuppa.

"Hi, Roberta," I say. "Do you mind if I sit here for a minute?" I just need to collect my thoughts.

"Of course."

"I'm out of money."

"I'll start you a tab."

The gesture gives me heartburn. I'm already in a lot of debt. I want to say yes, but I'm also like, *MIA, YOU IDIOT, HAVE YOU LEARNED ANYTHING?!*

"That'd be awesome." I really need a coffee. I'll repay Roberta before the bank. I have to, or I won't be able to get coffee.

She fires up the coffee grinder. While it works, which takes forever, she shouts, "I saw your guy this morning."

"Max? He was here?"

"Yeah, the good one."

I laugh. I wonder if she knows JP, too.

"He wasn't in the shop. I saw his video on Twitter, and OMG, he had me dyyyying!"

Twitter video? I take the coffee with mucho gratitude and sit down with my phone. I tap into the Twitter app and see that it's actually a Moment. I tap into the original tweet, posted by a handle I don't recognize, but I recognize the profile pic—it's that bro I met outside the lab.

Talk about another flashback. Max is sitting in front of the screens in the lie detector room and Chan is wearing the scanner. They're wearing the same outfits from yesterday so the video must have been recorded right after I left.

Max runs through a few questions to make sure the scanner is working, including Chan's name and birthday.

"It's working great." Max looks up at Chan. "Do you have the list of phrases that Fay programmed in?"

Whoever is recording—probably the bro—is trying to stifle laughter. They obviously know what's coming. They're setting Max up.

Chan groans. "Dude, this is awkward."

"Just read them. I have to know what she did so I can fix the program."

Chan looks like he'd rather cut off a finger. "Here goes. They're pretty personal. Brace yourself." He takes a breath and says, "Here's the first one: *Next Generation* is better than *Voyager*."

Max looks at the scanner. "Do you believe that?"

"Of course, Max. I'm not an idiot. *Next Gen* all the way."

"It's coming up as false." With a really confused look he says, "She bugged the software with lies about *Star Trek*? Any bug would mess with the software, but . . ."

The way Chan says, "It gets worse," I believe him.

"Fay think she's funny," Max says.

Fay is funny, I silently correct. This is the most ridiculous breakup stunt I've ever seen.

Chan reads the next one. "Fay likes *Star Trek*."

When Max looks at the screen he says, "But she does like *Star Trek*." Max looks indignant. "We watched it all the time."

Ouch—I'm guessing Fay watched Max watching *Star Trek* all the time.

Calmly, Chan says, "I think she's telling you that she doesn't like *Star Trek* and you never really knew her."

"Of course I knew her."[58]

Uh oh . . .

"It gets worse," Chan announces. "The next statement is: I like Fay for more than her Nobel Prize potential."

Max shakes his head and shrugs it off. "Whatever."

Chan takes a deep breath and I can feel something big coming. In a robotic voice, Chan reads, "The sex is great." He looks up at Max for a reaction.

....

[58] It seems like every part of their relationship was "fine" and Max didn't notice.

Max's jaw drops. "What the fuck? She came every—" Max looks up and realizes he's arguing with Chan about his sex life with Fay.

Chan holds up his hands defensively. "Dude, I'm sure she came. Girls never fake, right?"

I snicker. She totally didn't come. It's obvious. She probably should have mentioned that earlier, like during sex, rather than wrecking his PhD project a year later.

Roberta calls out over the grinder, "You just get to the sex comment?"

I nod and pause the video. "You might have to train Max up if Fay is right," she hollers.

I laugh. "I'm willing to put in some work. I think Fay had communication issues. I don't think she's empowered enough to be in control of her own orgasm yet. Maybe after this stunt, though."

"I'd make her a free coffee if I wasn't already on Max's side."

"She *is* clever." One half of the would-be power couple of the neuroscience community.

I hit play on the video. Chan says, "One more, dude. Hold tight." Chan looks directly at Max, like he's about to say something important. And he does. "I love you."

Max looks mad at this point. "I did love Fay. How dare she say I didn't?"

Chan just sits there. "I don't know man. I'm not her."

It's so obvious that Max should have been having this argument with Fay, probably when they were still together.

"Seriously, what is this? Why did she do this?"

I know why—Fay is a jerk, but she's also a genius. Max would never believe the lies in his own relationship without scientific proof. I guess this isn't exactly scientific proof. She just used science to make fun of him. But wait. Fay plugged "I love you" in as an automatic false statement. That means when I told Max I loved him, I wasn't necessarily lying!

Talk about an ex-girlfriend getting in the way. Fay takes the cake.

This isn't to say that I love him. Now that I think about it, the idea seems crazy, but . . . feelings are crazy. I completely grant that I love him at least partially because of my recent brain injury and consequent dependency issues, but . . . I wasn't necessarily lying. What is love anyway? Max is the only person I've been honest with, the only person I've been vulnerable with. I trust him.

After lying to JP, I think that's a precondition to love. You can't love someone if you don't trust them enough to show them your true self.[59] That's Love 101. Certainly someone has won the Nobel Prize in Romance for that, and I learned it from Lizzo. I'm not sure if you have to love yourself to love someone else, though.[60] Let's get real. That's way too high a bar. Just show them your unfiltered self and don't tell them you're a millionaire when you actually are in debt to a hot-air balloon company.

....

[59] For the sake of argument, let's pretend I know my true self.

[60] Sorry, therapists everywhere!

I text Max: I saw the vid.

It's not that bad.

He responds: 👋 It is.

I don't understand what happened.

I can feel the confusion coming through the text. Max has no clue what happened to him. I can totally see it from my vantage point, but he's too close. That Y chromosome doesn't help either.

If you want me to give you the CliffsNotes version, let me know.

Funny not funny.

I love you.

Funny not funny.

I know. Too bad you're bad at sex. ☹

OMG.

😂 I'll check in with you once you have some time to recover.

It's nice having the lines of communication open again. #happysigh.

I understand his relationship with Fay now, too. Even if her method was uncalled for, her point was strong. He didn't truly know Fay or see her for who she was. He loved a chick who he thought was basically Marie Curie. Instead, Fay was a chick with a sick sense of humor and not that much commitment to science. Not to blame the whole breakup on Max's caveman-level understanding of human emotion and women. Fay was complicit because she didn't make herself known. I get it, though. She probably just figured it out. Been there, girl!

I still don't know if I love Max, but at least he doesn't know my mind better than I know it myself.

———

While I'm texting everyone I know and straightening out my life, I text Kobra. The old Mia might have tried to finagle some money out of him to take care of the debt. It wouldn't be hard. Hell, he threw ten grand at me last time he saw me. The new Mia is going to work things a little differently.

Sorry about throwing all your 💰 in the street. My bad! Still wanna go out?

You crazy bitch! But yeah, sure.

I will text with time and place. Be there or be square. 👊🖐

Kobra is such an idiot.

I call Denise to fill her in on my game plan.

"Denise, I assume you left me a message earlier about the check fraud," I say like we're talking about which Chinese restaurant has the best egg rolls. Great Wall, BTW.

"Why yes, Mia, I did," she says, obviously amused that I think I'm in control. (I am in control, BTW.) "In fact, if you checked your voicemails, you'd find one from me waiting for you."

"I hit rock bottom," I say. "I don't have enough cash for the bus. Would you meet me at the coffee shop on the corner of Ocean and Linden? I have an idea."

"Really?" she says.

"I think you'll like it." My voice is chipper. "I know you like coffee. All cops like coffee. My treat."

"You've been watching too much *Law & Order*. And I don't even want to know where you're getting the money for my latte."

"See you there, Denise!" I say brightly.

———

When Denise arrives half an hour later, she looks like she's already had a day. I put a coffee and a croissant on my tab for her and then launch into my plan like I'm giving a PowerPoint presentation.

"I'm prepared to go to jail or do community service or probation—whatever. If that's what happens, so be it, but I'd like to bargain my time down, preferably to nothing."

"That's nice to hear," she says, sipping her coffee. The tone of her voice tells me that she doesn't care how I feel about the consequences of my criminal activity. She's going to like Kobra on a platter, though. I know it.

"I wrote some checks to a hot-air balloon company and Delta Airlines that I can't cash. Kobra is a meth kingpin, which is a lot worse." I describe what Crystal saw the other night and tell her I have a date with Kobra. "If I get you something you can use on him, will you let me out of the check fraud, or at least plea-bargain it down?"

"Mia, you should really have a lawyer for this. And the lawyer is supposed to talk to the prosecutor. This is not how it's done."

I shrug. "We can get it done this way, right?"

She sighs. "I think the idea is fine, if you can really pull it off. We can get the prosecutor to agree."

I end up going back to the station with her and figuring out all the details. They'll fit me with a wire, and some plain-clothes officers will be on standby in case I get into trouble. I'm not scared. I've only been alive for real for a few days—the life span of a fruit fly. The stakes aren't that high compared to someone with a real life. What have I got to lose? What has anyone got to lose if I die?

Denise has me text Kobra.

Meet at your place? Tomorrow?

10 pm. I'll pic u up. 🐍

Gross.

When I step out of the police department I know I've done the right thing.

———

I might not know who I was or what I wanted before, but I know who I am now. I was born last Tuesday, which makes me a Gemini. I can't remember the whole Gemini myth—something about Castor and Pollux and one of them dying. At any rate, Old Mia is dead and New Mia is #indahouse, cleaning up all the shit that Old Mia left lying around. That bitch was messy.

As for my love life . . . a part of me still thinks it's nuts to give up on a relationship with the most forgiving billionaire in the world, but New Mia wants to be with Max. I know that with absolute certainty. He's a little stupid, as Fay proved, and he might be bad at sex. But he's also the kind of guy who helps a deranged stranger solve the mystery of her identity without (too much) fuss, he knows where the best tacos are, and . . . I feel like myself when I'm with him. My *actual* self. Whoever she is.

I have a plan. I'm going to woo Max the same way I do everything: through Instagram, but with a radical new approach—at least for me.

No filter. No editing.

I take a selfie in front of the Long Beach Police Department. I look like hell and I know it. My face is shiny and my mascara is smeared. I'm still wearing my yellow dress. It is one of the hardest things I've ever done, but I use the first shot I take. I want to do another one at a slightly better angle, a picture where I'm making less of a dumb face, but I go with the first take.

To me, I look really bad, but in reality, it's how I look in this moment on planet earth. I look like reheated, six-day-old tater-tot casserole. That's literally what I am. It's not like I stick out. Most people look like warmed-up leftovers. That's why Instagram invented filters in the first place.

I type out my caption without overthinking it.

I am @Mia4Realz. I've been online for years, but this is the first time you're meeting me. Before, I was a fake. The new me is 100 percent honest, no filters, no Snapchat, no lies. Why the change? I woke up to find that I'm wanted by the police for check fraud, my bank accounts are empty, and someone tried to kill me. I'm a mess, but I'm going to get it back together. I will post pictures on my journey to figure out who I am and what happened to me. Follow along!

I immediately get a bunch of likes and lots of comments. Most of the comments are sad emojis. But I see a few comments on photos from the weekend, too. OMG, @BlackEinstein314 is sooooooo cute. Heart eyes heart eyes!

Good luck!

Following along.

I text Max with a link to my profile with an updated bio:

Criminal charges and debt: in progress

Love life: in progress

The rest: Our father who art in heaven, hallowed be thy name.[61]

Three dots appear and then they disappear. It's not a rejection. It's not approval, but I'll take it. He's thinking.

....

[61] Definitely Catholic.

CHAPTER

TWENTY-FOUR

As luck would have it, Denise is leaving the station at the same time as me and gives me a lift to GoldRush with a gruff "As long as I'm dropping you off at work." She seems thrilled (relatively speaking) to support me in: 1) moving on from the boyfriend she didn't trust, and 2) earning money at legitimate employment. When she sees where she's dropping me off, she sighs, looking a little disappointed and very unsurprised. "Jesus, Wallace. Try to keep your clothes on."

I point at the Prada gown that I've never been out of and say, "They'd have to pay me a lot to take this off, obviously," and she actually cracks a smile.

Before I walk in, I take a selfie for my honesty project. The GoldRush sign is lit up behind me. I caption it: I work here. I do the books. I can't imagine that "doing the books" is a full-time job. I tag Max. Now that I'm going full disclosure,

I consider explaining how I stole the name and advertising materials, but it's too much to get into.[62]

Inside, I find Crystal. She's wearing sequined lingerie and five-inch heels with the same level of comfort that a nurse wears scrubs. I wonder how she holds down two jobs, takes care of a baby, and still manages to keep everything shaved. Instead of inquiring about that, I ask how she's doing.

"Oh you know . . ." She shrugs. "Getting ready for work." She looks seriously unenthused.

"How's it going with Jules?"

"Mmm."

I take that to mean good.

I kick back in a chair and put my legs up on a low table. Crystal slides a plate of cheese sticks closer to me for sharing. "Thanks," I say. "I've been thinking about GoldRush. I'm really proud of it in some ways, but then again, it's basically just a way to get sugar daddies for us." I shake my head. "I don't know. I'm thinking it's missing something. Like . . . instead of marrying millionaires, maybe we should become millionaires." I'm joking but not.

Crystal laughs like I've said the funniest thing on the whole planet. "Girl, I can barely afford to get someone to sit for my kid while I'm working two shitty jobs. How in the hell am I going to make a million dollars?"

"I know," I say, "but still. It seems a little 1950s of us to

....

[62] Pretty sure I didn't go to college. Writing an essay seems like a stretch.

just try to marry millionaires. Like maybe we should go to college or something."

"Whatever. I'm just sick of taking the damn bus. Fuck feminism."

The bus does suck.

"What if I restructure GoldRush to be some sort of human capital investment thing? Like I could get the millionaires to invest in your ideas or something." I take a bite of a cheese stick while I wait for her thoughts.

"Ideas?" She laughs like it's the funniest thing she's ever heard. "I'm no dummy, but I ain't sitting on the next big app or anything." She locks eyes with me to communicate how serious she is. "Matchmaking is perfect. We got the booty and the ballerina credentials or whatever they want. They got the money. No one's taking the damn bus. Bam!"

I frown hard. There must be a better way, but she's right— the bus sucks and it'd be nice to be with a guy with money.[63] And Mia 2.0 might be friendlier than the original, but she doesn't have any better ideas. "I got a few more guys interested, so our pool of sugar daddies is growing. All thanks to Jules. His posts have really blown up."

"Sweet. Maybe we can do some more posts. Really make it look like the ultimate party life. I'll wear a bikini and splash in the water. Men love that sort of thing." With a laugh she says, "I have to make up for the posts from last night. I wore a shirt with pit stains, and I didn't have any makeup on. I don't

---

[63] Don't overthink walking out on JP this morning, Mia!

know why he wanted to go out with me or why anyone is liking these photos."

"It is subversive in an exciting way. I bet women liked it because you made it look like you were good enough as is."

"I am good enough, bitch." She flashes a *you wanna start something?* look and I choke on a laugh.

"Whatever. You know what I mean. We say we're good enough, but not really." We're totally not good enough. Let's get real. Actually . . . maybe that's our only option.

Crystal arrives at that conclusion at the same time I do. "Maybe we should just be more honest," she says. "Like instead of saying that Tatiana is a Russian ballerina, you could just describe her as a rich girl with daddy issues who only strips to pay for her Amazon addiction."

I laugh at the idea. For the first time, Tatiana sounds like someone I can relate to. That ice queen look might be sexy, but the sexy ice queen schtick is not the stuff BFFs are made of.

Crystal gets a spark of mischief in her eye. "And for Gigi—she'll spend all your money on a weave, but don't worry, it'll be worth it." Then, looking slightly more introspective, she says, "And I will be a single mother with two crappy jobs who recently moved back in with her own mom and doesn't believe in love."

"You're going to change your mind about the love thing, I think." I have a feeling about her and Jules.

"Maybe," she says, a sparkle in her eye.

"And to think, all you needed was a rich underwear model." I shake my head. "Talk about a tall order."

We might be in a dingy club eating bar food but it's a beautiful moment. Most of the time, the beginnings and ends of things blend into the rest and you never notice them. But this time, maybe because the world is so new for me, I can feel it. I know this is the moment we're creating something. This is the beginning of something better than what we had. Gold-Rush was good in some ways, but it's going to be better now. And I'm 75 percent sure I have a business partner in Crystal.

I sigh happily. Who would have ever thought of an honest dating site? It's the most counterintuitive yet most obvious thing I've thought of. "I really like the idea of making everyone's bio honest. No more fantasy fulfillment. We're real people. No more hiding it."

Come to think of it, that was what made me feel like a pimp before—not the matchmaking, but the false advertising. I'm only here to facilitate a match, not sell anyone a fantasy. I'm so excited about my new idea for GoldRush. Not lying probably isn't revolutionary, but it's the first time I've thought of it. I can't wait to get online and change it all around.

I head back to my office in the back of the club and go to work on the site. It's going to be brand-new by tomorrow. It's not like I have a life to distract me.

I put up a sign on my door like I'm running conferences. I'm going to meet with every girl at the club and call everyone else. I'll update all the bios and retake all the profile shots—no filters, preferably with no makeup. "Wear some sweatpants," I advise the girls. "Whatever you look like on Sunday morning, that's what I want on the site."

"So, hungover?" one of the girls says.

"That's fine. I want honesty."

She laughs. "Okay, hungover with false eyelashes glued to my cheek. You've got it."

Hers is going to be my favorite profile pic.

While I'm digging through the drawers for a pen that works, I find a lockbox.

I pull out my sparkly clutch. I have two keys—one to JP's house and another that I've never found a home for. I fish it out of the bottom and insert it into the lockbox. It fits perfectly. When I open the box I find a Crown Royal bag and I know what's in it. It's the thirty-five grand Kobra paid for his match with Crystal.

I scream.

———

When I'm cross-eyed from working all day as a business genius who just discovered a life-saving windfall, I come out of my office and sit on the stripper walkway, kicking my legs off the side and eating a fresh basket of fried mozzarella sticks. Life isn't so bad.

I check my Instagram and see a lot of love for my Mia 2.0 posts—and a lot of DMs from girls who are excited for me.

That French guy wasn't cute enough for you, girl! Love the new nerd!

Has he called yet? Stay strong!!

My phone rings. It's a number not stored in my contacts, but I pick up anyway. "Hello?"

"Mia?" It's a feminine voice. Tentative.

"Yes, who is this?"

There's a long pause before the woman says, "It's your mother."

I almost choke on a mozzarella stick. "What?"

"I'm sorry I wasn't there for you that night," she says.

"Wait. You know what happened to me?"

"I saw your picture on the *MySelfie* wall at the museum. I'm so sorry, sweetie. I wish I'd seen it sooner or been there for you." I was doing great this afternoon, rethinking the business and finding money. But a mom? That's next-level support. Yesterday I would have been full-out crying if she called. Not today, though. Just a few tears prick at the back of my eyes.

Someone keeps buzzing in with texts, but I don't answer. I'm not going to interrupt a reunion with my mom.

"I lost my memory that night. I don't know anything. I don't remember you."

I can hear her gasp a little. She's trying to hide it, but she's crying. "Where are you, sweetie? I'm coming to you now."

"I'm at GoldRush, that strip club down on the PCH."

There's silence on the other end of the line for a while. When she's processed my location, she sighs. "Okay, honey. I'm coming now. Give me twenty minutes."

I hang up and run screaming toward Crystal.

"CRYSTAL! My mom is coming! I know it might be a little weird, but . . . I think we've been estranged and now we're going to reconcile? I can't tell, but I didn't have her number in my phone and I get the feeling that something happened between us."

"Well, things might get a little interesting."

"What do you mean?"

"Kobra just texted and said he's on his way. Apparently he saw one of your Instagram posts. He knows we're here."

"What the? What's that dude's deal? Why won't he leave us alone?" I had crafted a leisurely takedown plan in which I would carefully extract a string of confessions from him and send him straight to jail.

Crystal says, "Either he wants another date or he wants to kill me because I'm a witness to that one dude's death."

I call my mom back. "Uh, Mom, it might not be the best time for us to hang out right now . . ."

"Why?"

I think about making up an excuse—I have to leave in a hurry, or I would prefer to visit her or . . . I have a headache. I can't come up with any good reason, though, so I go with the truth. "I was caught up with some bad people and I think it would be best if we catch up in a couple of hours or even tomorrow morning."

In the background, I hear the engine of her car roar to life. "I'm coming to get you, honey."

At this point, there's nothing to do but invite the police, too.

CHAPTER

TWENTY-FIVE

The music is pulsing and the lights are dim. One girl is doing a half-assed routine on the stripper walk for a single customer. It's like an episode of *The Sopranos*, except in this version I'm Tony Soprano—and I'm about to host an impromptu gathering with my mom and a drug kingpin. Either way, I guess a strip club is as good a venue as any. At least there's liquor. And lots of it.

Officer Denise explains, "I'm going to be in the dressing room listening in, so if you need me, I'll be just a second away."

"Try to get a selfie with the girls, would you?" I so want to post that picture on my Instagram tour of honesty. "Or is there some departmental policy against that?"

She ignores me. "Ask him questions. Get him to talk about reasons that Crystal might be scared. If we can get a confession out of him . . ." She takes a breath, as if putting Kobra away tonight will save the world a heap of trouble.

Maybe we can take a selfie after. An honest one.

"Don't worry. I'm going to keep you ladies safe," she reassures me.

I nod appreciatively and smile. I'm not going to rule it out or anything, but dying isn't my number-one concern tonight. It never is. That'd be no way to live.

Mostly, I'm preparing for the coming awkwardness. My mom—who knows what she's even like. Trailer trash is my number one guess, based on me. I feel like I'm always trying a little too hard, which smacks of someone who wasn't born into money.

"Do you think I have a dad in the picture?" I ask Crystal. Denise is there too.

"No," she says authoritatively. "You have daddy issues. He's either gone or an asshole. Do you know what your mom looks like?"

Trailer trash with daddy issues sounds about right. "I'm expecting a lot of wrinkly cleavage, platinum hair, at least twelve rings on her fingers, some on her toes, neon-green short shorts, skinny-ass legs, and a smoker's cough. Basically me in twenty years."

Crystal laughs. "What's the matter with you?"

I fan myself with a menu. "I'm sorry. This whole situation just has me sort of amped." I don't know what to do with my energy. My life has been insane since I woke up in the hospital, but this takes it to a new level. Luckily, if Kobra and my mom take long enough to arrive, I might be able to settle down a little. Now I know how I react to situations that I can't control—I get hyper.

Exactly twenty minutes after Denise sets me up with a vape pen fitted with a recording device, the door of the club opens and a patch of bright sunlight slants through the room, obscuring my view. My eyes have adjusted to the dark, windowless space so I can't tell if it's Kobra, my mom, or a regular old customer.

When the door shuts with a heavy thud and the light is gone, I recognize the woman immediately. She's Martha Stewart–level classy, but in yoga clothes. I whisper, more to myself than to Crystal, "Holy shit. I know her."

Crystal sighs and puts her hand over mine. "We all know our mamas, don't we?" She looks all sentimental so I don't tell her that I recognize my mother from photographs, not from my heart.

It's Lauren Montcalm.

The woman married to Frederick Montcalm is my mother.

I wasn't having an affair with Frederick. I'm not a gold digger (at least in this instance)—my mom is![64]

She walks tentatively into the club. When her eyes adjust to the darkness and lock onto mine, she doesn't smile. She breathes out slow and long. "Mia. Oh my God."

I walk slowly toward her. Is she happy to see me? Was she worried? She's standing stock-still, her posture perfect, her expression inscrutable.

....

[64] Guess I know where I got the idea for my business.

"When the housekeeper said you'd been by the house, I thought you were just there to ask for money again. I'm so sorry."

When I explain that I lost my memory, her face softens and she says, "I'm sorry. Can I give you a hug?"

"Of course." What kind of fucked-up relationship do we have that she has to ask for a hug?

When she wraps her arms around me she holds on tight for a very long time, tighter than necessary. My shoulder gets damp from tears, which is surreal. She's reconnecting with her estranged daughter, a lifetime of love, failed expectations, and hurt between them. For my part, I'm a mannequin standing in for the daughter.

"Why don't you two ladies sit down and I'll grab you both a glass of wine?" Crystal says.

I mouth, "Thank you" at Crystal and she disappears behind the bar, her butt wiggling in a G-string. She returns, in a satin robe this time, with two glasses and a bottle. She says, "Just so you two know, we're coming up to happy hour. I mean, it's not gonna get real busy but it's a strip club, so . . ."

I steer my mom toward a high-top table and give her the highlight reel of my life since Tuesday.

"I feel so bad. You came to that party to see me."

I can feel my eyes go silver-dollar-pancake big. I must be thinking about pancakes because I'm with my mom, though I suspect she doesn't make them. She and Frederick definitely have a chef.

"You apologized. You wanted to introduce me to your boyfriend."

JP. She would have loved him.

"But I didn't want to hear it. I thought it was just you upstaging my show, and my therapist wants me to focus more on me."

"How long has it been since things were . . . like this?"

She takes a heavy breath. "Years. I married Frederick when you were in high school, maybe ten years ago. I thought things would get better, but . . . they didn't."

I give her space to finish her story. She's emotional. For my part, I'm just filling in details.[65]

The DJ makes a loud announcement: "Our next dancer might be named Crystal, but she's a real gem, a genuine jewel. This gem's gots bills to pay so pull out your wallets and give it up for CRYSTAL!" He turns up the bump-and-grind music and Crystal struts out. She looks my way and mouths "Sorry" before she starts shimmying and running her hands up and down her body.

My mom's back is to the stage and she doesn't turn around. "You started ditching school more after Frederick moved in."

High school flunky, adult con artist—everything is adding up. There is probably a reason my mom isn't surprised to find me in a strip club—she probably saw this coming.

"You only graduated from high school because Frederick

....

[65] Looks like I can delay Botox. I'm even younger than I thought!

303

donated some money. College was a no-go. Pretty soon you stopped coming around and when you did you were . . . not yourself."

"I'm sorry," I say. Crystal, on the other hand, has nothing to apologize for. Right behind my mom, Crystal crawls on all fours across the stage and starts stroking the pole suggestively and makes a move like she's going to lick it. Someone yells, "Lick it before you climb it, baby!"

"What?" my mom yells. "I can't hear over the music."

From what I can hear, it seems like communication between us has been bad for years. Crystal is pulling herself up the pole. Her upper body strength is off the charts.

"I'm sorry," I repeat. I'm guessing I have a side to the story, too, but at the moment, it doesn't matter to me. "I don't know what happened before, but I could really use a mom now."

The waterworks really break loose for both of us. Through her tears, she says, "Of course. Frederick is pretty much not there anymore—dementia. You don't have to worry about him."

Crystal must have caught on that our conversation is going well and she smiles big at me from the pole.

"What?"

"Dementia!" she yells.

I'm starting to get the impression that Frederick was a perv—and that my mom didn't always side with me.

"I'm sorry that I wouldn't talk to you at the art gala. My therapist has been telling me that I need to establish healthy boundaries." Crystal slides down the pole upside down and my jaw drops.

Mostly, holy shit, Crystal! But also, my mom's therapist comment makes me wonder. Are her "healthy boundaries" impermeable?

"Your therapist?" A man's voice cuts into the conversation, and Kobra sidles up to the table. His shirt is open to show off his python tattoo, as per usual. He's strapped and there's a big knife on his belt. Creepy as all get out, he says, "Boundaries are important. Some people don't know when to stop."

Funny coming from him . . .

"My therapist never shuts up about boundaries," he says.

Other people's boundaries, I assume. "You go to therapy, Kobra?"

He chuckles. "It's California. Everyone goes to therapy. I got things I can't talk to the homies about." He takes a slow up-and-down look at my mom.

"I'm Lauren Montcalm. Mia's mother," she says formally.

"I'm Kobra. With a K. I'm one of her clients."

It sounds like "With a K" is his last name.

"Clients?" My mom clearly thinks he's a john. She can't take her eyes off of his snake tattoo.

"For the *matchmaking* service." I lean heavily on the word *matchmaking*. "Actually, Mom, I hate to break this off but I really need to talk to Kobra and I don't want to make you sit through it. Can we catch up again soon?"

My mom looks at Kobra and then back to me and says, "No, I'm staying as long as he is."

Crystal, thank God, hustles over to the table. "Lauren," she says, "I was wondering if you want a tour of the club?" I don't think her outfit helps convince my mom that we're not prostitutes.

"Crystal!" Kobra gives her stripper outfit a once-over. "What are you doing here? I thought you were an actress," he says. But he stands and reaches out for her.

Then he looks at me and tips his hat. "You charged me thirty-five grand to go out with a stripper from this joint?" He starts laughing. "You crafty bitch."

"Fuck you, Kobra," Crystal says, practically stabbing him in the chest with one of her fake nails.

My mom's eyes go huge. I don't think she's been out of Laguna Beach recently.

"Don't worry, baby. You're still my girl. If you can shake your booty, who am I to complain?"

Crystal cringes and makes a vomiting noise. "If you think you got a shot with me, think again. No way in hell am I shaking my booty for *you*."

"Baby, you can't blame me for that. Sheba was hungry and I wasn't watching. Those things happen. It was an accident."

"You have a twenty-foot hell-snake in a cage next to your TV and crates of drugs." She takes her attitude to full power. "Is that even the first time she killed someone?"

My mom gasps, but Kobra ignores her. "Pedro musta been messing with her. He was high as fuck."

I can see it now. Pedro was passed out in the corner and Kobra let his python out to impress Crystal.

"It's illegal to own those things. You should be in jail."

"Baby, you don't understand. That snake's an easy keeper. All you have to do is feed her once a month."

"Feed her what, your friends?"

"Pedro wasn't a friend."

"Like that makes it okay to feed him to your snake."

Kobra makes a face that suggests he thinks it was probably okay. "The snake always knows best. It's just a miracle that she didn't eat you. I think God was with us that day. She always spares the true and righteous."

The bootylicious—because let's get real, Kobra.[66]

Crystal gives him an *are you crazy?* look and says, "You know what I think, Kobra?"

We already know what Crystal thinks based on the tone of her voice.

I look at my mom and mouth, "Sorry," as if I'm serving her a luncheon and I burned the chicken. This isn't how I'd plan a reunion, but it's an accurate representation of my life. The closer I get to my true identity, the more chaotic and insane things get. It's no wonder I ended up in a coma.

My mom doesn't respond. She's as still as a field mouse, waiting for the whole thing to blow over. I wonder if that's how she approached my teen years . . .

"You know what I think?" Crystal repeats. "I think you're overcompensating for something with that twenty-foot snake."

....

[66] I don't think he likes Crystal for her moral pulchritude, which is a word I know.

He looks truly hurt. "How about we go in the back and you can find out for yourself."

"In your dreams."

This is going to play really well in court. They've gone over death by snake at least twice. Denise must think so too because she chooses this moment to storm out. "Kobra," she says in a cop voice, "you have the right to remain silent. You have the right to an attorney. If you can't afford one, one will be provided to you."

Does anyone ever listen to the Miranda warning besides lawyers? I'm taping it so Denise better get it right.

At that, Kobra bolts, and Crystal cheers, "Get him, girl!"

Denise unholsters her gun and takes off after him. "Don't run. We have you surrounded." Then she talks into her radio, just like a cop on TV. "Suspect approaching the front door."

Sure enough, when Kobra opens the door, another cop is waiting. That cop shouts, "Stop!" and raises his gun. My mom has hit the floor and is hiding under the table.[67]

Kobra makes a move like he's going to run anyway, but Denise walks up behind him and tases the shit out of him. I wish I'd gotten that job.

"God, maybe I should be a cop," Crystal says. "I think I would have shot him, though."

"You should be a cop," I say. "If it doesn't work being Mrs. JulesBrand Underwear."

She laughs. "I'm getting us a drink."

....

[67] This might delay our next reunion.

My mom is still cowering under the table, sweating through her yoga clothes. "Mia . . ." She obviously doesn't know what she wants to say.

I give her a hand up. "I'm super sorry about that. I really couldn't back out of the meeting with Kobra." It's true. "And I think it ended up going really well. Crystal got a great confession out of him." Today is going great! "Thanks so much for hanging in there." She doesn't say anything so I say, "He didn't respect the boundary I set, so we had to get serious."

I think my therapy joke is funny but she doesn't laugh. Maybe she will when she gets home and replays the whole afternoon in her mind. "I think I'm ready to go home now," she says. "Do you want to come with me? Are you safe?"

"Thanks so much, but I think I'd better stay." I look around at the chaos. "The police probably want to talk to me." And I still need to hand over my vape pen with a bug in it.

My mom looks relieved and I can't blame her. "Next time, let's meet somewhere else." She leans in. "I don't know who pushed you into the Cupid sculpture, Mia, but there was a hashtag for the event. You might want to look on social media to see if anything jogs your memory."

Apparently my mom also thinks like an Instagram sleuth. "Thanks for the tip, Mom. You name the place, and I'll be there." Before she leaves I snap a selfie of the two of us. She looks beautiful, if a little shell-shocked.

Mostly I'm happy because there will be a next meeting. I have a mom and I'm ready to craft a relationship governed by healthy boundaries.

After I talk to Denise and decompress for a while, I sit in a booth, just me and my phone. My mind drifts to Max and I decide to update my honesty project.

First, I post the selfie of me and my mom. We look quite a bit alike. I caption it, Found my mom! Talked for the first time in years. It's a pretty good picture, except for the stripper booty and the uniforms in the background.

This is the first photo that Max likes. Now I know he's paying attention and following along.

I post the picture of us on the scenic overlook over Laguna Beach. Me and Max. ♡ ♡ ♡

I wait for him to like that one.

"Oh my God, Mia. Stop staring at your phone like that. You're going to light it on fire with your mind," Crystal says.

CHAPTER

TWENTY-SIX

After the police clear out with Kobra in cuffs, I sit at the bar, order another glass of wine, and scroll through the #LBArt hashtag on Instagram. There are so many posts—and I have no idea how I'm going to get through them all. I hop over to Twitter and see a bunch of tweets and photos with the hashtag as well. It's like everyone at the party spent the whole time staring at their phones. Which is probably true, especially given the theme of the exhibition.

There are about five hundred selfies, most of which aren't interesting, until I catch a glimpse of myself in the background of one of them. I stare at the photo, zooming in and looking at it pixel by pixel. I see JP with me.

There's another photo of JP and me standing next to a table of appetizer trays on the museum's official Instagram account. I can see why they'd feature us. We're young and good-looking and that yellow dress photographs amazingly.

If only I still had the cape! But the longer I study the photo, the more it becomes clear how off it is. We're standing too far apart, our bodies stiff and our smiles forced. I've read enough of those *Us Weekly* sidebars about the body language of celebrity couples to know when I see a happy pair and when I see two people who are in the middle of a giant fight about intellectual property.

The post is time-stamped at 11:03 p.m. on Tuesday. I was admitted to the hospital not long after that.

Suddenly, I'm super weirded out. If JP had been there, why didn't he know about the head injury? Why didn't he follow me to the hospital? Why did I wake up alone? You don't just watch your girlfriend bash her head on an ice sculpture and then go to Switzerland to get clarity on a fight you had before the party. It's a damning photograph. If the trial attorney showed this to the jury, they would deliberate for all of five minutes and send JP to prison for five years, of which he would serve six months maximum because, let's face it, he's a billionaire.

I can't think of a good reason for him to pretend he didn't know about my injury. Was he hoping to come back from Switzerland and find me dead?

A chill runs up my spine. I do the first thing that comes to mind. I text Max.

Can you talk? You might have been right about JP.

He responds right away: RU OK?

Yes. In fact, I left JP's this morning.

I see three dots appear and then disappear.

Going to stay with Crystal tonight. Idk.

I wait a beat, hoping he'll offer to put me up now that I'm not with JP anymore. He doesn't take the bait.

Glad ur safe. If you need me 4Realz let me know.

Wow, I really expected him to jump for joy that I wasn't with JP anymore. Instead I get a *glad ur safe* like he's my dad or something? He still hasn't liked our Instagram couple pic and I'm pretty sure he's seen it by now. For some reason I feel worse about that than about the very real possibility that JP tried to kill me. Crushed, in fact.

―――――

I'm lucky that Crystal doesn't turn me down when I ask to stay with her—she's still riding high from Kobra's arrest. On the bus to her house,[68] I explain that JP might've tried to kill me. "It must have been him. We had a fight in the car on the way to that art gala about GoldRush. Then, we were at the party eating appetizers probably moments before I was injured." She nods to show she's listening, and I hit her with the clincher. "Then, he left the party by himself, went to Switzerland for a few days, and has been acting like he didn't know it happened. It *must* have been him."

Crystal is quiet.

"He probably thought I was dead and ran. When he didn't see my death recorded in the papers, he probably texted me to see if I was alive. When I answered, he had to act like

....

[68] She had to pay because LA Metro doesn't break hundreds.

everything was totally fine and that he missed me. Ugh, what a psychopath!"

Crystal murmurs something.

"I should probably call the police. Now that I've helped them catch Kobra, they owe me." How conveniently I've forgotten the whole check fraud business.

Crystal is dead silent.

"I was really hoping that Kobra did it. That would have been so easy. I'm not in love with JP, but I don't want to send him to jail. I don't want to think I was in an abusive relationship. But it can happen to anyone, I guess."

Crystal murmurs again. "It wasn't JP."

"What?" I turn the full force of my attention on her. "Did you see something?"

"JP wasn't there when you fell. He'd already left."

"How do you know that?" My jaw drops. "You were there? I had a memory of you storming in, but I wasn't sure if it was real or if I was conflating it with something else. How come you didn't say anything?"

She shuts her eyes and I'm pretty sure she's saying a prayer. "I was so mad at you about setting me up with Kobra . . . I left his place and went straight to the museum."

As she's talking, I cut back to my memory of the party.

I'm standing by the sushi table and I hear a woman yelling. "Mia, where are you, bitch?"

I set down my plate of sushi rolls and stare in the direction of the yelling. It's Crystal, dressed for the club, coming around the corner.

"*Crystal?*" *I don't expect to see her. I don't know why she's here. I'm here to support my mom and that's it.*

"*You just set me up with a drug dealer. Not even a low-level guy. A fucking kingpin!*"

My hand flies to my mouth. "*No, he's in international ship—*" *As the words come out of my mouth I realize that he's not even trying to hide it. He's probably shipping teddy bears stuffed with meth to Australia and Thailand.*

"*Oh, you knew. How could you not?*"

"*I didn't. I was stupid.*"

"*You know I'm trying to get away from that lifestyle,*" *she says.* "*I want someone who can be a good dad to Kai, not some fucking insane meth head tatted up with Bible verses and snakes.*"

"*I'm so sorry, Crystal. I can make this right.*"

She glares angrily at me. "*Don't even try.*"

"*No, really, I screwed up, but we can find someone good.*" *I gesture to the crowd.* "*Maybe at this party.*"

I click on the camera app of my phone and move over, closer to Crystal. "*You look so cute tonight. Let's just take a selfie for Insta. I'll get you someone better.*"

"*Don't, Mia.*"

As I reach to put my arm around her shoulder and smile into the camera, she recoils hard and shoves me. "*I said no! I'm pissed.*"

Crystal pushed me?

"I'm sorry, Mia. I didn't mean to hurt you," she says. "I mean, I pushed you, but . . . I don't know what happened.

You lost your balance and you fell right into that sculpture."

I can't even focus on her feelings. I just relived a near-death experience. Some smelling salts and a fainting couch might be nice right about now, but we're on the bus. The driver hits the brakes and we slow to a stop, and someone gets on and sits next to me.

"God, I hate the bus at night. So many weirdos out," he says.

I turn away from him but Crystal is on my other side, so I stand and hold onto a pole.

Crystal is still telling me she's sorry. "It was an accident, I swear."

I want everyone to shut up for a minute so I can figure out what to think.

Crystal pushed me. JP left the country to get away from me. My mom told me to back the fuck away and respect her boundaries. Not her words, but that's what she meant. Everyone hated me.

I move to an open seat and shut my eyes for the rest of the bus ride. Should I find somewhere else to stay for the night? It's probably weird to stay with Crystal after she just admitted that she shoved me into a sculpture of Cupid so hard that I lost my memory.

She's sitting across from me now, crying. "I'm so sorry, Mia. It was an accident. I didn't know how bad it was because I ran. I didn't even know you went to the hospital."

I should be furious with her, but somehow I'm not. From where I'm sitting now I can see that I sort of deserved it.

I didn't deserve to end up in the hospital, but she didn't deserve to go on a date with a violent creep and watch a guy die.

"It's okay, Crystal." It's probably weird to console someone who almost killed you and took all of your memories. Even I know this in the moment, but I can't just watch her cry without saying anything. "I'm sorry, too. I lost sight of things before. I never should have sent you to Kobra's house. I should have known better." I shake my head just thinking of it. "The tattoos alone."

When I think of it, Crystal saved my life. Sure, I'm broke and have no man and an uncertain future, but now I can finally live with myself.

I take her hand. "We all make mistakes."

We get off at her bus stop, exhausted but okay. Crystal's mom lives in a third-floor walk-up, the same place Jules picked her up from on Sunday, which was yesterday but feels like a lifetime ago. We climb a few flights of stairs to her apartment. All the lights are off except for a nightlight in the hall and one light over the cooktop. The smell of dinner lingers in the air, hamburgers maybe. After she checks on Kai, who is peacefully sleeping in a Pack 'n Play, she tiptoes into her mom's room and emerges with a few blankets. The apartment has two bedrooms, a bathroom, a galley kitchen, and a living room. "You can take the couch. I'm in the room with Kai."

"Thanks." I'm so grateful to have somewhere to be. As soon as I get my finances straightened out, I'm going to get my own place. "You want to get a place together?" I ask her, "You know, after I get the money from the new guys who signed up?"[69]

"Maybe," she says.

I assume her hesitation is financial and not due to the fact that she nearly killed me.[70] "I'll cut you in for a bigger share of the profits. I would rather run GoldRush together." Even though I've been struggling, it really is one of the hottest new businesses in SoCal. "We're going to make good money, which reminds me." I pull out the Crown Royal bag. "I owe you ten grand."

She takes the money and her eyes well up with tears. "Holy shit. I was wondering why you were carrying a bottle of booze around with you like some weird lush."

"It's Kobra's money from your first date. I said I would pay you, and I meant it."

"Are you serious about working together?"

"I need someone I can trust, someone who will shove me into an ice block if I get mixed up with any drug kingpins again."

She starts laughing through her tears "That would be amazing."

Then she gives me a once-over. "Are you gonna change?" she asks.

....

[69] I spent the last week looking for the person who tried to kill me. Now that I found her I want to be her roommate. This is Leo or Scorpio behavior.

[70] Pretty sure she's a Virgo.

I nod. "I mean, I'm trying to. I've already put a lot of work in!"

She laughs. "Bitch, that's not what I meant. I'm not letting you wear that raggedy dress one more minute."

I laugh. "I think I'm ready to say good-bye to it, too."

"You don't have anything to wear, do you?"

"Just this." I really got my money's worth.

She heads to her closet and gets a pair of sweatpants, a T-shirt, and cozy socks. I change in front of her and she gives me an approving nod. I've never felt so happy to wear sweatpants in my life. She heads to bed and I sit on her couch, wrapped in clean, comfy clothes. I pull up Instagram and see more comments than I can read. Lots of congratulations on finding my mom, some questions about where the hell we are, and more.

The shot of Crystal and me at the club is probably the most popular thing I've ever posted. The shot is only from the shoulders up, but we look like Charlie's Angels.

Max liked it, and it makes me smile.

Tomorrow, I'm going to track him down.

CHAPTER

TWENTY-SEVEN

First thing the next morning, I post a pic of @BlackEinstein314 and @Mia4Realz at L'Empire Tacos, the taco truck with the longest line ever. Maybe it was only three days ago, but it feels like a lifetime. It's the dumbest pic from that photo sesh, a selfie gone totally wrong. You can see part of the food truck, my thumb, and Max just about to take a bite of a taco.

Max, meet me at 8pm at that taco truck where the line is too long and they don't have the kind of salsa you like. I'm ready to live up to my Insta name.

The post immediately gets a ton of likes, though the comments are varied.

DO IT MAX!

SHE CUTE MAX!

Good luck Mia4Realz. You'll need it. (This one's from Fay.)

Stop stalking that man! (This one's from Crystal standing

ten feet away from me. I flag for discussion in the kitchen.)

So many heart emojis!

What you need a white girl for, Max?

Maybe I should have waited a few more days to let him cool off, but there it is. I've played my hand. I want Max. I think he wants me. All day today, I'll try to look casual and trustworthy, just in case he's watching.

Feeling dreamy, I wander into the kitchen. Crystal's mom is making breakfast and the smell of sausage fills the whole apartment. With her mom cooking and me wearing one of Crystal's old basketball T-shirts, it really feels like we're having a high school sleepover or something. "You must be Mia. Would you like some sausage?" Crystal's mom asks.

"Nice to meet you, and thank you so much for letting me sleep on your couch last night. But no sausage for me. I'm a vegetarian." #Brenda.

I zero in on Crystal. "What's with the cyberstalking comment?"

"OMG, girl. All the posts, tagging him all over the damn place. It's like you're Beyoncé asking him out with 150 backup dancers. Plus you got haters."

She doesn't understand. "I'm risking public ridicule. It's JumboTron-sized love. It means more that way."

"The dude is a lab geek and you're screaming from the rooftops after knowing him for five days." She gives me a hard, soul-searching look. "And girl, you still got stitches in your damn head."

"Uhhhh . . ." She has some good points.

"Just try not to scare him, Mia. You're kind of an intense person, in case you haven't figured that out already."

I exhale and accept her wisdom. Don't scare Max, don't scare Max, don't scare Max.

Crystal hands me Kai. "Will you give him a bottle while I eat?"

I hold him like a bomb, which confirms my suspicion that I have no experience with children. Crystal laughs at me. "My God. Relax."

I look into his fat, adorable baby face. "He's so cute . . . but I'm never having kids."

"Yeah you will."

"You think I'm maternal?" Maybe Crystal sees something in me that I don't see in myself.

"No, I just don't think you're that good at birth control."

"You have a point. I don't even know if I'm on it." Bad sex with JP flashes through my mind and I cross my fingers that I have an IUD or am naturally infertile.

Crystal gives me a look and I backtrack. "Not that a baby is the end. Babies are the beginning . . ." #not.

She shakes her head. "You just have to be woman enough to handle it." I think she's trying to convince herself with that statement but I give her a big "Whoop whoop, you go girl" kind of reaction.

In the interest of looking like I'm not spending all day obsessing about Max, I post a pic of all of us in the messy kitchen. Crystal looks like she's going to try to kill me a second time (that joke is never going to get old) and Kai looks angry.

"Hey, do you have to work this morning? Because I have a proposal." I wait for her to respond.

She looks up from preparing more bottles for Kai. The planning it takes to be a mom. Geez. "What's that?"

"Let's go shopping. My treat." After paying Crystal, I have twenty-five grand left in the Crown Royal bag. About another ten needs to go to the bank, and I owe Max for his "work," but I definitely have enough for new clothes. I've been wearing the same dress since I left the hospital. It's done good, but it's time to retire it.

After washing a couple of dishes, Crystal says, "Shopping sounds great. I have the day off. Actually, I have all the days off. I just quit Walmart, so we better get GoldRush off the ground for real."

I squeal and Crystal pretends to look exasperated.

Crystal's mom leaves the kitchen, muttering something about loud vegetarians.

Crystal bundles a sleeping Kai in a BabyBjörn and we ride the bus to the mall. We immediately buy lattes and take a selfie with them. Did you really have a coffee if you didn't post it online? I might be Mia 2.0, but some things haven't changed.

Crystal looks at it and says, "Um, how about a filter. That zit on my chin is . . ."

"Nope. This is Project Honesty. I'm changing my life completely. No filters. No lies."

Finally getting some new clothes. Good-bye yellow dress! Max likes that one right away.

He's thinking about me. He's following along.

Crystal rolls her eyes. "You've got it bad, girl."

"Tell me about it."

This shopping experience is much better than our last. Crystal doesn't storm out of the dressing room and put her Walmart uniform back on. "I'm glad to be rid of the damn thing!" she says.

"What store is the most me?" I ask Crystal. "I want to start life over as my true self."

"I liked that yellow dress. At least, I did a week ago.'"

"You're right. I'll just get a new one. It'll be my uniform, like I'm an adult Dora the Explorer."

Forever 21 turns out to be the ticket. They're all knockoff red carpet looks at a fraction of the price. What can I say, I might be real, but I'm a knockoff of the original.

I look for something similar to my beloved yellow Prada gown that falls somewhere between prom and sundress. I buy a whole bag of dresses, T-shirts, and jeans. I take a dressing room selfie. Finally changed clothes! Smell and look better.

Max likes it.

Crystal only buys clothes that go with four-inch heels and false eyelashes because that's the real her.

Standing in the middle of the mall, next to an obligatory fountain, I look into Crystal's eyes, madman-level intense—I can feel it. This is my *yippee ki-yay, motherfucker* moment. My voice cold as steel, I say, "This shopping spree ain't over yet, baby."

Her expression says *duh!* "Obviously. We haven't gotten shoes yet."

"True. We need shoes, but I'm thinking of something else. Something big." Nakatomi Tower big, and I am John McClane. "Jingle Bells" is playing in the background.

I text JP: I know things are weird between us, but I have a business proposition.

??

At least he's talking to me.

I respond. I'd like to make an offer on GoldRush. The building and the business.

I show Crystal the text and wait for her to get excited. Instead, she says, "Girl, are you nuts?"

"Maybe. It's a good idea, though. For one, JP can't sue us for stealing his intellectual property and all that. Two, it can be our GoldRush headquarters. We can have desks and fresh flowers and a coffee pot—it'll be our office. I'm thinking that we can phase out the stripping."

She laughs. "Phase out the stripping? How does that work? Like we move in some desks and a copy machine and only have stripping a couple of hours a day?"

"I don't know. We can work out the details later. And maybe that's a bad idea. You are reeeeaaaally good at it."

I already offered you the club. It's yours.

I like the price, but what strings are attached to that deal?

I want to buy it. You already gave me enough.

Haven't bought the yacht . . . yet.

Uh-oh.

He still thinks there's hope.

You're giving me GoldRush. Why?

You were right. Whatever happened to the employees at that place happened under my watch. I just wasn't looking.

I spend a crazy long time staring at that text.

He says, I know you'll do a good job.

I'll buy it.

You don't have enough money.

Technically true. I could put a lot of cash down with the money from the new bachelors Jules has brought in.[71] Maybe buy it contract for deed. I know that goes against the kind of advice dads give, but it's not like I care. No dad to object in this case.

No more discussion. I'll have the papers drawn up tomorrow. It's a gift. Do whatever you want with it.

I start to tear up. JP is being so good to me, so good to everyone. He doesn't seem to want to break up. I think he's trying to win me back and I'm posting selfies in the Forever 21 dressing room for a guy who might not want me.

I don't know how much that place is worth, but it's got to be at least hundreds of thousands of dollars—maybe even a million.

"Crystal, it's time to break out the champagne." I want to celebrate, but I also feel like the mantle of responsibility has been passed to me like I'm about to take my place on the Iron Throne. Is this moment too solemn for champagne?

....

71 Three so far! 35k × 3 = I'M RICH!

An hour later we're at our new office. I don't know what we'll do with it but it has a bar, a kicking sound system, and a stage. "I think we should keep the club running and maybe set aside a certain amount for office space," I suggest to Crystal.

"I like that. We could have singles' events."

It's going to be awesome.

I take a selfie of us making crazy excited faces and caption it: Guess who just bought a strip club?! 🕺 🍾 💼

"So should I quit stripping tonight?" Crystal asks.

"Probably wait until JP gives me the deed, or however that works."

Now that I almost own the property, I think it's fine for me to start a fire in the parking lot—just a small one, in a trash can. It's the last thing on my list for the day. I call out to one of the security guys, "Yo, do you have a light?"

"I got a book of matches," he says. Everyone who works at GoldRush smokes, which is fine by me. I'm not going to be a fucking health evangelist, even though I'm a vegetarian.

He waits for me to stick a cigarette in my mouth so he can light it for me. What a gentleman. "Can I just have the book?" He hands it over, mystified.

In one corner of the parking lot there's a metal trash can. It looks like an old oil barrel, black with bits of rust and empty except for some beer bottles that should have been recycled. Not a lot of environmentalists at the strip club. GoldRush 2.0 will have a recycling bin. #dolphins.

I hold the yellow dress close to my heart for a moment and shut my eyes tight against my emotions as I think about the last week, about the person I was. I'm not mad at her. She did the best she could and she brought me to where I am today, ready to officially move on. Hell, I already have moved on. I'm wearing a brand-new dress from Forever 21 and some pretty cute shoes. I'm a bona fide business owner and I have a damn good friend in Crystal, even if she did try to kill me. Even JP—I never expected him to care about something just because I do. Is that love, or just an awakening?

One kiss, and I drop the dress into the barrel on top of cigarette butts and Budweiser bottles, their blue labels peeling from exposure. I douse my old life in Everclear taken from behind the bar and light a match. The flame goes out before it hits the dress. I try again and again. By the fourth match, I'm practically in the trash can so I can hold the flame against the yellow fabric. It won't ignite. I'm getting streaks of rust on my new dress from leaning into the can to light the old one.

"Fucking dress!"

After I use the entire book, the dress looks slightly blackened in a couple of spots where some old paper burned on top of it, but the dress isn't going unless I take it to a crematorium, and it's not quite that serious. I really wanted to take a picture of the flaming dress for Instagram, but I have to settle for a plain old shot of it in the trash. I caption it: Moving on.

Maybe it's symbolic. The old me isn't gone. I just threw her in the trash with a few other bad habits—lying, cheating, and red meat.

I almost take the dress out of the barrel. Imagining the once-beautiful garment being picked up by trash collectors and tossed in with food waste and dirty diapers makes me cringe, but what am I going to do with a partially scorched Prada gown? It doesn't spark joy. My old self doesn't spark joy.

So it has to be good-bye. I have things to do and places to be. I blow a kiss to the can and walk away. I have a date at a taco truck.

CHAPTER

TWENTY-EIGHT

I can take the blue Metro Express bus most of the way to L'Empire Tacos, about a 90-minute ride according to Metro Trip Planner.[72] The homeless guy next to me smells so much like old piss and cigarettes I can barely breathe. Plus the bus fumes. It's time to hurry up on those zero-emission buses, LA! I miss my (JP's) Ferrari. But this is part of the process. If I embrace this cocoon of reality for long enough, I'm totally going to emerge a millionaire.

"I'm going to snap a pic, okay?" I tell the guy. I have to document this shit for my fans.

I smile with teeth and he smiles without. #Meth #ThanksKobra.

I erase and rewrite the caption approximately twenty times until I finally settle on: Bussing it to the taco truck date, Max.

....

[72] Next purchase: a car.

Stay away from meth, kids.

While deciding between the pink bubbly hearts and the red heart emoji—is the red heart too much like long-stemmed roses on the first date, because I think that would scare him away—I miss my stop. When I finally get off it's almost 8:30 p.m. What if Max waited for twenty minutes and left? I kick myself for not taking an Uber. I'm an idiot.

I run as fast as I can in my Payless heels. The sun is setting, and the stoplights seem to glow extra bright against the dusky backdrop like they're charged with the electricity of a summer night. I'm feeling it too. I'm electric blue against the evening sky. Everyone else is moving in slow motion in their booty-hugging shorts and bare-midriff tops as I race toward L'Empire Tacos.

Running in the heat has done nothing for me. I arrive out of breath and sweaty. Blisters are starting to form where the heel of my shoe cuts into my ankle, and Max is nowhere to be seen. I sit down at the communal picnic table to catch my breath. He's running late, too—no big.

The perpetually too-long line at the taco truck is, as expected, too long. That's part of its charm—twenty extra minutes to stare into the eyes of your loved one and talk about whether you're going to take a risk on an enchilada or get the tacos like normal. The parking lot is filled with the same amount of trash and janky cars as last time. There's no grass anywhere in sight. Unlike last time, my dress isn't splattered with blood from a recent head wound and I know who I am. I am prepared to be happy.

If Max comes.

He didn't respond to my Instagram post and I can't even be sure that he saw it. I feel like Meg Ryan at the end of *Sleepless in Seattle*. You might say the stakes were higher for her because she had to get from Baltimore to the top of the Empire State Building, probably in bad traffic. I think a 90-minute bus ride through iffy neighborhoods with a missed stop is probably about the same.

Mostly I hope that Max shows up, but I also hope that he has a car. It'd be nice if I didn't have to ride the bus back to Crystal's in the middle of the night. But I'm prepared. I burned my yellow dress today (sorta). I own a strip club. I can ride the bus after midnight. I'm one of the weirdos on the bus.

A bunch of other spicy nightlife types are sharing the table with me, the same table I shared with Max a few days ago. I stare at my phone and pretend they're not there, but I'm obviously way too cute to ignore. (I put in some extra effort for this date.) A guy starts talking to me. "You waiting for someone, mamacita? How 'bout you come home with me."

I respond, "Get out of my face, dirtbag" so fast, crowd management was obviously my first language. Two other guys get the same treatment. I ain't no ho—that's something I've firmly established over the last two days.

At nine-thirty I feel like an idiot. I've watched at least twenty people eat dinner and I can't take it anymore. I've made a fool of myself. Max isn't coming. Maybe he didn't even check Instagram. Who knows. My whole future could have died with Max's phone battery. Maybe he went to work and forgot his charger at home. My mind is trying to provide me with an explanation to save me from a total breakdown at the taco truck. Max would know about this because he studies brains. If he shows, I'll ask him.

Also, I'm starving. I think. At this point, I can't identify what's the matter with me. Just so I don't start crying from low blood sugar, I get in line. I thought Max was my real relationship, but maybe it was all in my head. When he said he didn't want to be together, maybe he meant it. Crystal is right and I'm just cyberstalking him.

I can add cyberstalking to my list of things to atone for: check fraud, theft of intellectual property, charging rich guys thirty-five grand to date strippers (I'm still kind of proud of that, though), and parking in handicapped spaces (in a stolen car). Speaking of which, I should make sure I'm cool with the police. I'm pretty sure I am, but Denise was too busy arresting Kobra to peace out officially. Maybe I still need to get a piece of paper with a stamp on it.

Crystal is right. I probably shouldn't have been in Max's face online. I probably should have . . . I don't know . . . joined the biology department and tried to get into one of his labs. No—that's stalking, too. It's like I only know how to stalk people. That's how I landed JP, too. I'm a stalker.

"Hola, what would you like?" a voice interrupts my shame spiral. Thank God, but also ouch—I'm at the front of the line.

"Um, I'm sorry, I didn't look at the menu yet." I glance around. "Is it on that board?"

He points and says, "Side of the truck." It's a giant sign.

There are a bunch of choices, but it's all confusing because it's half in Spanish.

"What do you recommend?"

"Depends on what you like."

Someone behind me says, "Jesus."

"I'll take the tacos," I say without even reading. There has to be an order of tacos. "Vegetarian ones." #Brenda.

I also don't know what sides or salsa I want. "Maybe I'll order for the guy I'm meeting." If he doesn't show I'm going to have to carry a bunch of tacos home on the bus . . . but if he does show, I'll have to wait in line for another half an hour. The guy behind me looks like he's ready to pull a gun on me so I just say, "And I'll take a burrito. Surprise me."

Now I'm sitting at a table with a bunch of people, a couple of dogs, and two plates. No Max in sight.

"Excuse me, someone's sitting here," I say to a guy about to sit in front of Max's plate.

He rolls his eyes and then saves about five inches on the end of the bench for Max.

"Are you gonna eat those?" another dude asks me. He can't get over the fact that I'm sitting in front of two plates of uneaten food. Neither can I.

"I'm waiting for someone."

He's not coming and all I can think is *What am I going to do with this burrito?* It was ten bucks. I might have Kobra's money but damn, $10 is a lot for a burrito.

It's shapeless and huge. Nothing to do but Instagram it. I don't even write a caption. The uneaten burrito speaks for itself.

Immediately, people start commenting with crying emojis. Crystal was right. These random people I don't even know are the only ones responding to my posts. My online shit did nothing but drive Max away.

I take a sad bite of my taco and set it back down. I don't think I can eat, but the taco is fucking amazing so I inhale it.

I refresh my Instagram just one more time. There are a ton of notifications, including one from @BlackEinstein314. My heart soars and my pulse races. It could be something bad, but I'm optimistic.

It's not a comment. It's a like. Instagram tells me that @BlackEinstein314 likes one of my posts.

Please let it be the picture of the two of us on the scenic overlook. Please.

It is! That's as good a declaration as any that Max is into me and that he has forgiven me.

So where the hell is he?

As I'm looking at the screen, he comments. I don't love you, too.

A smile breaks out on my face like the morning sun on a cold winter's day. I'm bursting—he doesn't love me. I'm pretty sure that means he loves me. Or maybe that he likes me. I don't know, but it feels good.

"Mia." I turn, half expecting Max, even though I know the voice belongs to someone else. I see JP, dressed casually, like he's about ready to drive to a winery in Sonoma. "Mia," he says again. "Thank God I found you."

"How did you know I was here?"

"You told the whole world, right? Instagram."

I don't know what to say. Why exactly is he here? He proposed. I left the house. I invited another guy out for tacos on Instagram. To me, it seems like we're done.

"I love you, Mia. I shouldn't have proposed the other day. I didn't realize how badly you were injured and how extensive your memory loss was. You aren't acting like yourself." He shakes his head as if confounded. "I saw your Instagram posts. Burning your clothes in a trash barrel and . . . taking the bus—I don't know what's happened to you, but I'm worried."

That's nice of him. "I'm fine, JP."

"I'm not even mad that you invited the house sitter out to tacos. I want to take you to a doctor and get everything back to normal, back to the way it was. I see now that you're just not yourself. That was a serious head injury."

"Going back to normal is exactly what I don't want. I'm not that person anymore. I don't even like her."

"I was only gone for five days, Mia. How could everything be that different?" He gestures to the crowd that doesn't include Max. "The house sitter isn't even here. You're waiting for no one. Please come home with me."

The Ferrari docs look good.

"Max is coming," I say. He liked that post. Any dummy could figure out what that means. He's coming and he's forgiven me.

"Everything was so perfect before. It was so beautiful."

I think for a second before coming clean with him. "JP, it was beautiful in pictures. But none of those pictures were true.

They were staged and filtered, just like my life. It was all spin."

He shakes his head. "No. Some of it was real."

Did he really not know? "I lied about everything. I lied *to you*. The business was all facade, my image was all facade, I was in trouble with the cops. I charged you for matchmaking and then set myself up with you."

He draws his eyebrows together. "You faked your way into my life. Sure, I was mad. But hey, it's what you do. It's what we all do. What am I? I was born with this money. I'm not brilliant. I pretend every day to be as smart and good as people think I am, but it's an act. You, though—you made it on your own. That is impressive. You faked your way to the top. I'm not mad. I'm proud of you."

Faked my way to the top—that *is* pretty cool. No one at the top deserves to be there, so what does it matter that I faked it? He's right.

"Just get in the Ferrari. Let's go get a cocktail somewhere nice and then go home. Tomorrow I'm going to find you the best doctor in LA."

If he had told me all this five days ago, if he hadn't been gone when I'd lost my memory, I would have fallen right back into my place at his side. But . . . I don't know now.

Max texts: If you're in line, I'll take the special! 😉

He follows it up with a pic of him in the helmet. On my way. Sorry I'm late! Have been in fMRI room telling the truth all day. Fixed lie detector. Learned a few things about myself . . .

I remember that there are no phones allowed in the fMRI

room. He didn't even find out about our taco date until the "I don't love you, too" text a few minutes ago.

I shut my eyes for a second. This is so intense. I try to remember all the feelings I've had over the last few days. I really connected with Max. A real connection. I connected with Crystal, especially after I repaired our relationship. That's real. The yacht, the fake bios on GoldRush—everything I arrived to on Thursday felt hollow, like a chocolate Easter bunny. You bite into it and it's just a waxy shell. That's my relationship with JP, a waxy shell of Jacques-o-late, beautiful but empty.[73]

"Mia?"

I turn and see the person I've been waiting for.

Max steps out of the passenger side of a Kia. His T-shirt is aqua (a great color for him) and says THE SQUARE ROOT OF YOU IS ME. He looks as confused to see me with JP as I feel about his T-shirt. Is it supposed to be romantic? Is it a math joke? Does he it mean he loves me? "I'm sorry, Max. I really wanted to meet you for tacos." I don't say "alone" but I think it's implied.

"Then what's he doing here?"

I exhale. *I didn't invite him*, I mouth. Then I say, a little too loudly, "JP wants to marry me and he thought he'd interrupt tacos."

JP looks from me to Max. "I didn't say that exactly."

"Oh, I guess I misunderstood," I say.

----

[73] Side note: JP should make Jacques-o-late bachelors! I would so buy.

"I mean, I do want to marry you, but I would like to get you back to normal before we make plans."

Wow. This nonoffer really seems to rely on me turning back into my former self.

Max walks over to us. "Well, I know we've only known each other for a few days, but I really want to sit down, have a burrito, and get to know you better."

JP says, "This is interesting and all, but . . . I think it's time to go." He gestures to the crowd, which looks a little druggy at this hour. "I'm not sure if it's safe here."

I look down at the burrito. It takes up almost the whole plate. I can't remember what's in it—some kind of fatty pork with extra guac and beans and special sauce. "I only have one burrito."

I look between them and I know what I have to do. JP might have been offered the role of *The Bachelor*, but he didn't want it. I do, though. I am *The Bachelorette*.

"There are two of you, but I only have one burrito. I could buy another one, but I want to make my choice now. Even though both of you are super awesome and amazing in your own way, only one of you can have the burrito."

Max squints at me, as if he's trying to make sense of what I'm saying. He's clearly never watched *The Bachelor*.

"JP, you are the most perfect man imaginable. You are beautiful and successful and nice, and you forgave me for so many bad things. For that, I am grateful. I'm grateful for everything you offered, but I don't love you and I can't be the woman you want anymore. It's time to say good-bye."

JP shakes his head. "Fine. I can't believe what you just gave up, though."

Me either.

I can tell JP is going to livestream his reaction, just like a rejected contestant on *The Bachelorette.* Crystal and I will watch it later with a cocktail.

I turn to Max. "Max, JP just offered me a cocktail and a ride in a Ferrari and probably a life as a lady billionaire, but I'm a woman of my word. At least, I am now. I invited you to tacos. I bought this burrito for you. I saved this seat for you. More than anything, I want you to give me another chance."

He smiles big. "Thanks, Mia."

I hand him the burrito. It's on a Chinet plate and has no garnish. It's better than any single, long-stemmed rose. "I know we've only known each other for a few days, but I don't care. All I want to do is get to know you better."

I still want to be a billionaire, obviously, but I'll figure that out on my own. I already faked it all the way to the top once and I'm only . . . twenty-seven? I can't remember. I'll need to double-check. At any rate, I'm super young. It's scientifically proven that thirty is the new eighteen. I'm barely old enough to vote.

"Did you already eat?" he asks.

"Yeah, I was starving. Do you need a fork?" I ask.

He nods. "Probably. And maybe you could get dessert or something?"

"Good idea." I don't want to just watch him eat like I have a fetish.

I look back at the Kia Max emerged from. I think I see Chan in the driver's seat. "Is he okay? Does he want some food too?"

"Chan? He's cool, he's just messing around on his phone."

"He's driving us home, right?"

"He better."

"We're definitely getting Chan a burrito." Then I remember how much it cost. "Or some chips at least."

While we stand in line, Max turns to me. "I'm sorry about the other day, Mia. At the lab."

My antenna goes up and I give him my best *do go on* expression. I can't wait to hear more about me. I could talk about my feelings all day long. Instagram is probably just an overflow.

"You have the right to feel however you feel. I promise not to tell you otherwise, even if my lie detector says you're wrong."

"Thank you," I say. "I really appreciate that. You might be right, though. We've only known each other since Thursday and it's Tuesday now." I shake my head.

"That's less than a week," he says.

"There are different kinds of love though. It's like going to a waterslide park. Sometimes you take the steepest, fastest slide and part of it is a dark tunnel you can't see out of. Just because it's too fast doesn't mean it's not as real an experience as the slower, twisty-turny slide, or even the lazy river." And that fast slide—*whooeee*—love is scary when you're on that slide.

"Just so you know, I'm still climbing the stairs up to the slide."

I raise my eyebrows.

"Don't get me wrong. I'm on the stairs and I'm going on the ride." He's so cute when he's trying to explain himself.

"That's okay," I say. "I already went down the slide once. We can go a second time together, climb the stairs, and hold hands."

Even though it wasn't a hint, he takes my hand. "I'm sorry I called you a liar, too. That was pretty harsh."

"But true." I have no qualms about admitting that.

"But it wasn't just you. I lied. We all lie. We decide who we are and act it out. In a world where we all get to be whatever we want, we have to fabricate an identity. When you don't live up to it, you're a liar, even if it's not malicious."

"I assume you're talking about Fay and your neuroscience power couple thing."

He laughs. "Yeah, I involved her in my lie. I was lying to myself there, and to Fay. She was right."

"No big," I say. "I'm the fakest person I know."

"No, you're the realest," he says. "Maybe losing your memory broke you loose from the Matrix so you can see everything. At any rate, I don't know who you were before, but you are sincerely trying to do your best and you have a beautiful soul. You only lied to me because you were embarrassed. I've done much worse without even being aware of it."

He squeezes my hand again.

The guy at the food truck window practically groans when he sees me. "You again."

I smile. "I'm back. Could I get a quesadilla, some chips, and two horchatas?"

Max and I toast with our horchatas and take a selfie. I don't use a filter so we look pretty realistic. Granted, we're both fairly good looking, but I look tired and my eye makeup is raccooning. He's making a weird face, like I caught him mid-sentence, but it's perfect. Neither of us knows exactly what's going to happen. We don't know how long we'll stay together or what we're doing. He has some cool research ideas. I have some cool business ideas. We might screw up. We might go bankrupt. I hope we don't break up at the end of the night, but I'm jumping into the deep end of reality.

Even without remembering most of my life, I know that I'm living up to my name for the first time ever. I am finally @Mia4Realz.

ACKNOWLEDGMENTS

Jhanteigh Kupihea, thank you for your insightful edits, the awesome title, and every great joke you added to the manuscript, not to mention all the bad ones you deleted. Somehow, with your edits, Max seems a little like my brother, at least according to my daughter, which is slightly disturbing but cool. Everyone loves him. While I'm on the topic, I should thank my brother for brainstorming with me from his fancy engineering job more than his boss probably knows. But back to Jhanteigh—thank you for trusting me to write this book and not hating me after you read it. And thanks to everyone else at Quirk, too—Brett Cohen, Jane Morley, Andie Reid, Nicole De Jackmo, Jen Murphy, and probably a bunch of people I've never emailed or twittered with. I'm so grateful for all of the support and the great work you all do!

And Barbara Poelle, thanks for signing me and repping this book even though you weren't there at conception. You rock my world.

Also, thank you to Blair Thornburgh, who encouraged me

to write this proposal in the first place, and who worked with me on the books that didn't take before this one. I still love Fantastic News.

Terrell, for taking me to Compton and Long Beach on the first weekend away I've had in forever. A beach vacation without any trips to the courthouse would have been nice, but I wouldn't have written this book without that craziness. And thanks for listening to me talk about my plot pretty much every day for the last year and offering so many good suggestions, not to mention opening up my eyes to more of the world. I couldn't have written this book without you.

Cristina Pippa, thanks so much for making me work on the SIRI proposal, for reading umpteen versions of it, for honest feedback, and for being available 24/7 for random questions. Also, thank you for telling me not to change Max to a herpetologist two weeks before the book was due. That was a close one.

Monica, thanks for watching my kids and being way more fun than me. (Kids, you got the dedication and Monica so you're out of luck here, but I love you.)

Carly Bloom, thanks for proofreading my acknowledgments and reminding me of all your contributions that I forgot, including: brainstorming, coming up with that alien spaceship angle I didn't use (thank God!), and reading the initial proposal. Mostly, thank you for not quitting writing and going full dance mom. And Roselle Lim, thank you for reading my proposal, brainstorming, and being available via text for writer therapy 24/7.

As always, I need to thank my dad, who provides medical advice for all of my characters. Thank you for stepping out on actual head-injury patients to answer questions about Mia's head injury while I was on deadline. And to my mom for buying me that super cute red dress that I'm going to wear to some sort of book event, and texting about fake people whenever I need her to.

Cuppa Cuppa, if this book makes it big and everyone starts asking for a maple latte that you don't serve—sorry. I guess she could have ordered off the menu.

Ingrid, thanks for dressing me up in some cute clothes and taking my author photo, and for moving back to Minnesota and buying a hot tub. Actually, I'm on the fence about the hot tub.

Now for the section about Max. I've never whined so much about a guy to so many of my girlfriends. Thank you to all the women who provided a shoulder to cry on when he was giving me trouble. First of all, thanks to Max's team of neuroscience advisers, in particular Dr. Emily Rosario and Dr. Katie Tschida. An actual neuroscientist would be lucky to have you two! And did you know that you both play French horn? Katie, if I'd given him one of your project suggestions, he would have been respectable. And Emily, thanks so much for taking a break from serious research to answer absurd questions about a scientist with girlfriend drama and for telling me what USC looks like.

Esther and Jeannine. You two helped me save Max that morning at Kopplin's just before I crossed the event horizon of despair at never being able to tie up all those loose ends. There were so many! Also, thanks to Esther's cousin, the snake charmer who made me think of Kobra.

And Liz, the funnest neighbor ever! Thanks for getting me a little drunk and talking through the last chapter with me the day before the book was due. It's so much better because of you. Also, thanks for the cardboard cut-out of Johnny Depp.

These seem long, so it doesn't seem like I could have forgotten anyone and it would be surprising if I thanked your perfect sister instead of you by accident after you read my whole book to offer a teen perspective (shout out Camille!), but it's so easy to do that. So I apologize if I thanked your sister instead of you or if I just completely blew you off. So this paragraph is for the forgotten ones.

And last but not least, thank you to anyone who read this book! And if you're still reading, I love you even more. Let's do this, readers. All the way to the bitter end!

SAM TSCHIDA (pronounced "cheetah") is from the wilds of Minnesota, where she lives with a motley crew of kids, dogs, and one handsome man. She is the cofounder of ManuFixed, an editorial consulting company and writing workshop that services the Twin Cities. In her spare time she runs, exercises, and watches Netflix.